Impala

Andrew Diamond

September, 2016 - First Edition (r3)

Paperback ISBN: 978-099635070

e-book ISBN: 978-0996350747

For Lindsay.

Part I
Absence

I

Shimmering pools of silver float above the pavement of Richmond's long, broad avenues on this broiling summer afternoon. The pools dissolve as I approach, and new ones form a little farther off, always within view but just beyond my reach.

When I catch a glimpse of my reflection in the shop windows, I see someone else going through the motions of my life. He is well liked, well mannered, and polite. He shows no outward signs of the deep downward currents of my mind. And yet he looks at me like I'm the impostor.

Jamie's car is in the lot up ahead, the little blue Ford by the repair shop entrance. The new tires are on, and a numbered ticket hangs from the rearview mirror. I step into the subarctic cool of the waiting room, with its gray tile floor and the table strewn with magazines beneath the muted television.

The mechanic in the oil-stained jumpsuit runs his blackened fingers line by line down the work order. "Tires, oil, filters, flush, and coolant."

"She'll make it to New York?" I ask.

"Oh, you could drive that baby straight to Costa Rica."

I stare at him for a few seconds, until he looks uncomfortable, and he says, "I say something?"

"No, it's just, why Costa Rica?"

"I'm just saying, that car'll go a long way before it gives you any trouble."

"Yeah, but why Costa Rica? I mean, you could have picked any place." I know I'm pushing it too far, but when someone hits on the exact thought that's at the top of my mind, I want to know how they got there.

The year before we got in trouble, the year before I ran away from San Francisco, Cred kept warning me: "He'll get you to do things you wouldn't do on your own."

impala

I knew that. Hacking into the big, high-profile targets was part of the thrill. Like walking a high wire.

I tried to brush off his concerns. "That's how you grow, right? Taking on big challenges."

"No," said Cred. "That's how you end up in jail."

We got stoned that night and went out drinking. At the end of the evening, it was just Charlie and I throwing darts in the back room of some bar I've never since been able to find. There was a map of the world on the wall, and Charlie handed me a dart and said, "Close your eyes and throw. We'll go wherever the dart lands."

I hit the coastline of northern Siberia and Charlie said, "Fuck that!"

I said, "When are we going to this place?"

And he said, "Not this year."

He closed his eyes and tossed a dart into the middle of the Pacific. When he looked at it, he said, "Shit! We're gonna drown."

Then I squeezed my eyes shut and threw the last dart smack into the little coastal town of Sámara, Costa Rica. Charlie looked it up on his phone and said, "Nice work, dude. The Mar Azul has four stars and a poolside bar. If we have to run, we might as well run to the beach!"

"Wait," I said. "Why would we have to run?"

A year later, when I finally did decide to run, I chose Richmond, Virginia. It's a full continent away from San Francisco. There's more going on here than you might think, and the pace is slow enough that you can enjoy it all.

And Charlie? I haven't talked to him in four years.

The mechanic says, "Shit, go to LA if you want."

"But I don't want to go to LA," I say. "I want to go to Costa Rica."

"Whatever, man," he sighs. "It's seven hundred thirty-three and tax. The keys are in the car."

Tomorrow, Jamie and I will leave Richmond at 5:00 a.m. and drive to Long Island, and I'll drop her off for a four-day retreat where she'll uncover her true self and develop the tools for a purposeful life of self-actualization. Or something like that. You have to read the website. It's full of testimonials.

I told Jamie I'd spend the night with her on Long Island and drive back Thursday. And I told my boss I'd be at work Thursday morning.

I did that on purpose. Overcommitted, so I'd be sure to disappoint someone.

2

ON THURSDAY MORNING, I'm back at work. After I dumped Jamie off on Long Island yesterday, I headed straight back down I-95.

Jamie, the cheerleader, the optimist, the sorority girl who can talk enthusiastically about anything, because it's all so exciting. Jamie who reads *Vogue* and *Elle* while she watches *The Voice*, and sits on the edge of her seat when the judges decide who will make it to the next round. Jamie, who needs her blush and mascara and eye shadow to be just right before she can even answer the phone. Who is sweet and kind. Who deserves better than me. She is in every way my opposite, the sunshine to my shadow. The dark currents can't pull me down when she's around, because she keeps us in waters too shallow to drown in. She is perfume and matching furniture and designer sheets; a lilting South Carolina accent, dark eyes, and a black band pulled across honey-blonde hair.

I'm sorry I was rude to her—and I really was rude—but she needed to know how I felt, and where we stood, and I didn't know how to tell her in words. So I just pulled up in front of the hotel, and I didn't even stop the engine. I didn't help her with her bag. I didn't say I love you or I hope you have a good time. I just said, "See you later."

"You're not coming in? You're not going to stay?" she asked, with a mix of bewilderment and…I don't know what that look was. It seemed like relief.

"No," I said.

"Okay, Russ. Maybe you need some time alone."

Maybe.

I gave her a little parting kiss that had no heart in it, and she turned away.

* * *

Work is a little software development shop in a one-story building that once housed an accounting firm. There are seven of us. Ethan, the

andrew diamond

founder. Thirty-six, short, skinny, and intense. Brad, the salesman and project manager, a tall, blonde-haired surfer boy with a square jaw, blue eyes, and a consistently positive attitude. He's my age. Twenty-eight or twenty-nine.

Trish is the office assistant, but don't call her that—and, no, she won't get your goddamn coffee. I like her. She's all efficiency and no bullshit. She's twenty-four, with a broad face, unruly copper-brown hair, dark eyes, and freckles.

We have two junior developers, Tom and Marty, who look like twins out of the J. Crew catalog. Then there's Karim, who's quite a seasoned programmer at twenty-six. I'm the team lead. I have a little office in back, next to Ethan's, with a window that looks out to the alley.

There's not much in the way of decor around here. The developer desks are all pushed together in the common area. Trish's desk is at the front. There's a big TV for doing demos and code reviews, two whiteboards, a couple of plants, and a kitchen. Nothing to distract us from getting work done.

Ethan started the company to build mobile games, but it was impossible to make a living because so many developers give away games for free. To make ends meet, he helped a local newspaper build a mobile app. That was *the pivot*, as they call it back in the Valley. The moment when you make the shift from doing what you thought your company was going to do to doing whatever will bring in the money.

Now we help established companies build mobile apps and bring their back-end systems into the twenty-first century. In the two years since I started, it's been stable and predictable. A big change from the old days in San Francisco, when Charlie, Cred, and I spent our evenings getting high and poking around inside corporate networks. The three of us made quite a team.

Cred, whose real name was Bill, was working at a start-up, building a mobile app to help people find parking spaces. The job bored the hell out of him, so in his spare time, he would disassemble commercial software and then spend days reading through the assembly code like it was Shakespeare. He had a knack for finding bugs. Every time he described a new exploit, Charlie and the other hackers who hung out in the IRC chatrooms would say his street cred just went up another notch. Eventually, they just started calling him Cred.

Charlie was Hatter, as in "The Mad Hatter." He picked up contract jobs here and there, working for a few weeks at a time, but he could never bring himself to be anyone's employee. No one was all that eager to hire him either, once they got a look at his code. Good developers try to write clear code, so that when other developers read it, they understand what the code is doing. Charlie liked to write obfuscated code, just to confuse other developers. It seemed like everything he wrote had to be a riddle.

In the evenings, he would hack into just about anything without regard to consequences. His recklessness, along with his intelligence and his disregard for the opinions of others, earned him an outsized reputation in the hacker community.

He was a tall, skinny guy, with long black hair that he rarely washed and was always pushing out of his face. He had an insatiable interest in software, painting, music, and film, and he could stay awake for ungodly stretches of time. He might code for twelve hours, take in a movie or two, go see a couple of live bands, and then drink until sunrise. I have no idea where that stamina came from.

He liked women too, and they liked him. He wasn't particularly handsome or charming, but he had this confidence that would infect everyone around him. It wasn't the kind of pep-talk confidence you get from the self-help gurus who pump you up with enthusiasm. It was more of a matter-of-fact certainty in his own abilities. He would say he was going to do something improbable, and he'd say it like it was the most natural thing in the world, because, in his mind, it was. And then you would buy into his point of view without even realizing you were doing it.

He was in an artist's studio one day, looking at this guy's paintings, and out of the blue, he said, "I'm putting together a show, and you're going to display these three pieces." He even gave the guy a date, which he just pulled out of thin air. Then he went around to a few other artists and said the same thing, telling them he had a bunch of bloggers lined up to promote the show. Which he didn't. Yet.

6   andrew diamond

He told the bloggers that the artists were on board, and they signed on and started writing about it. Pretty soon, there was a big buzz online. Only there was still no venue, so the bloggers couldn't tell anyone where to go. But that just added to the mystique of the event, and people all over town started talking about it.

Then he found this big empty garage in Oakland with a For Rent sign. The owner was inside cleaning up, and Charlie walked in with one of his girlfriends—not Celia, but whoever he had ditched her for that week—and he told her to sketch out where all the pieces would go, while he persuaded the owner to rent him the place for two weeks.

In the end, he got a few hundred people to show up, and a bunch of the pieces sold. Charlie didn't make any money off it, but he wasn't in it for the money. As far as I can tell, he was in it because he got an idea to have an art show and that's what he was going to do.

That was Charlie. Get an idea, talk it up, and then watch everyone fall in line to make it happen. But with his wide-ranging pursuits, he wasn't always the most dedicated person. He didn't even stay till the end of the show.

While his other enthusiasms waxed and waned, he maintained a consistent dedication to hacking, women, and drawing. Perhaps for the sake of efficiency, he combined those last two hobbies and started drawing nudes. He had a tremendous gift for it, capturing character and mood in sharp realistic detail. Maybe he was driven by love for his subject. Or lust. I never saw him draw any still lifes.

And then there was me, the last of the three amigos. By day, I was writing Rails code for a little start-up that could have become Tinder, if our founder had a little more business sense and our development team had a little more discipline. I could see early on the company wasn't going anywhere, so I didn't put much into it. Most developers at start-ups were working sixty-hour weeks. Companies would bring in lunch and dinner and let you have your dog in the office just so you'd never have to leave your desk. I used to walk out at 6:00 every day no matter what, and they wouldn't fire me because I still cranked out twice as much code as anyone else.

Charlie used to call me Genie, in part because of my middle name, Eugene, and in part because whenever Charlie hacked halfway into a system and then hit a wall, I could figure out a way around it. He was always amazed when I got past some seemingly impossible obstacle. He'd say, "You're magic, Genie! Fucking magic!"

In the beginning, we were like kids breaking into school on the weekend to go rummaging through the staff lounge. We played a few pranks, like posting fake announcements on company websites and forwarding internal corporate emails to the bloggers at TechCrunch. After a while though, Charlie started breaking into high-value systems like banks and government agencies that could get us into real trouble. We'd swipe a bunch of internal documents and dump them out on some public site. It was stuff even Wikileaks didn't want, because it didn't contain any useful information. We were just being dicks. Cred was the first one to get cold feet about it. And me...well, I can't say I had the best judgment in those days.

My problem has always been an obsessive persistence. I'm the kind of person who, if I see a piece of string on the sidewalk, I just start following it. If it goes through a wall, I find a way past the wall. I follow the string to the end, even if that's miles away, and when I get there, I'm done. There's no more mystery to solve, and I walk away.

But where I had only curiosity, Charlie had intent. Charlie would follow the string to see if it led to something he could take. If he couldn't reach the end, he'd dangle it in front of me, because he knew I couldn't rest until I figured it out. Compulsive curiosity and relentless persistence were the exploitable bugs in my nature, and Charlie took advantage of them when he could.

He was a brilliant social engineer. Cred said it best. "He'll get you to do things you wouldn't do on your own."

I think the guys at the FBI understood that too. That was part of the reason they let me go.

* * *

andrew diamond

At 3:00 p.m., I'm in Ethan's office, walking through the presentation I'll be giving at the developer conference on Friday. Brad, the project manager, is taking notes.

If we land either of the big contracts we've been chasing, we'll need to bring some new developers on board. My presentation, about a project we just launched, was designed to give us some cachet in the developer community, and maybe lure in a new programmer or two.

As I go through the slides, I start to get excited about the system we've built. I dive into the details of how we identified and fixed all the bottlenecks. Some of the solutions rely purely on good, solid coding and efficient algorithms. Others rely on the well-designed distributed architecture of the back end. It really is a thing of beauty.

It should take me about forty minutes to go through the slides. Brad is timing me. I'll have an hour at the conference, and Ethan wants the last twenty minutes to be open to questions from the floor.

I know the presentation is going well, because Brad is totally drawn in. As I reach the end, he stops the timer and says, "Forty-two minutes. You're right on target." He has a big smile on his face. When he's not worried, he loves his job.

Ethan, the owner, is not smiling. He leans back in his chair, measures me with a long stare, and finally says, "So what's it going to take, Russ?"

"What's what going to take?" I ask.

"What's it going to take to keep you on board?"

I don't have an answer for that. Has my restlessness these past few months been so apparent? Can everyone sense it? I look at Brad and see that he's uneasy. I look back at Ethan, and he's waiting for an answer.

I sigh and say, "I don't know, Ethan. I honestly don't know."

And then my phone chimes, and there's a text from Celia back in San Francisco asking if I've heard from Charlie. She sent me an email yesterday with the same question, and I realize now I haven't responded. So I type "No" and hit send. I don't have to say any more than that. She knows I don't talk to Charlie.

I wish she'd just get over him. The way he's been stringing her along all these years is disgraceful. She's his girl, his one and only, until she's not. Then he's off with some other woman and she's a crying, shaking wreck... who happens to produce a flurry of powerful, emotional paintings. And then when Charlie's done with his fling, she takes him back, and she's blissfully happy.

Some people—rational, intelligent people—are so damn stupid when it comes to love you just have to give up on them. All you can do is wait for them to come to their senses and try not to be too annoyed.

But I am annoyed, and I must look it, because Ethan asks what's wrong.

I tell him my lunch isn't sitting well and I need to use the bathroom.

Then I go around the corner and have a beer.

* * *

Someone's hand is on my shoulder. I turn from the TV, where the Nationals game has somehow reached the seventh inning, and Karim says, "Dude, what are you doing?"

"What?"

"How many pints have you had?"

"Three."

"Come back to work," he says. "Something's wrong with that code we deployed this morning."

3

IT TAKES ME TWO hours to figure out what's wrong, because I'm not really focusing. As it turns out, the problem isn't really in the code. The disk on one of the servers is full because we haven't been rotating the logs, and that makes the whole system slow as molasses. If we had a decent ops person or a system administrator, this would not have happened.

By 8:30, I have it all sorted out. I put my laptop into my shoulder bag, lock up the office, grab a quick dinner at the Thai place down the street, and stop by Tom's. He's playing *League of Legends* with Marty and Karim. We drink a couple of beers and smoke some really powerful weed that makes me feel slow and tired. When I leave there, a little after ten, I'm hearing echoes and feeling paranoid.

But outside, the air is moist and pleasant, and it feels really good to be stoned. Floating down the sidewalk, among the hydrangeas and fireflies, I catch little snippets of conversation drifting from the porches and balconies. I'm happy to be in Richmond, where life spills out of doors on these balmy summer evenings.

The blue and purple hydrangeas remind me to stop by Jamie's to water the flowers. That's a good long walk. But it's a beautiful evening, and I've shaken off the sluggishness I felt at Tom's. The last vestige of paranoia is this nagging feeling that the little guy with the funny mustache on the other side of the street is following me.

I ignore him. Sometime over the course of this twenty-minute walk, he'll turn off onto another street, and I'll forget he ever existed.

Summer nights in Richmond are almost tropical. The air is thick with a comforting moisture, and the chirping of the crickets, fast and loud, is an audible measure of the evening's warmth.

I close my eyes and pretend I've made it to Sámara, down on Costa Rica's Pacific side. The waves lap the shore in a soothing rhythm. The leaves of the palms rustle in the breeze overhead, and the air is thick with the perfume of salt and hibiscus. I'm stoned enough to continue the fantasy with my eyes wide open. My body glides down the street on autopilot while the rest of me is in Costa Rica.

Now I'm going up the stairs to the second floor of Jamie's building. Unlocking her door. Filling the black plastic watering can with the long, narrow spout. Crossing the big living room wearing the little green apron I found under the sink. I thought it would be funny to wear an apron while I watered the plants. It's such a domestic task. I should dress the part.

The flowers grow in planters on the windowsills. As I move from one lighted window to the next, the little man with the mustache watches from across the street, and a perverse little part of me feels vindicated. It says, *See, Russ. You're not paranoid. He really was following you.*

He's short and stocky with a dark, bushy mustache and curly black hair. If you put him in overalls and dropped a red cap on his head, he would look just like Mario from the old Nintendo games.

He turns and pretends to walk away, but he's obviously not going anywhere.

I look down at the flower I'm watering. With its tower of hanging purple blossoms, it's quite beautiful. Jamie has a dozen of them. What attracted her to these particular flowers? It must be the color. In daylight, they're halfway between light purple and her favorite pastel blue.

I rub the leaves between my thumb and index finger. What would Jamie say about that? "Don't do that, silly! Just water them."

andrew diamond

4

AT 10:45, I LEAVE Jamie's building. It's nine blocks back to my apartment, and Mario is still following me. I walk at my normal pace and he keeps a steady distance, about half a block back, on the other side of the street. He's talking quietly into the phone. I can't hear what he says.

Then, two blocks from my apartment, he disappears.

I round the corner toward my building, and the street is empty. Moths circle erratically in the orange halo beneath the street lamp in the middle of the block, and the neighborhood is silent except for the sound of crickets and far-away traffic and the thump-thump-thump of my shoulder bag as it bounces against my hip.

As I walk into the pool of light, I pull the keys from my pocket and turn to take one last look down the street. Nothing.

Then I turn forward again just in time to see the big guy with the fat shaved head skipping kind of sideways toward me with the two-by-four wound up behind him, ready to deliver the big blow. Picture a baseball batter running toward the pitch as he swings. I am the ball.

Time stops, and a number of thoughts go through my mind. He's wearing black pants and a black leather jacket, and it's way too hot for that. He's incredibly ugly, with rolls of fat on his bald head. His eyes are lost in shadow beneath a protruding brow. His size, his powerful build, and his ape-like brow make me think of Donkey Kong.

The blow is aimed at my stomach, and even though I'm stoned, my reflexes are surprisingly intact and my body recoils in anticipation. I bend at the waist, my head and shoulders going forward, so the target is moving away from the weapon.

Still, the two-by-four lands with more than enough force to knock the wind out of me. I crumple onto the pavement. Before I'm even down, he takes another swing. He might have been aiming for the back of my head, but I go down so fast, he winds up hitting me across the shoulder blades.

My face crashes into the pavement and hot blood gushes from my nose. I can't move or breathe. How badly am I hurt? There's no line between the fear and the pain.

My forehead scrapes the sidewalk as he lifts me by my belt and starts pulling stuff out of my pockets. He puts my phone and a little USB drive full of personal photos into his jacket. When he finds my wallet, he drops me, opens the wallet, and looks inside. Then he looks at my face and throws the wallet onto the sidewalk by my head. I'm just now able to get a breath.

He lifts me again by the belt with one hand, and I hang there like a rag doll. With his free hand, he grabs my shoulder bag and tries to pull it over my head. The strap catches around my left ear and chin. Instead of untangling it, he yanks the bag and wrenches my head around. It feels like he's ripping my ear off.

He drops me again and unzips the bag and looks inside. I guess he's satisfied with what he finds. It's a MacBook Pro, top of the line. Over two thousand dollars new, and easily worth twelve hundred on eBay. He puts the bag over his shoulder without closing the zipper.

Then he picks up his stick and he does something that really pisses me off. He has everything he wants, and for no good reason at all, he raises the two-by-four and brings it down hard across the back of my right leg. I don't know if you've ever taken a sharp blow to the hamstring, but let me tell you this: It really fucking hurts!

I'm not sure which I feel more, the pain or the anger. I watch helplessly as the big bald Neanderthal lumbers off into the dark with my stuff.

In a few minutes, I'll pick up my keys and limp back to my apartment, where I'll assess the damage.

But I don't want to get up just yet because, in addition to my bloody face and bruised muscles, I have a much bigger problem. The tingling in my right hand has moved up to my elbow, and I'm starting to feel sick. This isn't from the beating I just took. This started back at Jamie's.

I may have just done myself in. Tomorrow, I'll either wake up in pain or not at all.

andrew diamond

5

I WAKE UP AT 8:30 Friday morning. My abdominal muscles are bruised and sore. My hamstring is worse. I have to pee, but I'm afraid to move. I roll slowly onto my side, drop my feet to the floor, and push myself upright with my right arm.

As I cross the apartment, I'm pleasantly surprised that my stomach doesn't hurt as much as I had feared. The leg, though, is bad. I hobble into the bathroom and check my face in the mirror.

By the time I arrive at the office at 9:30, the ibuprofen has kicked in and the scrapes on my face are cleaned up, but I'm still limping, and my nose is swollen. Trish is talking on the phone and stops mid-sentence when she sees me.

"Oh my god! What happened?"

Karim and Marty and Tom and Brad all look up from their monitors.

"I got mugged."

They want to know the details. I tell them this big guy clocked me with a two-by-four and took all my stuff. A crude, strong-arm robbery. I don't tell them about Mario.

They ask what the robber looked like.

"Like the guy you root *against* in professional wrestling," I say. "Big and ugly and hairless. Like someone spilled Nair on Donkey Kong."

Trish wants to know why I didn't report it to the police. Mostly, it's because I don't like talking to cops when I'm stoned. But I tell her I was too traumatized and just wanted to go to sleep. Trish calls the police, and while we wait for them to come and take a report, everyone starts telling stories about how their brother or their uncle or their friend once got jumped.

After the cops interview me, Brad drives me to Best Buy to pick up a new MacBook. He asks if there was anything important on the stolen laptop. I tell him no. Some source code, but that's all on GitHub, so it's easy enough to get back.

"What about the presentation?" he asks.

"I was using Google slides, remember? It's all up in the cloud."

I can feel him relax as we turn into the sprawling parking lot.

But one thing about last night keeps bothering me. I don't want to think about it, but I can't *not* think about it. I need something to take my mind off that thought. I need to get back to work.

Apparently, I said that out loud.

"Yeah," says Brad as he pulls into an empty space by the big yellow Best Buy sign. "Work will take your mind off last night."

As we make our way to the back of the store, I run through the presentation in my head. I have the last slot of the day: 4:00 p.m. I want to touch up two slides, but there should be plenty of time for that.

We look at the MacBooks, and I decide I want an Air this time. The MacBook Pro is too heavy.

Brad catches a salesman and asks for an Air with 8 gigabytes of RAM. Then he says to me, "Don't worry too much about the presentation."

"I'm not worried about it."

He grins and says, "All you have to do is walk through it like you did yesterday, and I think we have a good chance to sign both contracts."

"You mean all I have to do is not fuck it up."

"Exactly. The recruiter has a bunch of candidates lined up for the new developer positions."

While Brad charges the new laptop on the company card, I browse through the mobile phones and choose a new Samsung Galaxy. I tell the sales rep my old phone was stolen, and she says she'll get my number transferred to the new one. Brad comes over just as she's ringing up the purchase.

When I take out my wallet to pay for it, Brad gives me a curious look. For a second, we just stare at each other. Then he says, "Why didn't he take your wallet?"

I don't know. Why didn't he take my wallet? Or the ninety-two dollars inside?

This is what I was trying not to think about. Something is wrong here.

6

I SPEND THE NEXT TWO hours back at the office installing developer tools on my new laptop. Git, Emacs, Clojure, Postgres, Elasticsearch. Then I'm about to start loading apps onto my phone, but the cheap plastic feel of the rear panel annoys me. I rip it off and look inside. More white plastic, and a battery. I pull the battery out, and what's underneath? More plastic. White, like the wheels that move the paper inside a laser printer, but it's even cheaper and flimsier.

My father helped design those cheap printer wheels when he worked in Palo Alto years ago. They wanted to replace as many metal parts as they could, to bring down costs. Dad was leading the team that was doing the work, but it wasn't going well. The stress tests showed that some parts would wear out before the warranty was up, and others wouldn't behave when the printers got too hot.

I remember coming home after the first day of high school, when Dad was sick from months of stress at work. He was in the kitchen, talking to his boss on the speaker phone, when I heard him say, "I'm not going to rush my team to push out a crappy product that's going to piss off our customers."

The stern, emotionless voice that came back through the speaker said, "Look, John, we gave you the numbers. We gave you the target date. *You* make it work."

My father started to argue, but the man cut him off with a final command. "Do your job!"

That was one of the few times I ever saw Dad upset. Later that evening, his hands and his voice were shaking when he showed me two gearshifts he had pulled off the bikes out back. One of the shifters was disassembled. The other was broken open.

"This is Campagnolo," he said, pointing to the disassembled shifter. "Built to last a lifetime. You can take it apart, replace what's worn, put it back together, and it's good as new.

"And this," he said, picking up the other one, "is what's taking over

impala   17

the market. It's mostly plastic. You can't disassemble it. If anything inside it breaks, you chuck the whole thing in the trash and buy a new one."

He pointed back to the Campy shifter and said, "In engineering school, we learned to build things like this. But now...Do you see what kind of world we're building here? What kind of world we're leaving you? It's a world where nothing can be repaired. It all has to be replaced."

Two weeks later, he was dead. After years of putting on weight at his little desk beneath the fluorescent office lights, he had his first and only heart attack in the company parking lot.

Things at home fell apart pretty quickly after that. Mom, in particular, started falling apart, and I started looking for a retreat. Pot worked okay, but it wasn't quite what I was looking for, and I didn't like having to be around a bunch of idiots to smoke it. Alcohol worked okay too, and if the people drinking around me were idiots, I didn't really care.

But the best escape of all was the computer. I had been programming since middle school, writing little games in Python, and poking at the hardware in C, but I had never really spent long hours at it. In high school, when everything at home went to hell, I buried myself in the machine. Here was a world utterly unlike the chaotic and unpredictable one we lived in. The rules were crystal clear, everything was logical and consistent, and I was in control. When I thought of something I wanted to create, I just had to describe it in a way the computer understood, and the machine would bring it to life. It was magical, watching those little universes of my own design blossom into being.

Programming kept my mind off the thoughts that kept bubbling up from the gaping hole at the center of our broken world: Why is it all so fragile? You remove one piece, and the world that once seemed so permanent barely held together. Was it really ever as solid as I imagined? Or is this appearance of order, this illusion of wholeness, just a thin veneer over a hopeless void waiting to swallow us all?

I tried to talk about this once with my mother, in the summer before sophomore year.

She was standing by the sink in the kitchen with a glass of wine, staring quietly out the window. I should have left her alone, because

andrew diamond

I knew we were thinking about the same thing. But I was stoned and caught up in my own thoughts, looking at things from an intellectual perspective instead of an emotional one. And the words didn't come out quite right.

"It's funny how things work," I said. "You remove one variable from the equation and—"

She turned on me fiercely and said, "Goddammit, Russ, the world isn't a fucking math equation! There is no fucking algorithm and there is no fucking answer! You do your best, no matter how bad you want to quit." Then she started sobbing.

She couldn't have chosen a more stinging response. Because at that time, when I was so intoxicated with technology and all its possibilities, I really did believe that our algorithms and what we built from them would change the world. I had invested the little bit of hope I had left into the orderly, predictable machine that had never let me down. But my optimism was no match for the power of her raw emotion, or the reality of the world that had wounded her.

A few weeks after that conversation, I read an article about SQL injection. That's a little trick hackers use to get a website to expose sensitive information. Most websites display data from databases, and if the website is poorly built, as many were back then, you can tack some extra database instructions onto the end of a URL, and the database will execute them.

For example, when you search for boots on a shopping site, the end of the URL might look like this:

```
?category=boots
```

That tells the web server to display a list of boots from the database. In a SQL injection attack, you add something like this to the end of the URL:

```
?category=boots&%27%3B%27select%20*%20from%20employees
```

That says, "Show me some boots, and while you're at it, dump out a list of all the company's employees." That was a simple attack that worked against only the most amateur of sites. I spent a few hours hunting around online for some of those sites. And I found them.

And that opened a door I wanted to step through.

Within a few months, I was performing much more sophisticated attacks against more sophisticated corporate sites. I did it in part out of curiosity, just to see how far I could get. But there was some malice in it too. My father was dead, and the whole world kept chugging along as if nothing had happened, and that made me angry. That was the archetype of all injustice: that what mattered more than anything didn't really matter at all in the end.

I wanted to pull back the veneer of all those shiny companies that had made it through the dot-com bust, just to prove that, underneath, they were weak and flawed, like us. Out of petulance and pettiness and spite, I wanted to show how so much of what we depend on in this world is fragile enough to be shattered by a single well-placed blow. I discovered it's really not that hard to take down a website. It's really not that hard to expose a company's secrets. And that bothered me even more.

I was offended by how easy it was to hack in to the big-name companies that commanded such respect throughout the Valley. I was offended by their sloppy programming and their disregard for their own safety.

How can you not plan for the obvious threats, I wondered, *when there are so many dangers you can never even anticipate? Why should I have any pity for you, if you won't even make an effort to protect yourself?*

I've never been able to dislodge from my heart the bitterness that took root all those years ago, and I've been of two minds ever since. Half of me wants to walk the narrow road of responsibility. To find the right woman, settle into a routine, and build the life my family should have had. And half of me wants to destroy everything. Because it's all so flawed. It's all so broken. Nothing can be repaired. It all has to be replaced.

* * *

At 3:15, Brad says it's time to go to the conference. The other developers have been there since noon. I put the pieces of my phone back together, and we get in Brad's car. On the drive over, Brad talks about the job candidates and says he wants me to go up to DC to do the technical interviews.

Just as we're parking at the hotel, I get a call from Cred back in San Francisco. We chat occasionally online, through a private IRC channel, but he only calls me once or twice a year. And never during the day.

"Hey, Cred."

"Hey, Genie. Who was that Spanish guy who answered your phone?"

"What Spanish guy?"

"I called a few hours ago and some guy answered in Spanish."

"I got jumped," I say. "They stole my phone."

"Oh, shit. You okay?"

"Yeah, I'm okay. What's up?"

"I found a new zero-day."

"In what?"

"The Windows JPEG library."

"No shit. Is it bad?"

"Really bad. Lets you execute code with full admin privileges. I'm going to send a proof of concept to Redmond in a few days."

A zero-day is an attack that exploits a previously unknown bug. It's a bug the software vendors have had exactly zero days to prepare for. Hackers sell these exploits on the black market, and the price varies, depending on how many computers are affected and how bad the vulnerability is.

Software vendors now pay "bug bounties" for zero-days. To get the bounty, you submit a description of the problem and a proof of concept—a POC—which is a short program that shows how to exploit the vulnerability. You agree not to tell anyone about it until the vendor has had sixty or ninety days to fix the problem. The bounties can be quite high for really dangerous bugs.

Cred works at Google, doing security research and analysis, which also happens to be his hobby. He says he found this zero-day on his own time, while playing with a Windows laptop over Memorial Day weekend.

He tells me the bounty will pay for his summer vacation. Then he says, "That's not really why I'm calling. I was wondering if you could give Celia a call. She's kind of beside herself."

I don't like talking to Celia when she's beside herself because that means listening to her dump out all her anxieties and neuroses. I just want to shake her and say, "Forget about Charlie! Move on!"

"What's wrong with Celia?" I ask. As if I don't know.

"Charlie's not talking to her. She says it's been like ten days."

I sigh. "Okay. I'll give her a call."

"Thanks, Russ. She listens to you."

"Does she?"

"Also," Cred adds, "she's driving me crazy."

That part I believe.

"I'll talk to her," I say.

I hang up and a minute later, I run into Trish in the lobby. She says, "You're not going to present looking like that, are you?"

"Looking like what?"

"Those scrapes," she says.

"What?" I ask defensively. "I cleaned them."

She sighs, pulls out a little compact, and says, "Close your eyes."

As she dabs the powder on my face, I feel like a politician being prepped for a TV appearance. When I open my eyes, she has this big smile on her face, like it's funny putting make-up on a guy. She says, "You want some lipstick?"

I don't answer that. I head into the banquet room where a hundred or so people in folding chairs sit facing the podium.

andrew diamond

7

WITH MY SLIDES PROJECTED on the screen behind me, I describe how we rewrote an existing system to scale to more than one hundred times its former capacity. I get animated as I dig into the details. I can see that my audience is interested and engaged. Some are taking notes on their laptops while others are looking directly at me.

I know most of these people. The tech community in Richmond is small enough that you tend to see the same faces again and again. But there's one guy sitting in the back I haven't seen before. He wears a suit and he has this bored, detached look that just rubs me the wrong way. He looks a lot like my dad's old boss. Probably in his late fifties, with the same deeply-lined, immobile face. I hear that voice again coming through the speakerphone: "Do your job!"

I look at the guy, and I think, *Why are you here, if you're so fucking bored?* He looks me up and down in an arrogant way and types some notes into his laptop. Everything about him annoys me.

I get through the slides in forty minutes, and then the questions flood in. This is a good sign. The first thing people want to know is why we chose to write the system in Clojure. I spend a few minutes praising the extraordinary elegance of that language.

As we approach the end of the hour, the last question comes from one of those complacent cubicle-dwellers you find in big corporate development teams. There's a certain type of programmer who doesn't want to learn anything new. He wants to be the guru of the old technology. The indispensible holder of the system's secrets. He is the opposite of what we hackers consider to be real programmers. Real programmers always want to learn.

The guy says, "Why did you use that wonky VTD XML parser?"

"Because it's the only one that parses fast enough to keep up with the load we have to handle."

"Yes," he says, with a slightly smug expression, "but then you can't use the Web Services Description Language to automatically generate the parser."

"That's right," I say, as I unplug my laptop from the projector. "You can't."

"So then," he says, as if he's got me now, as if he's going to expose me for a fool, "you have to parse the XML by hand?"

I shut down the slide presentation and behind it is my email window, and just at that moment, a new message comes in. It says, "For Sale - 1967 Chevy Impala - Cherry Red." My heart skips a beat. I stare at the message in silence for several seconds.

Suddenly, words I said four years ago are coming back to me, and I am full of regret. I worked hard to build this quiet life. And even though I'm not really sure I want to keep it, I've done my best to hold on for four years now.

And this...this is a mess I really don't need.

I click on the link in the email and there's the Craigslist ad with a photo of a cherry red 1967 Chevy Impala. The price is $26,000. The phone number has a 212 area code. That's New York.

I save the ad and the photo. I know they'll both disappear in a few minutes.

I hear a rustling and look up to see the audience staring expectantly. What are they waiting for? Right, there was a question. My heart jumps. Is my email window showing on the projector? The cable is unplugged, but I turn and check the screen, just to be sure. It's blank. I breathe a sigh of relief.

I look instinctively to the man in the suit and our eyes meet. The email has caught me off guard and I have the guilty look of a child caught stealing.

I turn my attention back to the developer who asked about the XML parser and I say, "Um. What was the question?"

This guy who was so smug a moment ago sees that I'm shaken, and he doesn't know what to make of my sudden change. He hesitates for a moment, then repeats his query with some uncertainty. "You have to

andrew diamond

parse the XML by hand?"

I respond absently, "Yeah. You have to parse the XML by hand." And then I add in a quiet voice, "That's our job, right? We write software." And I leave the podium.

The conference organizer takes my place at the mike and tells everyone where to go for food and drinks. Brad catches me near the front of the room and says, "You did great, man! You killed it!" Then he adds, "You got a little lost there on that last question, but everyone was thinking about beer by then anyway."

I glance at the back of the room, but the bored man in the suit has disappeared. I click again on the link in the email, but of course the ad and the photo are gone.

Before leaving the conference, I stop at the hotel desk and ask to borrow the phone for a call I don't want to make from my cell. I dial the number in the ad, 212-571-2404, hoping someone there really is selling a cherry red 1967 Chevy Impala.

A woman answers and says, "Bank of America. How may I help you today?"

"You can't." I hang up.

I promised Cred I'd call Celia, and now I regret that. How should I tell her? Best to just say it straight out. Charlie is dead.

8

WE SKIP THE CONFERENCE social hour and go back to the office to drop off our laptops. Brad wants to take us all out for shots, so we walk to the bar around the corner.

Brad orders a round of tequila and tells the team we're days from signing both of the contracts we were after. "In a few months," he says happily, "we'll be in a bigger office. Maybe with a pool table." After the second round of shots, Marty and Trish start telling college stories.

I order the third round. Trish and Marty pass, so I drink theirs. They're laughing about something, and when they quiet down, I say, "Do you know how they used to keep the locomotives from running away back in the old days, when the engineers used to get shot?"

Trish turns to me and says, "What?"

"The engineers. They used to get shot. You know, with the train robbers in the Wild West. Jesse James and those guys."

"What are you talking about?" Trish says. "We were talking about tailgate parties in college."

"They had a dead man's switch," I say. "It's a little pedal on the floor, and you have to keep your foot on it."

Marty says, "Hello! Earth to Russ: We were talking about football!"

Trish corrects him. "Tailgates!"

"Same thing," Marty says.

"The point is," I say, "when the pressure on the pedal goes away, it means the operator is no longer in control, and the whole system comes to a stop."

Tom laughs. "Dude! What the fuck are you talking about?"

"Because the system isn't smart enough to run itself. So it has this safeguard. If it can't detect the presence of the operator, it powers down and comes to a stop."

"Oooh-kaaay," says Marty. "And your point is?"

Brad says, "His point is, he wants another shot!"

That isn't really my point. My point, which I keep to myself, is that

Charlie set a dead man's switch on whatever system he was running, and when he didn't log in for ten days, the switch posted the ad on Craigslist. He set up a little bot somewhere that's probably been checking for that ad every five minutes for the past four years. The email came from the bot.

Four years ago, the night before I was leaving San Francisco, Charlie showed up at the bar where my friends were throwing my goodbye party, even though no one had invited him. He walked in with this surly bald-headed guy, and the two of them went straight to a corner table and sat drinking beer in front of an open laptop.

The rest of us were drinking and laughing and taking photos, while Charlie and his buddy were hacking NATO for all I know.

After the bald guy left, I told Charlie that his friend with the shaved head and scruffy beard and cold blue eyes looked like a white-supremacist prepper from backwoods Idaho. Charlie laughed and said, "Sixx? He's definitely not a white supremacist. But a prepper?" He thought for a moment and nodded. "I could see that."

At closing time, it was just Charlie and me at the bar, drunk as hell. He kept pushing me to join him in a new venture, and I kept refusing.

He said, "Come on, man, can I get you to say yes to anything?"

"Maybe another shot."

Charlie bought two shots of tequila as the bartender rang the bell for last call. We toasted and tossed them back, and Charlie said, "This is your last chance. I'm letting you in on the ground floor."

"No."

He let out a little sigh and said, "Okay, dude. But if I fuck it all up and I send you a message, will you read it?"

"Sure, Charlie. I'll read it."

He smiled and patted me on the back. "Russ, my man, that's all I wanted to hear." Then he told me to look out for a cherry red '67 Impala. "Make sure Celia has enough to get by," he said. "And then you can run the show."

"Whatever," I said, not understanding and not wanting to.

I forgot about this conversation until this afternoon, when it came back to me at the podium, in front of a crowd of people. And now, here I am, four years later, drinking the same silver Patron tequila and acting just as stupid.

By 7:30, everyone has left except me and Tom and Karim. We have one last beer before heading back out into the heat. Tom walks home, and Karim and I walk to the office to get our laptops.

andrew diamond

9

"SHIT!" I SAY AS we enter the building.

"What?" asks Karim.

"I forgot, I have to call someone in San Francisco. This is not the kind of call you make when you're drunk."

"Call him tomorrow," Karim says.

"Her," I say.

"Call her tomorrow."

Karim flips his laptop open and looks at Hacker News. I slide my new MacBook into my shoulder bag, ready to head home. The tequila is making me sleepy.

Karim says, "Who is Charlie Taylor?"

"What?" I'm surprised to hear the name of the person I keep thinking about, and paranoid thoughts go through my head. Is Karim reading my mind? Or have I been thinking out loud?

Karim, still staring at his screen, asks again, "Who the fuck is Charlie Taylor?"

"Hatter?"

Karim looks up. "You've heard of him?"

"Yeah. Why?"

"There's like four stories on Hacker News saying Charlie Taylor is dead."

10

FOR A WHILE, CHARLIE was on this kick of hacking into home computers. He'd get into someone's laptop and turn on the video camera, just to see the look of blank confusion when the user noticed the little green light next to the camera lens peering out at him. You could see the questions slowly unfold in their minds. *Why is my camera on?* Because Charlie turned it on. *How long has it been watching me?* Only Charlie knows. *Who is watching me?* Charlie is watching you.

Isn't that funny?

Not really. It's actually pretty fucking rude.

Most home computers are easy to break into, but every now and then you run across an impenetrable fortress that piques your interest. If someone's taking that much trouble to protect their machine, they must have something valuable in there, right? Or something they want to hide.

It took Charlie two full days to break into one guy's machine in Silver Spring, Maryland. Turns out, the guy was a system administrator, and a pretty good one at that.

This was back in April 2011. Charlie was sitting at the desk in my apartment, digging through this guy's system. Cred and I were drinking beer and smoking pot, making fun of an old sci-fi movie where a whistling sound preceded the arrival of the UFOs, and the robots had little banks of flashing lights on their chests.

After an hour or so, Charlie said, "Check this out." And he showed us a black terminal window with a list of files.

"What's that?" Cred asked.

"This guy in Maryland. He has full access."

"To what?" Cred asked.

"He's a sys admin for the FBI," Charlie said. "I'm in, with full admin privileges!"

"Not from my place," I said. "You're not hacking the feds from my Wi-Fi!"

"Relax, man," he said quietly. "It's all going through Tor."

Tor is The Onion Router, an opaque network of interconnected computers that allows you to do things online anonymously. You connect through an entry node, then your connection bounces through an unknown number of other computers and comes out an exit node thousands of miles away to reach your target. It's impossible to trace a Tor connection from the exit node back to you.

Tor is a product of the US Navy and DARPA, the Defense Advanced Research Projects Agency. The US government uses it for diplomatic and intelligence communications. Dissidents living under oppressive regimes use it to hide online activities they might be persecuted for. Every year, the State Department pours money into strengthening Tor, while the NSA puts its best minds to work trying to break it. Two departments of our government are locked in an arms race. So far, the State Department is winning, and we are the beneficiaries.

Charlie was on my computer until 2:00 a.m., poking around the FBI's network. A system like that has intrusion detection, audit logging, and tripwires everywhere. You don't poke around in there without someone finding out.

But whatever. I told myself they couldn't trace it to me. Thanks to Tor, I slept soundly that night.

But at 9:00 the next morning, someone knocked at my door. Softly at first. Then with a little more authority. When I answered, I saw four agents. The one in front said, "Can we come in, or do you want us to get a warrant?"

I said, "Come in."

They took my laptop and started combing through the apartment. One said, "We want your hard drives, SD cards, phones, cameras, anything with memory."

They didn't handcuff me on the ride downtown. The guy who asked for the hard drives said, "Thanks for making it easy." Then he held up a piece of paper and said, "We already had a warrant. But we weren't going to be dicks about it unless you were."

We walked down a white-walled corridor in the FBI building. Charlie was in the first room on the left. Cred was in the first room on the right.

In the conference room at the end of the hall, one of the agents told me they ran into a dead end at the Tor exit node, so they couldn't trace the attack back to me. But Charlie stole exactly three files from their system. The dossier on Charles Allen Taylor, a.k.a. Hatter, and the dossiers of William Barlow Wilson (Cred) and Russell Eugene Fitzpatrick (Genie).

What kind of person engineers a brilliant, untraceable hack and then incriminates himself by stealing his own file? Charlie fucking Taylor. The Mad Hatter. You don't run into many people like him, because nature has a way of taking care of them. People who do stupid things like that eventually remove themselves from the gene pool. Charlie was a Darwin Award waiting to happen.

I spent a couple of hours in an interview room answering questions about buffer overflows, SQL injection, DNS cache poisoning, and other types of attacks. When I asked for a lawyer, they told me this was only an interview. I wasn't being charged with anything.

At noon, two agents took me to lunch at a teriyaki place, and the questioning continued. Then we went back to the office, and they asked me who I knew and what kinds of projects certain people were working on. I got the sense they wanted to know if I'd be a useful informant.

When I finally left the building, a thick, cool mist was rolling in from the bay. Cred was standing on the steps out front, shivering. We looked at each other but didn't say a word until we got to a bar a few blocks away. I took a sip of my beer, and Cred let out a long sigh and said, "What the fuck?"

Charlie was still in the FBI building.

KARIM AND I READ the first Hacker News story together. Charlie's rental car went over a cliff in Colombia ten days ago. It burst into flames at the bottom of a ravine, and his body was charred to the bones. The authorities say the hole in the side of his skull was caused by a bullet. There were more than a dozen bullet holes in the side of the car.

Below the article is a flood of comments from the hacker community. Most of them along the lines of "the guy was brilliant" or "brilliant but misguided." One person wrote, "We loved you, Charlie, but we all knew you'd never make it to thirty. Intelligence without judgment is worthless. Sorry, Charlie."

I'm sorry too. No one should have to go like that. But then I think Charlie would have appreciated a quick, dramatic exit and four stories at the top of Hacker News. He always did have a certain flair. If he had the chance to script his own demise, he would have come up with something just like this.

Now that the news is out, I don't have to call Celia. That's one less thing to do before bed. Tomorrow, when I'm sober, I'll call Cred.

12

A WEEK AFTER MY FIRST interview back in 2011, the FBI asked me in for a second meeting. Two agents told me there was nothing incriminating on any of the devices they seized from my apartment.

"I could have told you that," I said.

One of the agents gave me a compliment. "You're quite thorough. Good job."

Then he showed me some photos that were posted that morning on 4chan and Reddit. Me walking into the FBI building. Me chatting with two agents in FBI jackets as we waited for a table at the teriyaki restaurant.

"What's all this?" I asked.

"Check the comments."

The comments said I'd become an FBI informant.

"What the fuck? *You* posted those photos. That was *you*."

He smiled and said, "You're tainted, Genie. No one's going to trust you now."

"Why would you do that? That's just wrong!"

He said, "You're hanging with the wrong crowd, and you're doing stupid shit."

Then the other agent added, "So we thought we'd give you a little nudge in the right direction."

"We like you, Russ," the first agent said. "You have a good head on your shoulders."

And the second one interjected again, "This is a good time for you to walk away. Before you do something stupid and fuck up your life. Stick to your day job. A Rails coder with your skills can make an honest living anywhere. And grow up, will you?"

I left there feeling relieved. Like I had been given permission to go out and live the life I wanted to live.

In my heart, I was sick of doing things I wouldn't want other people doing to me. I was sick of the guilt and anxiety, sick of sneaking around, habitually covering my tracks, even in matters that didn't need to be hidden.

And I didn't want to see Charlie anymore. I told myself I'd go somewhere far away and start all over. Some idyllic Sámara maybe, or perhaps just a sensible mid-sized city on the other side of the country.

13

TEN DAYS AFTER THE FBI first hauled him in, Charlie returned to San Francisco. He told us he'd been in Washington, DC, sitting in a room with the system administrator whose laptop he'd hacked into. They gave Charlie some systems to crack, and according to him, he cracked them all. As he walked them step by step though his exploits, his audience kept growing.

Then they showed him some systems that had been compromised and asked him to work backwards from the evidence to figure out how the intruder got in.

Charlie said, "There are some clever people out there exploiting stuff I hadn't even thought of."

We were sitting on a bench outside the botanical garden in Golden Gate Park on a Saturday afternoon, and Charlie was drinking a beer.

"Why did the FBI let you go?" I asked.

He took a swig from the bottle and said, "They don't want to prosecute me. Imagine that trial. Guy hacks into the FBI and steals his own file. How's that gonna look in the press?"

"So they just let you walk?"

"No. They want me to be a snitch."

"You gonna do it?"

"I'm not going to rat on anyone I know. But they have me watching these right-wingers who want to take down the power grid around Chicago. The FBI calls them domestic terrorists, but they're just a bunch of racist idiots.

"I'll tell you something, though," he said as he took another sip of beer. "If anyone ever does go after the grid, we're fucked. There are so many ways to take that thing down, I'm surprised it hasn't happened yet. I could black out Chicago in thirty minutes."

I laughed and said, "Charlie Taylor, Mister Responsible, is helping the FBI catch terrorists!"

"They're not terrorists," Charlie said. "Just a bunch of Nazi script kiddies who can't get a date. But the feds keep asking me about a bank heist too. Someone swiped a bunch of cash and left zero evidence of an intrusion."

"You have any idea what happened?"

"Oh, I know exactly what happened. And who did it. Sixx hacked a router in the bank's data center and set up a man-in-the-middle attack. Then he waited for the system administrator to log in from a machine that didn't know the server's SSH key. You know that message you get that shows the key's fingerprint and asks if you want to accept it? Well, who the hell reads that? The admin accepted the key. Sixx injected some commands into his session and transferred a bunch of cash to a money launderer named Mr. Greene. Then he deleted the man-in-the-middle app from the router and got away without a trace."

"How'd you figure that out?"

"We were chatting on IRC while he was doing it."

"You know Sixx? Nobody knows Sixx. He's a ghost."

Charlie shrugged.

I thought through the logistics of a man-in-the-middle attack. A hacker gains control of a computer between you and whatever remote server you're connecting to. As the communication flows through the machine that the hacker controls, he can read and even alter the messages going back and forth. That kind of attack is hard to pull off, because it changes the encryption key that the server uses to secure the communication. The administrator's computer would recognize the bogus key, cut the connection, and warn him of a possible man-in-the-middle attack. All computers do this. Unless you happen to be using a new computer that's never seen the server's encryption key before.

"Wait a minute," I said. "How did Sixx know the guy was going to login from a new machine? That's the only way the hack would work."

"He made sure the guy got a new machine."

"How?"

"He followed him to the PATH station in Hoboken. When the guy put his bag down to take off his raincoat, Sixx *accidentally* knocked it onto the tracks."

Charlie went on to explain one of his principles of successful hacking. I'd already heard this lecture a dozen times. "You can't leave an end-to-end electronic trail," he said. Some essential element of the hack has to happen outside of cyberspace, among humans, who are careless, forgetful, and unobservant.

This part of the hack, the social engineering component as Charlie liked to call it, should look insignificant and random. Like, for example, a laptop falling onto the train tracks. Or a for-sale ad for an old Chevy Impala.

Charlie always ended this little lecture with the paranoid mantra that Cred and I liked to tease him about. "There are no coincidences," he said. "Anytime a series of unlikely events produces a meaningful outcome, it's not a coincidence. It was meant to happen."

I'm not sure if that was his true worldview or just a statement about the way he worked.

"So, are you going to tell the FBI about Sixx?" I asked.

Charlie says, "Hell, no. That guy's a psycho."

Then he said, "Dude, I get how the feds work. Those guys are smart as hell, but they're stuck in this bureaucracy that slows them down. We can work around them with Tor, and Bitcoin, and virtual servers that we can spin up anywhere in the world. I know how we can make some damn good money." He threw his empty beer bottle into a bush.

"What the hell?" I said. "Put that in recycling."

"It'll decompose," he said.

"That's glass, asshole!"

"You gotta take the long view," Charlie said as he opened another beer. "In a million years, it'll turn back into sand and no one will know it was ever there."

"Yeah, but until then, everyone has to wonder why some dickhead is ruining their park." I picked up the bottle and put it in the recycling bin.

"What do you say, Russ? You want to make some money?"

"No."

"Yeah you do. You just don't know it." He took a sip of his beer. "As

andrew diamond

long as we keep moving, we'll always be three steps ahead of law enforcement."

"I don't want a life where I have to stay three steps ahead of law enforcement."

"What are you gonna do then? Write JavaScript for some start-up? Build Android apps? Dude, you're gonna be bored as hell. Because you're just as devious as me."

"No I'm not."

"Yes you are. The only difference between me and you," Charlie said, "is that I embrace my inner deviant, and you run from yours."

"I'm nothing like you, Charlie."

"You're exactly like me, and that's never going to change, however much you want it to. If you don't take a risk and challenge yourself, you're gonna get bored and go crazy. So, you want to hear my idea?"

"I'm not interested," I said. "I will never be interested." And I started to walk away.

Charlie said, "You can't say never. That implies that you know the future, and you don't."

I turned back and said, "I'm leaving. I'm going East and starting over. I'm done fucking around."

"What are you gonna do?" Charlie asked.

"Build a real life. Keep my nose clean."

Charlie said, "BOR-ING!" and took a swig of beer.

"When I'm thirty, I'll have a wife and kids. And you'll be dead."

I regret saying that now.

Charlie just shrugged and said, "At least I'm not running from life."

14

AFTER FIFTEEN MINUTES OF reading through Hacker News, Karim closes his laptop and says, "I'll see you Monday."

"Yeah. Have a good weekend."

"You too. You'll lock up?"

"I'll lock up," I say.

I watch him leave, and I wait a few minutes to be sure he won't be walking back in. There's a six-pack in the fridge. I carry it over to my desk and pop one open.

Mark Twain once said that good decisions come from experience, and experience comes from bad decisions. I can take that a step further and add that bad decisions come from alcohol.

I am drunk. I am about to make a bad decision. This will lead to an experience. Whether that experience will one day lead to good decisions, I don't know.

I open the photo of the Impala in an image editor called the GIMP. When the photo appears, I go straight to the application menu and click *Image Properties*.

I look for the EXIF data, which is automatically embedded in the photo by most cameras and phones, and will tell me where and when the photo was taken. But this photo has no EXIF data.

I click on the Comment tab to see if anyone has added a COM marker into the file and secretly embedded a message. Someone has done exactly that. This is what appears beneath the comment tab:

```
-----BEGIN RSA PRIVATE KEY-----
MIICXAIBAAKBgQDVZymCYEgwFpqoGvicGls6BQuolT7tRhUWxHkxsACPoVLN2tZ9
sTTBqLl5G5MY90kiHeoH7s+NmuJRDM3Qzsnanj+O2yqSO2Kd9HPF6ntc+TFk/VMp
uvJjc/OOwkQ7cIlv5BjATueGSWR//aPIvosel00HXcDOko9xhEosApjcaQIDAQAB
AoGAZVLnHZUzkUmaQwkTU6Mb/49XusKqLySgbL/6vOHO8mNpmn42a1WRNAY1kjAq
hqcbHUzQytVzzMtme481xdf5dKqCNgifUnlO3spkopW4msmOxlQCusf/aPhwbIFO
FdNeumPrvKYanlIhsayjkJSEHHvxq9FEVC1Ti3DR3kuulHUCQQD17D3HaWY6MlD4
rIylhGXEPSo4A4vDDKEViN6srDQ67D8A50sDJ/qDL6woEhdhduMzv5u0gAbpaVjj
SeoQvDgzAkEA3iXIsOunyHoe84GuUgcUBDqhCuLqTQM6is1tPJwXCvF/L9XDb/gl
zdMPKix7d77Ne9ZYxb4ZRmTeyCJmFN5s8wJAHUALHRPRP+zKKrnDRNCZlhy8T8tE
```

```
LV/sLPaJnbohwDxnRgE8r9RqfH4IGQAF3ebZIUeSCocLy2lnVClveKwadwJAerO2
CXrwvvwtMmUzyx0bwkY8A45Yylb5NAfJyYuR8rp3fQ1+mM8psNlea/YL8JVUXI2F
1RuuTEKVB0hwyCAfXwJBAOe3ZX79x18E1+9FZKhsDSPqmZmSHs61+tTWnS/ysHd9
gskB9YWbkOmiznnA2/MPoqBwUotrteXz5u4mi/x+Jco=
```
-----END RSA PRIVATE KEY-----

This is the private half of a 1024-bit RSA key pair. It will allow me to open a remote, encrypted SSH connection to some server out there in the Internet. But which server? I take another look at the advertisement. That number I called from the hotel…it's not a phone number. Put the dots in the right places, and it becomes an IP address. 212.57.124.4.

When it comes to sharing secrets, I prefer cryptography. If you use it correctly, it is very secure. Charlie uses cryptography when he must. But there's another way of sharing secrets called steganography, which is the practice of hiding information in places people wouldn't think to look.

A for-sale ad on Craigslist, for example. There's nothing to distinguish it from the millions of other ads that run every year. Why would anyone look in there for secrets?

They wouldn't. Unless they got drunk one night, a long time ago, and agreed to be the recipient of the message sent out by a dead man's switch.

I save the RSA key in a file called ~/.ssh/dont_do_this. The IP address 212.57.124.4 belongs to a server in Moscow. I type this command to initiate the connection:

```
ssh -i ~/.ssh/dont_do_this root@212.57.124.4
```

Then I see this message:

```
Enter passphrase for key '/Users/genie/.ssh/dont_do_this'.
```

What passphrase would Charlie have set? Well, since he set this up just for me, I type "genie." The connection opens up and I see this:

```
CentOS7 - GNU/Linux 3.10.0 x86_64

System information as of Fri Jun 24 23:59:12 UTC 2016
System load: 0.0   Memory usage: 5%   Processes: 63
```

```
Usage of /:  15.9% of 7.74GB   Swap usage: 0%  Users logged in: 0
Last login: Tue Jun 14 20:46:34 2016 from 152.201.7.3
```

I'm a little surprised by the login message. I wasn't expecting CentOS. The weakness of the encryption key also seems a little strange. 1024-bit keys are at least theoretically breakable, and most of the world has moved on to 2048 bits or stronger. It's not like Charlie to skimp on security. But I push these thoughts aside and explore the system.

The last login on this machine was on June 20th, a few hours before Charlie's car went over that cliff. That login came from 152.201.7.3, which is an IP address in Bogotá, Colombia. You can look it up on iplocation.net.

I run *netstat*, which shows me a list of open network connections. There is only one active connection, and it's me. But port 443 is also open, which means this machine is running a secure web server.

I look at the list of running processes. Nothing much going on there. Nothing of interest in the file system either. There are no external drives attached. This is a bare-bones server that's just sitting idle.

I pop open a second beer and start looking through the Apache web server logs, which are littered with the usual requests: web crawlers, log spammers, and WordPress hackers. Every entry has a 404 response code, which means the requested file does not exist.

Except one.

The one successful response was for an image called impala.jpg. The log says 9.1 megabytes were sent successfully. That's a very high-resolution photo for an ad. The timestamp on that request is 8:55 p.m. UTC, which is 4:55 p.m. Eastern Daylight Time. That was me, standing at the podium at the developers conference.

I look again through the file system, but the photo, impala.jpg, has been deleted. Probably right after I looked at it. By now, I'm into beer number three, and my vision is a little blurry.

I poke around a little more, and in the /usr/bin directory, I find a program called *deadman*. That's not part of the standard Linux system, and it was created just a few weeks ago. A recently installed custom program. Hmm...

andrew diamond

I type *deadman* at the command prompt, and I see this:

```
> Are you sure? [y/N]
```

Am I sure of what? It's hard to be sure of anything in this world. But the alcohol gives me a sense of confidence, and I think, "Sure, I'm sure." I type *Y*, and I see this:

```
> sending kill to load balancer
> sending kill to commerce-east-01
> sending kill to commerce-east-02
> sending kill to commerce-west-01
> sending kill to commerce-west-02
> vault has been spared
> deleting deadman
> deleting bash history
> check /usr/local/data/
```

What just happened? It looks like I shut down a bunch of servers somewhere. Then the program deleted itself and any traces that it was ever run. But what is *vault*, and why was it spared?

I check the /usr/local/data directory, and I see three dozen files: 01.dat, 02.dat, 03.dat, etc. I run the *file* command to see what type of files these are. *Unknown binary data.* They're encrypted. I don't like this.

Screw Charlie and his little game! I'm not going to play. I know better than to get involved in his mess, even when I'm drunk.

I cut the connection, close up the laptop, and put it in my shoulder bag. When I get home, I'll wipe this entire hard drive and re-install the operating system. The ad and the photo and the SSH key make the whole machine feel dirty.

I'm sorry you're dead, Charlie. But you had it coming. Everyone told you so.

Rest in peace.

15

I LOCK THE OFFICE DOOR on my way out, and as I stumble over a crack in the sidewalk, I realize I don't feel much like walking. It's muggy, and I'm drunk, and it's a long way to my apartment. Cool air drifts through the open door of a bar as I pass. I go in and sit on a stool. But I don't know anyone here, so I leave after two beers, and hello! What's this? Someone has left a bicycle in the middle of the sidewalk. A new blue bicycle, with a headlight and a taillight and a rack with a zippered nylon bag on top. Someone has been very careless!

I don't see anyone wearing a helmet around here. The owner of the bike must be inside somewhere. I flick up the kickstand, put my foot on the pedal, and fall over. A passing couple gives me a sideways glance. I get up and try again, and this time I get both feet on the pedals before I fall.

One more try! Start with a push. Yes! I'm moving now. A little more speed, and I have my balance. But then the buildings disappear, and I'm looking at the stars. The spinning rear wheel clicks beside my ear. I sit up. Who knew there was a mailbox there?

In a few minutes I'm back in the saddle, pedaling down an empty street. I can't keep a straight line, but I can keep the bike upright. The trick is to ride right in the middle of the street and to keep a decent pace. If I slow down, I'll go right over. If I get too close to the side of the road, I'll hit something.

As I round the corner onto my street, I see the red brake lights glowing on a little black Honda parked by the entrance to my building. Arms hang out the windows on both sides. They bend back inside. A puff of smoke blows out each window, and the arms extend again, the tips of the cigarettes glowing orange.

I'm still sore from my beating the other night, and I don't want any surprises. So I loop around into the alley and drop the bike by the little green dumpster next to the back door of my building.

The Honda turns into the far end of the alley and rolls quietly toward me with its headlights off. As I pull my keys from my pocket, the car stops twenty feet away, and two guys get out. They leave the engine running. Both of them are bigger than me. They wear dark clothing, and their hair is cut short, military-style. They flick their cigarettes to the ground as they approach. I remember now that I don't have a key to the back door. I never have.

I make bad decisions when I drink.

The one with the gun approaches more quickly and with a palpable intent. The taller one lags behind. I smile and say, "Is that a hybrid? It's very quiet." Always be polite when you first meet someone. It sets the tone for the whole relationship.

In one smooth, efficient motion, the guy with the gun grabs my right arm and twists it up behind my back. He spins me around, and now he's behind me, holding my wrist up between my shoulder blades as he presses the gun to the back of my head. He's breathing hard into my ear, like an angry bull.

I want him to calm down, so I say, "I was talking about the car."

He grunts and says with a Russian accent, "No talking, eh? Only shut up!" The adrenaline pumping through my veins is making me a little less drunk, but I'm still a long way from sober.

The second guy, the tall one without the gun, takes a moment to examine my shoulder bag. He unclips the strap at one end and gently slides it across my shoulder as he puts the bag up on top of the little dumpster and opens it up.

I'm glad he didn't hit me with a two-by-four. I'm glad he didn't wrench my head around or almost rip my ear off. I say, "You are very considerate." Continuing the thought, I think, *I wish all assailants were as thoughtful as you.*

I am being very quiet. The guy with the gun must be pleased. I want to say to him, "This is going pretty well, isn't it?"

I'm not really sobering up. I am very, very drunk.

The guy with the bag pulls the computer out and opens it up. The one behind me, still huffing in my ear, starts twisting my arm harder. He pushes the barrel of his gun into the back of my head and turns it like a

impala   45

screw, tearing my scalp. I'm starting to get angry.

The guy with the computer holds the laptop out to me and says, "Password."

I say, "It's *genie*, all lowercase."

He looks at me with an indifferent expression, then sets the computer on top of the dumpster and types in the password. He's in. Now he says, "Genie is weak password. Is bad security. Where is key?"

I'm about to tell him, "It's—" when his friend twists my arm a little harder, and I change my mind because I don't like people twisting my arm. So I say, "What key?" And the guy behind me gives me a kick.

The other guy shuts the laptop and takes a step closer and says, "Why do you hesitate? You have key?"

"I don't know what you're looking for. Just take the damn laptop." Then to the one behind me, I say, "Goddammit, stop twisting my arm!" I really have to pee.

The guy behind me doesn't like my outburst. He gives my arm another twist and says in a menacing snarl, "We check computer. If you have key, we kill you. If no key, we kill you."

I'm sorry, but when I see logic like this in someone's source code, it sends my blood pressure through the roof. Before I can stop myself, I blurt out, "That makes no fucking sense! If you're going to kill me either way, why not just do it now?"

I can see that the guy with the computer thinks this is a perfectly reasonable question. He looks at the guy with the gun as if he's waiting for a response. There's this awkward silence for a couple of seconds, and finally the computer guy says impatiently, "Answer him!"

The guy behind me cracks the butt of the gun straight down on the crown of my head, and says angrily, "No more question!" The blow sends a shock wave down my spine and my knees buckle. In the movies, when this happens, the guy who got hit goes unconscious. That's not what happens now. But I wish it had, because that really fucking hurt, and I'm actually starting to cry a little.

The computer guy puts my laptop back in the bag and carries it toward the car. He says something in Russian. The guy with the gun

andrew diamond

rams me face-first into the side of the building and gives me a hard kick in the back as I fall.

I feel helpless, violated, and angry. I can't let them leave me in this state of humiliation. When they open the car doors, I say, "I'm telling the FBI about this!" I realize I sound like a six-year-old.

The guy with the gun lets go of the door. He walks back to me with slow, deliberate steps, boot heels clomping against the pavement, sand grinding beneath his soles.

He stands over me and says, "What you say?"

"I said I'm telling the FBI."

He squats and puts his face near mine, and he smiles. His face is square, like an Easter Island statue, with deep lines going from the sides of his nose to the sides of his mouth. He says, "You tell FBI, Yuri says hello."

Then he laughs and I can hear a little rumble in his lungs from the cigarettes as he walks back to the car.

They drive slowly down the alley with the headlights off.

After they're gone, I find my keys, and I pick up the bike and wheel it around to the front of the building. There's no elevator, and as I go up the stairs to the second floor, I realize just how heavy this bike is.

I roll it right into the middle of my apartment and flick the kickstand down. And I say to myself, *Tonight wasn't a total loss. Yes, I lost another computer and got hit on the head, but I didn't get shot. And I didn't get hit with a two-by-four. And I got this awesome new bike!*

I want to call Jamie and tell her. What kind of bike is it?

I look at the letters painted on the frame, but they won't stay still. Something has me seeing double. Maybe it's the beer, or the tequila, or the blow to the head. I make a resolution. In the future, I will not get drunk and get my head smashed in. This is by far the best decision I have made since I started drinking today. But I know I'm going to forget it tomorrow. For a moment, I'm sad to think how many great ideas we conceive in drunkenness only to forget in sobriety.

But this is no time to be sad. I have a new bike. What kind of bike is it? My vision is clearing up. The white letters painted across the top of the frame say *Police*.

16

THE PHONE WAKES ME on Saturday morning at 8:30. It's Celia. I can't talk to her. I let it ring.

I'm on the unpleasant cusp between very drunk and very hung over. What the hell happened last night? This is not a normal hangover. Why does the top of my head hurt?

There's a bike in the middle of my apartment. Where did that come from?

Holy shit! It's the cops!

I sit up and look around. The room spins for a few seconds, and the crown of my head is throbbing. When I put my hand up there, I feel a hot, oozing crust.

Wait. The Russians! Why were they after me? Oh, the encryption key. They want to get into that server. I logged in to that server, didn't I? Why did I do that? Because I was drunk.

Something is different about this hangover. I have moments of clarity interrupted by waves of nausea and confusion. Maybe that blow to the head did more damage than I thought. The big bloodstain on my pillow is brown around the edges and dark red in the middle.

I turn away from the sunlit windows and put my feet on the floor, but I can't stand up just yet because I'm dizzy. After a minute, I'm up and fairly steady on my feet. I need to get rid of that bike.

Then there's a space of blank time and I'm no longer in my apartment. I trip on the second-to-last step in the stairwell and fall on top of the bike on the landing. The chain comes off, and my fingertips are covered with black grease from putting it back on.

I haul the bike out the front door and admire it once again in the golden morning sun. It really is a fine piece of machinery!

The flat streets of Richmond make for easy riding, and as I round the corner, I'm aware of nothing but the breeze in my hair. I'm enjoying the ride so much, I decide to continue on to the diner. I have a hangover craving for eggs and sausage and bacon and hash browns.

As I coast up to the diner, I see Trish and her boyfriend walking out. "Hey!" I yell. "Hey, Trish!"

They both look at me, and, *shit*! I'm going to run into them. I hit the brakes and turn to the right just as Trish jumps out of the way. I'm almost at a stop when my front wheel hits the base of a lamppost. I bump against the handlebars and fall over sideways, in slow motion.

In a second, I'm sitting up, and Trish is looking at me funny. She says, "Russ? Are you okay?"

"I'm fine," I say from the sidewalk. But I'm not, really. A sharp, cracking pain like lightening pulses through my head, and I keep having this feeling that I'm fading back into reality without any recollection of having faded out.

"Russ," she says. "Your head is bleeding."

I touch my fingers to the wound and examine the blood, which is diluted with a thin yellow ooze.

Trish looks at the bike, then back at me with an expression of concern. "Where did you get this bike?"

"I found it on the sidewalk," I say as I stand up. "Can you believe someone just left it there?"

I read the word *Police* on the frame, and I say, "A cop, no less! I'm surprised they're allowed to have bikes if they can't be bothered to lock them up. I guess this'll teach them."

Trish's boyfriend whispers something to her, and she says in a low voice, "I don't know. He got really drunk last night. We were talking about football, and he starts, like, talking about locomotives and Jesse James."

Trish says, "What happened to your head, Russ?"

"I got jumped."

"Again?"

"Yeah. Except this time, they had a gun."

"The same guy?"

"No," I say. "These were Russians. Not the Spanish guys from Nintendo. And the one who wasn't bashing me on the head was very thoughtful."

andrew diamond

"Are you still drunk?"

"I think so."

"You need to see a doctor, Russ. Your head shouldn't be oozing like that."

Trish takes my left arm and her boyfriend takes my right. As we walk to Trish's car, a police cruiser pulls up behind us and I hear the cop say, "Found it!"

I'm in the back of Trish's car. She drives, while her boyfriend looks out the window. Every now and then, they look back. No one is talking, so to keep from getting bored, I play a game with myself called *Where are we going?*

It takes some thought, but I'm able to solve the riddle again and again. Each time I solve it—and the answer, by the way, is "the hospital"—I forget, and then I get to play again.

When we pull up to the ER, I'm eager to break the silence. I lean forward and say, "Do you guys think this is where you'll have your baby?"

Trish hesitates for a moment, then says, "You know this is my brother, right?"

17

On Sunday morning, Celia calls again. This time, I answer. She doesn't sound hysterical. Just sad and tired.

"I suppose you've heard about Charlie," she says.

"It was all over Hacker News," I say.

Wait. Why am I in a hospital bed?

It sounds like she's holding back tears when she says, "We're having a memorial for him next Saturday, here in San Francisco. You'll come won't you?"

Oh, my head! I got stitches in the ER. And an X-ray. And an MRI. The doctor wanted to keep me overnight. Someone kept coming in and waking me in the dark.

And the Russians! A little shiver runs through me.

"Wait, what time is it?" I ask.

Celia says, "Five a.m. Eight your time."

"Why are you up so early on a Sunday?"

"Because I've been up all night, Russ. I'm heartbroken. What the fuck do you care why I'm up?"

I say, "Hey, uh...do you know what Charlie was doing when he died?"

"He was driving," Celia says.

"No, I mean, like, what kind of business was he in?"

There's a long silence, and finally Celia says, "I don't really know for sure, but even if I did, I don't think I'd want to say it over the phone." But something in her tone tells me she does want to say it. She wants to get this off her chest.

"He was really paranoid in the last few months," Celia says. "And I guess he had reason to be."

"Yeah, well, um, it's probably not a good time for me to come out."

"But I want you here, Russ! I know you two weren't close these last few years, but you once were. He once considered you his best friend."

This is news to me. "Really?"

"Yes, really. And he still talked about you that way, even to the end."

In the brief silence that follows this remark, I feel a sense of duty. This woman who considers herself Charlie's widow wants to bring his community together one last time to honor him and help her through his death.

"Sorry, Celia. It's not a good time." The dull background pain inside my skull occasionally pulses like hot lightning.

"Why not?" she asks angrily. "Is Charlie's death an inconvenience to you?"

Actually, yeah.

"Should he have scheduled it to coincide with your vacation?"

"No, it's just...I think some people are following me, and I don't want them following me out there. I don't want to drag you into all that."

"Do you mean the FBI?" Celia asks with impatience. "Or the Russians? Because they're already here. Or do you mean the Colombians?"

"Wait, I thought they were Mexican."

"I don't know what they are, but they trashed my apartment. They're looking for something. What a fucking mess Charlie left! I can't believe he did this to me!" And when she starts to cry, I see my mother in the kitchen, crying by the sink. I can't say no.

"All right," I say. "I'll be there. Just hold tight, okay?"

She sobs and says, "Thank you."

"I'll see you soon."

"Okay," she says. "Oh, and Russ?"

"Yeah?"

"Do you know what a dead man's switch is?"

I'm silent for several seconds, until finally she says, "Russ?"

"Yeah?"

"I think Charlie set a dead man's switch on whatever system he was running."

"Yeah?" I say slowly, and it's hard to push the next few words past the big lump in my throat. "What makes you say that?"

"Did you see Reddit yesterday? Or Twitter? Or Hacker News?"

"Yesterday? No."

"All the Twilight servers shut down on Friday night. They all went offline at once."

Oops.

"Take a look at Twitter when you get a chance. Hashtag twilightbazaar and hashtag hatter. The tweets overlap."

My head and back ache as I lay staring at the ceiling. Celia says, "Now do you see, Russ? Do you see what he was up to?"

The Twilight Bazaar is where people buy and sell heroine, cocaine, stolen credit card numbers, zero-days, and anything else they can't trade legally. All transactions are in Bitcoin. This online black market, I now realize, is the business idea Charlie was referring to that day in Golden Gate Park.

After the call, I check the comments on Twitter and Reddit. They're mostly jokes.

```
No more #twilightbazaar heroin delivery? What's the point of hav-
ing an internet if I have to buy this stuff on the street?
```

```
#hatter dies, #twilightbazaar disappears. Coincidence?
```

That one has some replies.

```
#hatter was the only one who could keep #twilightbazaar running
and avoid the feds.
```

```
@kr3bz0s: Ur idiot. Sixx could do it. Mad skillz and untraceable,
like a ghost. Feds worst nightmare.
```

On Reddit, the initial speculation was that Twilight was unreachable due to a denial of service attack. But after a few hours, people started speculating that someone took the whole thing down on purpose. One comment in particular has me thinking.

```
Sooo...you all know The Twilight Bazaar ran on an escrow model,
right? Whoever ran the site held the keys to the escrow account.
I have a feeling that not all the funds made it out of escrow.
That'll earn you a bullet to the head.
```

I had heard about the escrow model. A buyer wants drugs, and a seller has them available, but neither side trusts the other. So the buyer puts the money in escrow and Twilight tells the seller the funds are there. The seller makes the shipment, and when the buyer confirms he's received it, Twilight releases the funds, minus a little cut off the top.

That's a much nicer system than what's on the streets, with buyers and sellers ripping each other off and killing each other. Twilight is downright gentlemanly compared to that.

Maybe Charlie did steal the funds. He obviously made someone angry.

And I start thinking…If you were holding other people's bitcoins in escrow, where would you store them? Not on the same server that's running your site. Hackers would be after that. You'd hide them somewhere safe. In a vault. And when all the other servers self-destruct, you'd make sure the vault is spared.

I drift back to sleep.

18

THE NEUROLOGIST LETS ME go a little after noon on Sunday, and Brad drives me back to my apartment. He says, "Tomorrow, you're going to talk to the police."

When I get home, I book a ticket to San Francisco on my phone, which takes close to half an hour. My eyes don't want to focus, and my head still isn't clear. It's hard to compare the departure times, the layovers, and the costs. Finally, I just pick a flight that gets me in Friday afternoon and returns the next day. I don't want to be there any longer than I have to.

I spend the afternoon sleeping and Trish stops by at 6:00 p.m. with a couple of Cokes.

She says, "You haven't called Jamie since you dropped her off in New York."

I think back through the days. "Huh! You're right."

"I told her you got jumped. I told her about the concussion. That you were in the hospital."

She watches me uncomfortably, as if I'm supposed to say something. I just drink my Coke and wait for her to go on.

"Has she called you?"

"Nope."

She takes a breath, as if she's going to say something, but then she stops and folds her arms across her chest. After a few seconds of silence, she finally says, "You need to call her, Russ."

"Why?"

"What do you mean, why? She's your girlfriend, and you haven't talked to her in four days."

I shrug, and she gives me this look, like, *What the hell?* Then I see a spark of understanding in her eyes, and she says, "Oh. I thought it was just her."

"You thought what was just her?"

"That it was just her who was drifting. But...how have you guys been?"

"Oh, you know Jamie. Every day is rainbows."

"Seriously, Russ."

"Seriously. That's how she is."

Trish takes a deep breath and says, "Call her, will you? She's been hanging out with this guy, and I don't like where it's going."

"What guy?"

"She met him at the retreat. Rod. From the way she talks, it sounds like they're inseparable."

She sees from my look what I'm about to ask. Her hand darts forward to my shoulder and she says, "No! No. It hasn't got that far. I'm pretty sure she would have told me."

"Okay, Trish. I'll give her a call."

At 8:00 p.m., I go to Jamie's and take the mail upstairs. Her building is freezing. That's always the first thing I notice when I walk in. Half of Richmond is so over–air-conditioned in the summer, you need a sweater or a jacket just to go inside.

The floor of the corridor is covered in white dust, from the dry-wallers in the apartment across the hall. The door is half open, and their conversation echoes in the empty rooms. I close Jamie's door behind me and drop the mail onto the table. I think about her as I water the flowers.

You can see the essence of our relationship in our Sunday breakfast conversations. She talks and talks and talks, while I read the news online, not listening. Then I start reflecting on an interesting story and my mind moves outward in ever-broadening circles from the particulars of the story to the really big questions: *What are we doing? Why are we here? How should we live?*

Jamie says, "A penny for your thoughts."

I say, "Do you think there's any point to this life?"

And she gets frustrated and says, "Why do you waste your time with questions like that? Come back to earth, Russ. Focus on what's in front of you."

"But I am focused on what's in front of me," I say. "That's where all my questions come from. And they all lead back to that one."

Every time she tries to stomp down my wandering mind, she tells me how much she cares for me. Maybe she thinks she's saving me from myself.

I could see the difference in our temperaments the day we met. But it was her simplicity and cheerfulness that attracted me. She was this big shiny helium balloon that just couldn't be pulled down. Not even by me.

When I'm done with the flowers, I put the watering can away and call her. Since Trish filled her in on my recent dramas, I don't have to go too far into that.

Jamie tells me about her new boots, but her voice is uneasy. Something is on her mind, but she has to get out all the chatter first. So I settle in while she rambles on about the new concepts she's learning. The workshop is all about "potentializing" and "actualizing," which, as far as I can tell, means setting and achieving goals.

Finally, she starts moving toward the heart of the matter. "Do you remember two weeks ago? When we were invited to that party?"

"Yeah."

"And you wound up staying home because you wanted to finish that book?"

"That was a really good book!"

"That's not the point," she says. "The point is, everyone was going to be drinking and dancing. And you wanted to read a book. A book, for Pete's sake!"

This conversation is going in exactly the right direction. I decide to cut right to the chase.

"Trish tells me you have a new friend."

She lets out a little gasp, followed by a pause. "Um, what did Trish tell you?"

"Just that you're hanging out with some guy at the workshop. A lot."

She says cautiously, "That's right."

"What's his name? Dick or something?"

"Rod."

"Whatever. He sounds like a tool."

Jamie says, "See, Russ. There's that negative attitude. That's what

andrew diamond

holds you back. That's why you're stuck writing software instead of doing sales. Do you know Rod started as a sales rep a year and a half ago, and he spent six months potentializing a BMW in his mind, and then he actualized one! And it wasn't the little 3 series. He went right for the 535! Because he thinks *that big*!"

"Have you reached down his pants yet? Maybe he really is *that big*."

"Russell Fitzpatrick! What has gotten into you?"

"He just sounds so perfect," I say. "And you guys are up there all alone in that big hotel."

"Okay, since you're being so glib about it, I'm just going to tell you straight out. We're through, Russ. You and me. We're done."

I pump my fist in the air and say a silent "Yes!"

"Russ? Hello?"

"Yeah, I'm here. To tell you the truth, I was kind of on the same page. I mean, you've been really good to me, but I don't think we have a future."

"Oh, I can't tell you what a relief it is to hear that!"

We're both quiet for a moment, and then she says in a tentative voice, "Can I say something?"

"Go for it."

"And this is for your own good, Russ. I'm not doing this to be mean, so take it as constructive criticism."

"Okay."

"Well, Rod is like a BMW 5 series, power everything, leather seats and sunroof. And you're like...Well, I hate to put it so bluntly, but... you're like a book. One of those huge books that has so many words, it just makes your heart sink. Like F. Scott Hemingway, or *Who Killed the Mockingbird*, or one of those stories no one would ever read if their teachers didn't make them."

"Wow!"

"You know I would never say anything to hurt you, and that's not what this is about."

"No, no. I get it. I'm just amazed. It sounds like you're really getting to know yourself up there."

"I am, Russ. And I wish you were here, because I think it would really help you. But here's where I'm going with all this. What do you potentialize for yourself over the next four years?"

This question stops my brain cold.

"Russ?"

"Yeah. I, um…You know, I ask myself that question a lot. But…I have no idea. I don't know what I want or where I'm going."

"Oh, Russ!" There's that sweetness in her voice. "You need to fix that. Because you will never actualize anything until you potentialize it first."

"You're right. You are absolutely right."

"Listen, when I get back, we can talk through some of this stuff. Maybe I can help you figure out what you want. But I want to stay up here an extra week so Rod and I can…"

She trails off uncertainly, and I finish her sentence. "Get to know each other?"

She lets out the breath she's been holding and says nervously, "Yes."

"You want to potentialize your new relationship?"

"Don't make fun of me, Russ. This is hard."

"Oh, you two should just actualize it right now. You know, I really appreciate your honesty. This is the most real conversation we've ever had."

"Isn't it great? I wish you were here at the workshop, honey. It's, like, this real *all day!*"

andrew diamond

19

ON MONDAY, I GET up around noon, feeling fresh and well rested. Brad picks me up and we go out for lunch before heading over to the FBI office on East Parham Road.

"I thought we were going to the police," I say.

Brad says, "Come on, Russ. First you get robbed by a gang of Argentines."

"They're Mexicans!" I say. "And they're from Panama."

"Whatever. They were only after your computer. And then you get mugged by Russians, who are also only after your computer. Obviously, this is a case of mistaken identity."

He pulls into an empty parking spot. "A guy from the FBI came by the office this morning. He said they wanted to talk to you."

Just inside the glass doors at the building's entrance, I see the guy in the suit from the developer conference. He leans against the wall, watching us approach like he's been expecting us. He has the same bored, arrogant expression, and it still makes me want to punch him in the face.

A few minutes later, I'm in a little conference room with him and an agent named Steinmetz while Brad sits out in a waiting area.

Steinmetz is efficient and businesslike, but still friendly, asking simple, straightforward questions.

"Are you, or were you, personally acquainted with Charles Allen Taylor?"

"I was."

"When was the last time you saw him?"

"Four years ago, at a bar in San Francisco."

"When was the last time you talked to him?"

"Four years ago. Same night."

"And there's been no communication between you two since then? No email? No chat?"

"No," I say. "We have not communicated."

Steinmetz looks over at his stone-faced friend, who is sitting to my right with his laptop open, as if he's there to take notes. Except he hasn't typed a thing since the interview began. He also hasn't introduced himself. He just sits there staring at me.

Steinmetz says to him, "That right?"

"That checks out."

I say, "Wait, are you guys still snooping on me after all these years?"

Stone Face finally speaks to me. "We've been watching Charlie, when we can. He's a slippery guy. We have no record of him contacting you."

Steinmetz says, "Do you know what Charlie was doing when he died?"

"He was driving," I say.

"No, what was he doing online?"

"I don't know."

"Have you heard of The Twilight Bazaar?" Steinmetz asks.

"I've heard of it."

"Describe the Colombians," he says.

"What Colombians?"

"The ones who took your computer last week."

I look over at Stone Face, who hasn't spoken again, and I say, "You know, when you sit there just staring at the person right next to you, it starts to get kind of rude."

No response.

So I say, in a slightly obnoxious tone, "What's your name?"

"Special Agent Jack Hayes."

"Special Agent?" I say in a mocking tone. "Your first name is Special Agent?"

Steinmetz says, "Let's stick to business. The faster we get through this, the sooner you can leave."

I describe the Colombians and the Russians. I tell them what was on the two stolen computers, which is to say, nothing of interest to anyone except my employer.

"Do you still talk to Cred?" Steinmetz asks.

"Once in a while."

"How? Phone? Email?"

"Through IRC. We chat a few times a year."

"Why do you use an encrypted channel?"

How do they know this?

"Because that's where Cred hangs out," I say. "He's a security analyst. You know that, right? He's legit."

"Yeah, we know. What did you talk about with Celia?"

"Fuck! How do you know I talked to Celia? Are you recording my calls?"

Jack continues to stare at me, and I want to put my fist into his face.

"We're not recording anything," Steinmetz says. "We pulled your call logs from Verizon with a warrant related to the Twilight investigation. We're just doing our job."

"Are you putting Cred and Celia through this bullshit too?"

Steinmetz folds his hands and explains patiently, "We're interviewing people known to have associated with Charlie. Did Celia tell you her apartment was broken into?"

He gives me a pointed look and adds, "Charlie left a big mess. We're trying to make sure innocent people like Celia don't get hurt."

I relax a little bit, and as the questions continue, my mind wanders back to that server I was looking at the other night. Again, I wonder why Charlie chose a weak 1024-bit encryption key.

Steinmetz asks if I know of any particular black hats that Charlie associated with.

"You mean criminals?"

"Yeah."

I say, "Come on, it's been four years since I talked to the guy."

Jack Hayes says, "That's not an answer. Do you or don't you?"

Actually, I do know. But the fact that Jack asked the question—and the rude way he asked it—makes me not want to respond. I decide this piece of information isn't relevant to their investigation.

"No."

The other thing that bothers me about that server is the operating system. When Charlie had to use Linux, he chose CentOS because it's stable and secure. But when he was doing meaningful work, he always used OpenBSD, the operating system of the truly paranoid. It's the only one that was written from the ground up for security. Charlie wanted to make it hard for other Charlies to intrude upon his realm.

Jack Hayes says, "Are you sure? You went from not knowing to 'No' pretty quickly."

"If I remember anything, I'll let you know."

Charlie's server must be a ruse. The little clues he left—the weak encryption key and his second-choice operating system—are only clues to someone who knows him well. An investigator would overlook them, just as all but one person in the world would overlook that Impala ad.

After twenty more minutes of questions, Steinmetz says, "Thank you very much, Mr. Fitzpatrick. If we have any further questions, we'll be in touch."

He gives me his card and stands to leave. Ricardo Steinmetz. I picture him eating bratwurst tacos. Jack Hayes gets up and throws his card onto the table.

I stand and put both cards into my pocket as Steinmetz leaves. I start to walk out without saying goodbye to Hayes, but he grabs my arm and pushes me down into a chair. Then he shuts the door and turns his laptop to me and says, "What's this?"

I stare for a second, blinking stupidly, and then I say, "That's a 1967 Chevy Impala. It says so right there. Is there anything else you want me to read for you?"

This is the first time I've really looked at the photo. When I saw it at the developer conference, I was too stunned to examine it. The next time I was drunk, and I looked at the data hidden inside instead of the image itself.

I don't want Hayes to see me stare, but in the second my eyes are on the photo I notice some details I'd overlooked before. The car is parked at the curbside, on the wrong side of the street. A woman is walking by, to the right, with her back to the camera.

The car is polished to a brilliant shine, but there's a garbage bag in front of it, which seems out of place in a for-sale photo.

andrew diamond

As I stand again, Hayes looks at me with that stony, impassive face and says, "Genie, you're in more trouble than you know."

"And you're a fucking dick," I say.

"I can help you out of this."

"Fuck off."

When I leave the room, I see Steinmetz down the hall talking to another agent. He shrugs and says, "Nothing really. Four more to talk to. Two in the East, two in the Bay Area."

When he sees me, he says, "I'll walk you back up front. Your friend is waiting."

Brad is talking to a young woman in the waiting room. I think he's hitting on her. When he sees me, he looks up at the clock and says, "Half an hour? That wasn't bad."

Special Agent Hayes comes into the waiting area, and he and Steinmetz walk us to the front of the building. As we leave, Steinmetz says, "If you have any more information, don't hesitate to reach out. We'd like to wrap this up sooner rather than later."

As he says this, I'm already turning away. But I pause as I recall another little detail from that server the other night. This one is bad, and it has me a little scared, because it confirms my instinctive distrust of Jack Hayes. I know I shouldn't tip my hand, but I hate that arrogant dickhead cop, and I want to crack his smug façade. So I turn and I say, "Oh, yeah. There is one other thing."

"What's that?" Steinmetz asks.

I look Jack Hayes right in the eye, and I say, "Yuri says hello."

Steinmetz looks to Hayes with this expression that says, *What's that supposed to mean?*

Hayes is staring back at me, and finally I see a little emotion in that face. A tinge of anger piercing the cold indifference.

As we drive away, I think, *I shouldn't have said that.* I could have walked away with the upper hand. I really do have to practice more restraint.

Brad says, "Back to your place?"

"Best Buy," I say. "I need a cheap Windows laptop."

"Windows?"

"Yeah. That's what Hayes is running."

20

THAT NIGHT, I FIND Cred on IRC. I ask him through an encrypted channel to send me an explanation of his Windows exploit, along with the proof of concept.

```
Cred: Getting back in the game?
Genie: Just curious.
Cred: Curiosity killed the cat.
Genie: Do you remember Whisper?
Cred: Yeah.
Genie: Any idea where the source code went?
Cred: Probably still in the old BitBucket repo. What are you up
to?
Genie: Nothing.
Cred: Bullshit.
Genie: It's a white-hat job, I swear.
Cred: There are no white hats. We're all just shifting shades of
gray.
Genie: Sounds like a song.
Cred: Seriously, what are you up to?
Genie: Just taking back something that was taken from me.
Cred: I have a bad feeling about this.
Genie: Me too.
```

I'm burning with desire. Charlie has dangled this thread in front of me, and I have to know where it goes. The server is a red herring. The thirty-six encrypted files were meant to keep someone busy. The real clue is in the photo, which I must have back. Nine megabytes is too big of an image for a simple for-sale ad. Charlie wanted that high resolution for a reason.

Cred sends me his write-up and the proof of concept for the Windows exploit. This bug lets you slip executable code into memory and then run it with full administrator privileges.

After a brief search, I find the Whisper source code languishing on BitBucket. Charlie, Cred, and I hacked this together years ago, when we were trying to resurrect an ancient network protocol that predated the hardware of today's Internet.

By the time I find the code, I don't have the mental energy to review it.

My discharge papers from the hospital say the aftereffects of concussion may include headache, moodiness, restlessness, irritability, and difficulty reasoning. I've been having those symptoms for months.

At 1:00 a.m., I'm past the point of fruitful work. This is one of those nights where I'll fall asleep as soon as my head hits the pillow.

21

On Tuesday morning at 8:00, I call Brad to say I won't be coming to work. Then I hunker down and focus on reviving the Whisper code. It takes about twelve hours to get a solid build that will pass all my tests. After I have it running on the PC, I read through Cred's proof of concept, which shows exactly where in the JPEG image file to inject my data, and the magic sequence of bytes that will trigger the bug.

I leave the apartment only twice: once in the morning to get coffee, and once at lunch to pick up a pizza that I'll finish cold for dinner. This is an old-fashioned hackathon. Charlie, Cred, and I used to do this all the time. It feels good to be back at it.

I spend an hour fiddling with compiler options to reduce the program size. By 8:00 p.m., I'm able to slip my little program into a photo and test it out. I download the free versions of McAfee, Norton, and Kaspersky anti-virus software. If I've done this right, my image won't trip the virus scanners.

None of the anti-virus programs pick it up. Cred was right. This is a bad bug.

At 9:00, I download the Android Native Development Kit and start working on the other half of my hack. By 11:00, I'm wiped out and I go back to sleep.

22

I awake on Wednesday and check my phone. No one from the office has called. So I call Brad, who is up in DC with Karim interviewing developers.

"I don't know if I'll make it in today," I say. "I'm still not feeling so hot." And that's not a lie. My head hurts, and I feel slightly hungover, even though I didn't drink anything last night.

Brad says, "Don't sweat it. There's not much going on anyway."

I spend the next eight hours building and testing Whisper on my phone. It runs, but my integration tests reveal bugs in both the Windows and Android code. By the time I have those fixed, it's almost midnight, and my head is pounding.

The last thing I need to do doesn't require much mental energy. I log in to the old Flickr account I haven't touched in years, and in memory of Charlie, I upload a dozen photos. Charlie and me. Charlie and Cred. Charlie, me, Cred, and Celia.

And then the one with my poison payload: a picture I took in a bar four years ago at my going-away party. It shows Charlie sitting in front of a laptop at a table strewn with empty beer bottles. Beside him is the elusive black-hat whose real name no one knows. In his rare appearances online, he goes by Sixx. This will be the second known photo of him, and it's sure to be of interest to a great number of people that these two ever met.

Sorry to drag you into this, Sixx, but I didn't ask to be a part of it either. Still, you'd be proud to know I used your face for this brilliant piece of social engineering.

andrew diamond

23

On Thursday morning, as expected, I get a call from Agent Steinmetz.

"I saw you posted some photos in memory of Charlie."

"Yeah."

"There's one we want to talk to you about. Do you have a few minutes?"

"How about if I stop by this afternoon?"

"Why don't you make it around four? Then Hayes will have time to come down from DC."

That's what I was hoping to hear.

When I get to the FBI building, Steinmetz leads me to a conference room in the basement. Jack Hayes is already there, sitting at the table with his laptop. He is listening to an agent with a bulletproof vest and a German Shepherd tell a story about the training exercise they just completed. The dog is still panting from the heat. He makes me uneasy, but I'm not sure why.

"I'm going to change," says the guy in the vest. "You want to hold him till I get back?"

Steinmetz says, "Sure."

The guy leaves, the dog stays, and Steinmetz shuts the door.

I take a seat next to Jack, who says, "Quite a gallery you posted last night."

"Old friends," I say.

Steinmetz takes a seat to my left, and the panting dog stretches out beside him to absorb the cool of the linoleum floor. I take out my cell phone and when I look at the screen, Jack says, "You expecting a call?"

"No."

"There's no reception down here."

I lay the phone on the table and Steinmetz says, "We just want to verify the identity of some of the people in these photos."

"Okay."

Jack turns his computer to me, and there's my Flickr page with all the photos. I glance at my phone. Nothing.

"This is Charlie?" Steinmetz asks, pointing to the first photo.

"That's him," I say.

"And this is Celia?"

"Yeah."

"She's Charlie's girlfriend?"

"On and off for the last six years." The LED light around the main button on my phone pulses red. Now we're on! And immediately, the dog stops panting and sits up at full attention. *Shit!* This is why I was uneasy.

"Who's this?" Steinmetz asks.

"That's Cred. I thought you were already talking to him."

"Just checking," Steinmetz says.

"Why don't we cut to the chase," Jack says as the dog stands and cocks his head from side to side.

Jack clicks on the photo of Charlie and Sixx and says, "Tell us about this guy."

The dog moves toward the table and starts to whine. My armpits are sweating and so are my palms. When I wipe them on my pants, Jack says, "You nervous?"

"Dogs make me nervous." Actually, this isn't true. I like dogs. Just not this one right now.

Steinmetz pulls the dog back and tells him to sit.

"Who's this?" Jack asks.

"He goes by Sixx," I say, and Jack shoots Steinmetz a look. "I don't know his real name."

"When was this photo taken?" Jack asks.

"Four years ago."

The dog keeps interrupting his panting to cock his head and listen, and I keep glancing at him from the corner of my eye. I'm starting to think I made a mistake. I should have left this alone. I should not have come here.

Jack looks at the sweat beading up on my brow and says, "You feeling okay, Genie?" I can see his mind working.

Steinmetz says, "Did Charlie and Sixx hang out a lot?"

I rock forward and rub my sweaty hands on my jeans. There's no clock in here. That photo of the car is pretty big, and with the primitive networking protocol I'm using, it might take ten minutes or more to copy. I need to stall.

"Hey, um. Can I get some water?" No, I need to ask for something that will take a little longer to get. "Actually, a Mountain Dew."

Jack looks at Steinmetz, who starts fishing through his pocket for change.

"I'll be right back," Steinmetz says.

This whole idea, what I'm doing now, came from an article that Charlie showed us a few months before our first run-in with the FBI. A security researcher at an anti-virus company was disassembling a particularly nasty virus. He had it quarantined to a single laptop inside a safe room that Wi-Fi and cell signals couldn't penetrate. He even took the extra precaution of physically removing the network and Bluetooth radios from the infected laptop, so the virus couldn't spread.

A computer that has no way of connecting to any network is called an "air-gapped" machine. So the guy is in a safe room, picking apart the virus on the air-gapped machine and writing notes on his regular laptop.

The next day, he finds that his regular laptop is infected. He assumes the virus came in through his home network. He removes it, and just to be safe, he shuts off all the network interfaces on his laptop before returning to work.

As he digs into the air-gapped machine again, he finds the second part of the virus. In addition to the piece he has been studying—the payload, with its malicious code—he finds a separate piece with some sophisticated low-level assembly code that scans the computer's hardware. He's not sure what this code does, but when he takes a break, he finds his regular laptop has been infected yet again, despite being air-gapped itself.

That's when he has the a-ha moment. The second piece of the virus is its transport mechanism, and it's been running on both laptops, undetected, for some time. The virus on the air-gapped machine emits ultrasound through the speakers to transfer its malicious payload to his work laptop. His work laptop picks up the ultrasonic instructions through its microphone and gets infected.

This was all happening right in front of him, and he never knew. For a hacker, the big bonus of ultrasound networking is that, because it doesn't go through any routers, none of the traffic is logged. So there's no evidence that any communication ever occurred.

When Charlie and Cred and I read about this, we were blown away. We did a little research and learned that some software developers back in the 1960s had built sound-based networks inside their lab.

We spent a few weeks hacking together our own ultrasound program called Whisper, which we thought was pretty cool at the time. But we had no practical use for it, so we forgot about it.

Today, I've found Whisper's ideal use case. I'm in with my target, and my code has been running on his machine since he opened the photo of Charlie and Sixx, which was probably hours ago. Before I even got here, my program searched his hard drive and found the file called impala.jpg, and the HTML page that references it. Since then, the program has been waiting for me to show up. It knows I'm here because its microphone picked up the little ultrasonic hellos from my cell phone.

The problem is, the dog hears the hellos too, and he's trying to tell us something's going on. His little whimpers are starting to irritate Jack. When Steinmetz returns with my Mountain Dew, Hayes says, "Where's Fred? This dog has to take a shit or something."

"I'll get him," Steinmetz says.

Steinmetz leaves. Jack relaxes back into his stone-faced stare and says, "Tell me about Sixx."

The room is quiet for a second, and then the fan on his laptop kicks in. That shouldn't happen when a computer is idling. It means the CPU is working hard. I glance at Jack to see if he notices that his machine is behaving oddly. But I can't read his face.

"I know nothing about the guy," I say.

"Where was this photo taken?"

"In San Francisco. At a bar. At my going-away party."

Jack says, "It was taken on an Android phone at a bar in San

andrew diamond

Francisco called Salobreña on May 30, 2011. It's tagged in the metadata."

Shit! How far has he looked into this JPEG file?

"Well, if you knew that," I say, "why'd you ask?"

"I like to hear you talk."

I glance at the phone on the table, and Jack follows my eyes. The dog whines as I rub my palms on my jeans. Then I open the Mountain Dew and take a sip.

"Who invited Sixx?"

"No one," I say. "He showed up with Charlie. Charlie wasn't invited either."

"What did they talk about?"

"I don't know."

Jack takes a deep breath through his nose, then exhales loudly and says, "Do you have any reason to believe that these two may have done work together, or formed any kind of partnership?"

"I have no idea. That's the only time I ever saw the guy. And that's the last time I saw or talked to Charlie."

From the corner of my eye, I see the little LED light on my phone emit three green pulses. That's the signal that the transfer is complete. The dog quiets down. I relax. Jack quietly observes the change in my demeanor. He also saw the green light pulse.

Without taking his eyes off me, he picks up my phone and says, "You couldn't have gotten a text. There's no reception down here." He hits the button and the screen lights up. "Zero bars. No signal." Then he says, "You don't use a passcode?"

"No."

"Anyone who finds your phone can see all your information."

"I have nothing to hide," I say. "I don't care what anyone sees."

For a second, it looks like he's going to swipe the screen and start digging through the phone. But instead, he presses it against his palm and holds it there for a second. Then he hands the phone to me. "Why don't you put that away?"

As I slide the phone into my pocket, I feel how hot it is. My Whisper program uses a lot of processing power, and that warms up the whole

impala

device. An idle phone should never be this hot. That's why Hayes pressed it into his hand. He knows something's up.

Steinmetz is back at the door with the dog's handler, who has exchanged his uniform and bulletproof vest for civilian clothes. He takes the German shepherd.

Jack says, "So you met this guy once, and you didn't talk to him, and you've had no contact with him or Charlie for four years?"

"Right."

"You could have told us that over the phone. What was the point of coming down here?"

"I didn't know what you were going to ask," I say. "Is there anything else you want to know?"

"Not really."

"So we're done?"

"I'm done," Jack says. "Are you?"

I don't like the way he says that, or the way he measures me with his stare.

I say, "I'd like to get going if you don't mind."

Jack nods to Steinmetz, who says, "I'll walk you out."

Steinmetz walks ahead of me, and as soon as he is out the door, Jack says quietly, "It's not too late to make a deal, Russ."

"I'm not an informant," I say. "And I don't have any information anyway."

Hayes shakes his head. "That's not what I'm talking about."

"Then I don't know what you're talking about."

I turn and leave.

24

I PICK UP A SIX-PACK on the way home, against doctor's orders. When I get to my apartment, I boot the Windows laptop from a USB stick that runs the Tails operating system. Tails is a secure version of Linux that provides anonymous Internet access through Tor.

I copy the image I just stole from my phone to the computer, extract the RSA key and try to connect again to that server I logged into last Friday. This is what I see:

```
Permission denied (publickey).
```

Someone has changed the key on the server and locked me out. Of course. They want privacy while they dig around in there.

Then I take some time to study the photo. It's a front view of a cherry red 1967 Chevy Impala parked with the driver side toward the curb, on a street lined with shops. The three small trees along the sidewalk in the background are just beginning to bud. It's springtime, and a woman in a light-colored sweater is walking by.

Because of the angle, I can't read any of the signs painted along the storefronts. The store at the end of the block may be a pharmacy. Above one entrance midway down the block, I can see the spiraling red and white stripes of a barber's pole.

Why is that garbage bag in front of the car? If you're trying to sell a car, wouldn't you want to move that before you took the photo? The garbage bag obscures most of the license plate. I can see the first four red letters of the state, "Cali", but not the actual license number. Is the garbage bag there to hide the plate number? Or is it a clue?

Charlie used to say, "Anyone can hack you from anywhere. Put your important information where a computer can't reach it or can't understand it." He also used to say, "Computers don't get low tech. That's their weakness."

A computer doesn't know to ask why the car is red, or why there's a barber pole in the photo. It doesn't know that in the context of a for-sale

impala   77

ad, a garbage bag is out of place, or that a for-sale photo doesn't need nine megabytes of resolution.

Another thing strikes me. Charlie and I had more than one conversation about the importance of storing encryption keys outside of the computer. But we never had these conversations around Cred or anyone else. Was this a secret between us? Was Charlie grooming me for this task? Maybe I'm just overthinking this.

The most interesting element of the photo is the woman walking to the right of the car. She wears a long white sweater that goes down to her knee. Her left arm and right leg are extended in mid-stride. Her back is to the camera, and her straight brown hair is tied in a half ponytail.

The only part of her face that is visible is the edge of her left cheek. When I zoom in, I see the flesh along the cheekbone is pushed up, as if she's smiling. Perhaps the photographer just said something to amuse her. I zoom in further. Her skin is smooth. This woman is young. And the white sweater is not entirely white. It has tiny flecks of color throughout.

The woman was turning away from the camera when the photo was taken. I know this because she wears a Navajo-style silver eagle earring in her left ear, and the little bits of silver that would normally dangle from the bottom of the eagle's wings swing out to the side.

I imagine she is beautiful, and I feel a pang of longing for this creature frozen in the moment of departure.

Then I look out my window, and I see the little black Honda parked across the street. The Russians sit inside, smoking. The flashing lights on my wireless router show a flurry of activity as alerts appear on my monitor reporting blocked attempts to access a number of ports on my computer. The Russians have hacked into my Wi-Fi network and are trying to get into my laptop.

I open another beer. I'd like to go out somewhere, but I lock the door instead. This is one part of the hacking life I really don't like: hiding, wondering who's after you, living on the defensive. *Better get used to it,* I tell myself, *because I know that I can't let go of that thread Charlie dangled in front of me.*

andrew diamond

For the next hour or so, I watch the router lights flash. The Russians are being very crude about their work, and the alerts continue to pile up.

Finally, they drive away.

I drift to sleep and dream of the woman in the photo.

25

FRIDAY IS QUIET. A big line of thunderstorms swept through in the middle of the night, bringing in fresh, dry air. It's twenty degrees cooler than it's been. I open the windows for the first time in weeks, and it seems like everyone in Richmond is out walking beneath the drifting cotton-puff clouds.

I call Brad and tell him I'm going to San Francisco for a memorial service. Then I log into IRC and find Cred. It's 7:00 a.m. in California.

```
Genie: You ever see Wisp these days?
Cred: Ha! Haven't seen that guy in years. But I hear he's still
around.
Genie: Still doing what he used to do?
Cred: Um...what's going on?
Genie: Not sure.
Cred: First the zero day, and now you want Wisp?
Genie: Can't hurt to have some ID.
Cred: You coming out here?
Genie: Yeah. Today. And Wisp?
Cred: He's around. He might be at Charlie's memorial. Keep me out
of whatever you're doing.
```

On the way to the airport, I stop by the bank and take out five thousand dollars. The Russians have me on edge. I keep looking over my shoulder, and the fact that no one's there just makes me more paranoid. If I knew who was following me and where they were, I wouldn't have to keep guessing.

At the airport, I send the envelope full of cash through TSA's X-ray machine in the same bin as my wallet, shoes, and phone. No one says a word about it.

Just as the plane is about to board, Cred texts me a link to a reporter's blog. This guy has been investigating The Twilight Bazaar and a couple of similar sites for an upcoming book. The article lays out the details I already know: Twilight includes product photos, ratings, buyer and seller reviews, and everything else you'd expect from an online retailer.

The article notes that most transactions on these sites are small, in the hundreds or low thousands of dollars. The drug cartels don't sell through Twilight, because they already have an infrastructure built on trusted face-to-face connections. And it's one thing to send half an ounce of blow through the mail, quite another to send half a ton.

The last section of the article mentions how Twilight began to set itself apart from the other black market sites by becoming "the ATM of the dark web," converting Bitcoin into cash with quick turn-around, delivering anywhere in the world.

In the last few weeks, there's been some chatter on IRC and in the Dark Web forums about two big players, "the heavyweights," pushing more and more Bitcoin through the system to get cash out the other end. The article speculates that they're international criminal organizations, and that they each had a number of transactions pending in the days before the system went down.

One paragraph near the end of the article sends a chill down my spine:

The Twilight Bazaar has been operating for years in plain view. No government has been able to stop it, and now, the mobs and cartels who may have been using it as an online bank find themselves in the same position as law enforcement. Who do you go after when you want justice?

I'm shaking and sweating when the gate agent takes my boarding pass. In the gangway, I feel claustrophobic as I scan the line of passengers, looking for the Russians and South Americans. The heavyweights, out to recover their money. Jack Hayes's words come back to me all at once. "You're in more trouble than you know, Genie. It's not too late to make a deal."

For a moment, I think of turning and running through the terminal, all the way back to East Parham Road.

"Tell me what to do, Jack. Just tell me, and I'll do it!"

I can see the smug look on his face. I can hear the note of triumph in his voice and his arrogant, condescending words. "I knew you'd come running back!"

impala   81

"Fuck you, asshole!" I shout aloud.

The guy in front of me spins around and something in his hard, angry face tells me he's used to dealing with people who talk to him like that. Before I can stop myself, I say, "Are you a cop?"

He looks me up and down, as if to see if I'm a criminal, and he says, "Yeah."

Part of me wants to hold his hand; I'm so fucking scared right now. He sees me shaking, and I say, "Sorry. My meds haven't kicked in yet. And... and...Tourette's!"

He doesn't buy it. But he doesn't want to be bothered with me either. He turns his back and walks onto the plane.

andrew diamond

26

AFTER A BRIEF LAYOVER in Chicago, we land in San Francisco around 4:00 p.m. An hour later, I'm walking out of the BART station at 16th and Mission. I forgot how cold San Francisco can be in the summer. Coming from Richmond, it feels downright frigid. I also forgot how filthy this part of town is.

I walk over to Wisp's place on the edge of the Mission, but he's not in. I catch a young woman on her way out of the building and ask if Wisp still lives there. "Skinny guy," I say. "Pale skin, with long blonde hair."

"Oh yeah," she says. "He doesn't get out much. But I saw him a week or so ago."

Now it's 5:30. I should go by Celia's. She told me she'd be home.

I get an Uber over to Alamo Square Park and walk up Grove Street, arriving at Celia's a few minutes after 6:00. She has the second floor of a row house. A young woman who I've never met before lets me in, and I discover this is one of those old San Francisco houses that looks skinny from the street but extends back and back and back. Even with seven of us in the living room, it doesn't feel crowded. Celia is sitting on the couch, wearing a black sweater and leggings, playing the role of widow, graciously receiving condolences from the guests.

"Russ!" She stands and hugs me.

"Hey, Celia."

"I'm so glad you made it."

"How are you holding up?"

"Good," she says, with a smile and a little tear in her eye.

In the center of the living room, two low green couches and two cushioned chairs surround a coffee table of dark brown wood. Three bottles of wine sit uncorked on the table beside a number of glasses.

I don't know any of these people. They're all women. They must be friends that Celia has picked up over the last four years.

The room is strewn with sculpture, masks, instruments, paintings, and drawings, in that casual West Coast way that I prefer. In an East

Coast living room, these items would be carefully arranged like artifacts in a museum, each the precious centerpiece of its own inviolable little space.

Celia introduces me to her friends and asks if I'd like some wine. One of the women pours me a glass of red.

Celia and I sit on the couch, while two women browse the artwork, and she gives a little narrative of the pieces they linger on. Then she turns to me and says, "I'm going to have to give all this up soon. I can't afford it, now that Charlie's gone."

"He didn't leave you anything?"

She waves toward a sculpture and says, "Some art. And a criminal investigation."

I feel pity for her as Charlie's words come back to me. *Make sure Celia has enough to get by.*

"He didn't leave anything from…whatever he was doing?" I ask.

"No. And I wouldn't take it. That money is tainted."

She lowers her voice and says, "He was drinking a lot in the last year. The last few weeks especially. He used to be able to hold his liquor, but that changed. And he started getting strange."

"Like how?"

"Like, he was always hiding things. His keys. His wallet. My wallet! He'd lie about pointless little things, like whether he went to the drug store or not. And he was paranoid when we went out. We'd be in a restaurant, and he wouldn't even look at me. He'd scan the other tables, checking to see if people were watching him. I thought maybe he got roped in by the FBI again. Remember when they forced him to be an informant?"

"Whatever happened with that?"

"Six months of hell. He was irritable all the time. He hated being a snitch, even against those radical wackos. And he was frustrated at how stupid they were. He basically had to show them how to knock the power plants offline, because they weren't smart enough to figure it out. The FBI arrested them before they could launch their attack, and they all pled guilty because Charlie had gathered so much evidence. He never even had to testify."

"You ever think he would have been better off if he did testify? Then no one would have trusted him again."

Celia says, "I've thought of it often. He would have had to go straight and make an honest living."

"Ha! Could you imagine that? Charlie the security consultant?"

She gives me a sharp look and says, "Why's that so funny? Cred did it."

"Yeah, but Cred's a nerd. Could you really see Charlie sitting in a cubicle answering to some manager with half his intelligence? Could you see Charlie answering to anyone?"

A sour expression comes over her face. I suppose these aren't the right things for me to be saying just now. She's quiet for a moment, watching her guests, but I can tell her mind is elsewhere.

"I'm cooperating with the FBI," she says. "I never wanted to think about where his money came from. I never wanted to ask. Did you see the storm on Reddit and Twitter after Twilight shut down?"

"I did."

"It hurts to lose your ignorance," she says, sipping her wine. "Especially when you've worked so hard to maintain it." She has the faintest hint of a slur in her speech.

She drifts off into thought again, and when one of the other women starts talking to her, I get up and examine the artwork. The sculptures and masks are African. The paintings come from all different traditions. Some of the cruder works might even have come from garage sales.

I pick up an instrument that looks like a primitive black ukulele and pretend I'm fascinated by it because this whole scene is uncomfortable and I don't want to talk to anyone. Celia is halfway across the room behind me, on the couch, describing the day she came home to find her apartment ransacked. "That! On top of everything else!" She sobs quietly on someone's shoulder. I can't make out her muffled words.

I strum a few notes on the ukulele, hoping someone I know will arrive. Instead, I get sucked into conversation with some woman whose name I forget as soon as she says it.

She works at a restaurant, but she's really a sculptor, and if America could just get past the antiquated conventions of representation-al art, everyone would recognize she's at the forefront of her own self-absorption. She's cute, and a little on the chubby side, which makes her even cuter, but she's talking about all these artists and musicians from the local scene that I've never heard of. Four years ago, I would have known some of the names. It's pretty obvious from my responses that I'm not following what she's saying, but she just keeps talking.

At some point, I let out an audible sigh, and she shuts right up and gives me this offended look. "Oh, am I boring you? I'm sorry."

She doesn't wait for me to respond. She just turns and walks away.

I continue browsing, wondering how soon I can leave without seeming rude. Another woman arrives, and Celia and the group welcome her. In a few minutes, they're all gathered around the couch, telling funny stories about Charlie and laughing.

On a table in the corner is one of Charlie's giant sketchbooks. He used to carry them out to some art studio in Oakland to draw nudes.

I open up the pad and flip slowly through the pages. The models are all women, drawn hastily in charcoal with no shading and little detail. But he has all the lines right. He understands the planes of the body, and the perspective and proportions are correct even when the models are reclining.

Seven or eight pages in, I find a woman drawn in pencil, in great detail, with full three-dimensional shading. She's nude, sitting with her right leg pulled up against her breast. She has a heart-shaped face, and she looks out at me with lids half-closed over big clear eyes. She's young, maybe twenty-five, with full lips that show no particular emotion. Her hair is tied back, with a few stray wisps framing her face.

On the next page is another pencil drawing of her. Again she is nude. She sits at the foot of a four-poster bed with one missing post. Her feet are on the floor, her hands are on her knees, and she looks out at me with cool, sleepy eyes. There is a hint of satisfaction in her smile. Some-one has just made love to her.

Celia startles me when she says, "She's pretty, isn't she?"

"She's beautiful."

"You notice how much time Charlie spent drawing her compared to the other women?"

"Yeah."

Celia takes a sip of her wine and says, "He called her his muse. Which was kind of a joke, because her name is Calliope."

I turn the page, and there she is again, sitting upright on the floor. She is broad-shouldered, with the strong, athletic build of a gymnast.

"You know, the muse, Calliope, from Greek mythology?" Celia says. "But no one calls her that."

The model's head is turned to the right. She has the high, round cheek of the woman striding by the Impala in the photo.

"She goes by Cali," Celia says. "C-A-L-I."

And she's wearing the same Navajo eagle earring, with the bits of silver dangling from the wings.

Cali. Charlie put her name right in the front of the photo. Right there on the license plate. The first four letters of California are the only legible text in the picture.

"Will she be at the memorial service?" I ask.

Celia hears the excitement in my voice and asks in a mocking tone, "Are you in love with her already, Russ?"

When I turn to look at her, her face has a cold, unfriendly expression, and she says, "She knows not to show up there."

I turn my eyes back to the drawing.

27

THE MEMORIAL SERVICE STARTS at 10:30 a.m. on Saturday, at a bar near the baseball stadium. More than a hundred people show up. I'm there with my backpack, so I can head straight to the airport for a 2:00 p.m. flight.

Celia gives a rambling speech about Charlie the caring boyfriend, though she acknowledges that their life together wasn't all roses. She tells us what a well-rounded person he was. The artist and the software engineer who was interested in everything and could take orders from no one. She tells a few stories, and then invites everyone to share their thoughts and memories.

From the stories people tell, it seems Charlie got around quite a bit. Everyone knew him in a different context. I don't hear many women sharing memories, probably because their stories aren't appropriate for Celia's grieving ears.

I scan the crowd for Wisp, but he's not here. I see a few old friends from the developer community, and Cred is standing by Celia on the far side of the room. After the public reminiscence is over, the beer and wine start to flow, and the place gets noisy. This is what Charlie would have wanted.

I'm at the bar when Cred sneaks up and puts his hand on my shoulder. When I turn to greet him, he's smiling. He gives me a quick bro-hug and says, "You look exactly the same, man! Exactly the same."

I get him a beer and say, "You've put on a few pounds."

He pats his stomach and says, "Google keeps us well fed. Did the FBI talk to you?"

"Yeah. You?"

"Yeah, but I talk to them all the time anyway. My team consults with them on forensics and emerging exploits. They're the ones who helped me get the job at Google in the first place. Remember that big shitstorm Charlie got us into when he stole our files?"

"I remember."

"Fuck, I was pissed! That has to be the stupidest thing anyone has ever done."

"He liked to provoke people," I say. "Just to see what would happen."

"Yeah, fucking dumb-ass." Cred raises his glass for a toast and says, "To Charlie!"

"To Charlie!"

He takes a sip, and I swig down half my glass.

"Hey, you know..." Cred looks over his shoulder, then lowers his voice and says, "a couple of guys I know are helping the FBI with forensics on this whole Twilight thing."

"Yeah?"

"No one knows for sure whether it was Charlie, but all signs point that way." Cred takes a sip of beer and says, "That whole system was really well thought out. There was a load balancer in Iceland. The FBI actually located it right before it all went dark. It was routing traffic to application servers in Europe and Asia. Each application server had a backup, so if one went down, the load balancer would just route everything to the other one. Hey, what happened to your face?"

"What?"

"You have some scratches on your face."

"Oh, that's from when I got jumped."

"You ever find out who did it?"

"No."

"Anyway," Cred says, "the FBI found the load balancer, but before they could get their hands on it, a kill signal came in from some other server, and the system wiped itself out. All the application servers went down at once. And they had dedicated solid-state drives with ATA Enhanced Secure Erase, so good luck recovering that shit."

"How do you know all that?"

"Because the FBI has the hardware back in DC. They pulled the servers from data centers in three different countries. This guy Jack Hayes is running the investigation."

"That dude's a dick."

Cred laughs. "He's not the most personable guy. I talked to him for about an hour when he was out here. I think he talked to Celia too. I probably shouldn't be telling you this. We're not exactly suspects, but we're... what's that term they use? Persons of interest."

"Jack seems to think I have some big secret."

"Do you?"

I shrug. Cred lets out a little chuckle and says, "Yeah, right. You're the one who ran all the way across the country just to keep his nose clean." He gives me a pat on the shoulder and says, "It's good to see you again, man! How long are you here?"

"For another half hour or so."

"That's it?"

"That's it," I say. "Is Wisp around?"

Cred gives me a serious look and says, "Come on, Russ. What do you want from him?"

"I told you, I need some ID."

"You running from something?"

"I might be soon." I put my beer down and point to the scratches on my face. "You should have seen these when I got them." Then I tilt my head forward and point to the stitches in my scalp and say, "This came from the butt of a gun."

When I straighten up, I see a look of concern on Cred's face.

"I don't like getting beat up or pistol whipped," I say. Suddenly, all this emotion creeps up on me, and there's a little break in my voice. "I don't give a shit about my job, and my girlfriend left me for some other guy. Why should I stick around? I can code anywhere."

Cred says, "Sorry, man. I'm sorry to hear all that." He pauses for a second, then says, "Where do you think you'll go?"

I almost say Costa Rica, because the idea's been stuck in my head for so many years. But I don't want to let that little bit of information out. Charlie was the only other person who knew about Costa Rica, and now that he's dead, the secret is all mine. So I just shrug and say I don't know.

Cred gives me a long, probing stare, and says, "Russ, Jack Hayes has asked me about you three times now. You got jumped twice, and then you asked me for a zero-day exploit and the Whisper code. What are you up to?"

"Nothing!"

My response is a little too quick and emphatic, and I can tell Cred isn't buying it. He says, "I hope it's nothing, Russ, because I'm a bad liar, and he keeps asking me questions."

He drains the rest of his beer in one long swig and says, "I'll let you in on another little bit of information."

He leans in and lowers his voice. "The kill signal that took down Twilight came from a server in Russia. The FBI found the key to that server and they copied down the whole hard drive, including thirty-six encrypted files. I know the guy who's heading up the decryption effort."

He slides his empty beer glass onto the bar and says, "He cracked the files yesterday morning. You know what was in them?"

"Porn," I say.

Cred cocks his head and gives me a funny look and says, "How did you know that?"

"I didn't. I just figured that's the kind of joke Charlie would pull."

"But how did you know the files would be a joke?"

"I don't know," I say. "That's just what Charlie would do."

"It is," says Cred. "But it's funny you knew that right off the bat. And it's funny you're so sure it was Charlie. Anyway, it wasn't quite porn. Just a bunch of nudes."

I finish my beer and say, "We shouldn't be anti-social. We're here for Charlie, after all. And Celia."

I turn to walk away, but Cred pulls me back and says, "Do you understand what I just told you, Russ?"

"What?"

"That server was a ruse. Charlie probably thought it would take three months to crack those files. But now they're cracked, and everyone knows this isn't the server they're looking for. Whoever's after you is going to come after you again. They're all looking for a server called the vault, and they all seem to think you know where it is."

He looks at me as if he's waiting for me to deny it all. But I don't.

Cred shakes his head and says, "Don't talk to me, Russ. I don't even want to know what you're up to."

We drift apart, and I spend the next twenty minutes talking to programmers I used to work with. They're all writing JavaScript these days. It's a fine language for small tasks, but not for big systems. That's my argument, anyway. They think otherwise.

I don't really have to listen to them talk, because they all tell the same story. They're working sixty, seventy hours a week, waiting for their product to take off, for their options to vest, for their little company to be swallowed up by Google or Facebook.

While I half-listen, I scan the crowd, hoping to catch a glimpse of Charlie's beautiful muse. But she's not here. And I'm sad I won't get a chance to meet her. I've been thinking about her ever since I got that first little glimpse of her cheek.

28

AT A QUARTER PAST noon, after three beers, I say good-bye to Celia. She's already drunk. She gives me a hug and asks me to keep in touch. I tell her I will.

As I head for the door, I'm thinking about Wisp. I won't have time to make it to his place, which was the whole point of this trip, as far as I'm concerned. Just before I reach the exit, I overhear a little snippet of conversation between two women:

"Of course she's not here."

"I don't see why not. Half his other girlfriends showed up."

"But they're from years ago. She said she wouldn't come. She's working anyway."

I can't help butting in. "Cali? Is that who you're talking about?"

I addressed my question to the dark-haired woman with the short skirt and fishnet stockings, but they both turn to look at me. The other woman is short, with a round freckled face and blue eyes. Both look surprised at my intrusion. But they're tipsy, and the short one says, "You know Cali?"

"Yes," I say. "No." I don't know which answer is better in this situation.

The dark-haired woman looks me up and down and says, "Who are you?"

"An old friend of Charlie."

The shorter one leans in and says, "She wouldn't come, out of respect for Celia."

"Where is she?" I ask.

"Waiting tables at Chez Guevara."

"Where's that?"

"Right by Berkeley."

The dark-haired woman wants to talk, so we chat for a few minutes, but I don't like her vibe. She asks if I have a girlfriend, then wants to know why not. She seems somehow needy and bitter all at once. And she's drunker than I thought. Her friend can see this isn't going well, and eventually steers her toward the bar for another drink.

I leave before anyone else can pull me into conversation. I can take the train to the airport, but I'm cutting it close.

Three steps out the door, I see that Cred was right. The ruse of the Russian server has been exposed, and somehow the Latin Americans have found out about it. The little guy sitting on the bench at the bus stop—that's Mario. And he's looking right at me.

I head toward the BART station, keeping a good pace on the long walk up Second Street. I look back every now and then to check on my pursuer. He has a hard time keeping up on those short legs of his, and I can see he's relieved when I slow down where the street crosses beneath the Interstate.

I wonder where Donkey Kong is. I really don't want another one of his surprises. I don't think he'll come at me with a two-by-four in broad daylight on a crowded street, but I can't help looking for him among the faces of the homeless people beneath the underpass.

At Market Street, I get the train for San Francisco International. Mario sits in the next car back, and we have an uneventful trip.

He follows me into the terminal and watches me get my boarding pass at the check-in kiosk. He watches me go through security, but he doesn't follow. He must not have a ticket. As I put my shoes back on, I see him talking into a little flip phone. Probably calling ahead to Richmond to set up my welcoming party.

I turn away and disappear into the crowd.

When I arrive at my gate, the attendant is calling for volunteers to give up their seats on the overbooked flight in exchange for a later flight and a voucher.

I think again about Wisp. I really could use some ID. If Mario followed me all the way to San Francisco, maybe the Russians did too. And the FBI must have been watching who was going in and out of that memorial service. I would rest a lot easier knowing I had some way to slip past all of them and get out of this mess.

I walk up to the counter and tell the gate attendant, "I can take another flight."

andrew diamond

She looks at my ticket and says, "It may be a few hours before the next plane."

"Just give me the voucher," I say. "I can go tomorrow."

I get my voucher, and a nervous-looking old man is suddenly relieved to know he'll be getting home tonight.

I turn off my cell phone so no one can track my location, and I stay at the gate until the plane takes off, just in case Mario is still hanging around the terminal.

At 2:35, I catch the shuttle train back to the BART station and buy a twenty-dollar ticket with cash. I tell myself I'm going to Wisp's, but I'm lying. I know exactly where I'm going.

At 3:25, I watch the train doors close at Wisp's stop at 16th and Mission. Then we roll through the Civic Center, Powell Street, Montgomery, Embarcadero, and on over to the East Bay.

When that woman said the restaurant was "right by Berkeley," I assume she meant the university. If she had meant the city, she would have said "in Berkeley." Walking out of the Downtown station, I resist the impulse to turn on my phone and check Google Maps. I stop a stranger and say, "Do you know how to get to Chez Guevara?"

andrew diamond

Part II
Presence

I

CHEZ GUEVARA IS A fifteen-minute walk from the station. When I arrive, the place is empty, except for the bartender and two women at the bar in back. This is the post-lunch, pre-dinner lull.

Except for the mural of Ché Guevara on the wall, this place looks like it hasn't changed since the 1930s. Old wood tables with old wood chairs sit on a worn wood floor. The bar, with its brass foot rail, is made of better wood than the rest of the place. It looks like mahogany at first. But as I get closer, I see the varnish is wearing off, and the wood underneath is too light to be mahogany.

And then…there she is, in a light olive paisley blouse and jeans, counting out her tips next to another waitress who is doing the same. She wears silver bracelets on her left wrist that clink together as she counts the bills. The wide one with the big turquoise stone has a flatter sound than the thin round ones.

I catch her face in profile for just a second when she looks at the other waitress. Then she turns to the bartender, who says something to her as he wipes down the bar. She sips ice water through a narrow black straw as she listens.

I'm seven or eight feet behind her, standing among the bare wood tables that have all been wiped down. I don't realize how brazenly I'm staring at the back of her head until she turns around and looks me square in the face with those big, sleepy green eyes.

She has a slowness about her, and the soothing calmness of one who is at ease with the world. Her face at first shows no expression. Then a little smile appears. A delayed reaction. It grows slowly into a genuine, warm, friendly smile, and I feel like the sun has come out just for me.

The other waitress turns and looks at me. "Oh, I didn't even see you come in. The kitchen re-opens at five, but you're welcome to have a drink."

The bartender says something to Cali, and she turns back to continue their conversation.

andrew diamond

"I, um..." I stare for a second, not knowing what to say.

I can't play this cool because ever since I studied the Impala photo I've been weaving fantasies about this woman, and I've managed to whip up quite an infatuation. Charlie's drawings only fanned the flames. He did a good job of capturing her slow, cool, unpretentious sensuality.

"You can have a seat at the bar," the waitress says.

I sit three stools down to Cali's left, and the other woman goes back to counting her tips. When the bartender asks what I'd like, I order an Anchor Steam—one of the many great things to come out of San Francisco over the years. Then I look again at Cali. In profile, I can see her lips move as she counts out the bills.

What do I say to this woman? "Hi. I'm a friend of the dead guy who used to draw naked pictures of you. You're so beautiful and intriguing, I just had to come stare at you in person. Will you marry me?"

The bartender brings my beer, and the other waitress gets up to leave.

"I'll see you tomorrow," she says. Her eye catches mine, and Cali turns to see what her friend is looking at. Once again, she catches me staring.

I am not Mr. Smooth. The way I'm acting right now, I'm halfway between Mr. Lost and Mr. Restraining Order.

Cali turns back to her friend, who is already walking away, and says, "Bye, Casey."

She stands up and slides her cash into the front pocket of her jeans. Then she pushes the glass of ice toward the bartender and turns to go.

Only, she doesn't turn toward the door. She turns toward me. I can't look away from her, but I still don't know what to say.

She walks right up to me, her sleepy green eyes unfazed by my stare, and it occurs to me now that she's stoned. A big warm smile spreads across her face. The kind of smile that rises inexorably from real feeling. And when the first hint of bashfulness appears—when her head bows just a little bit, and she looks toward the ground, and her shoulders roll ever so slightly forward—I wonder if she's feeling the same thing I'm feeling.

She looks back up at me, and she says, "Hi, Russ."

2

SHE ASKS IF I'M doing anything right now, and if I don't mind going to Oakland with her to pick something up. I don't mind at all. I'd go anywhere with her right now.

"It's only a few blocks from the train," she says. "It won't take long."

Take all week, for all I care.

She goes into the kitchen and I pay the bartender. When she returns, she doesn't just walk by and say, "Come on, let's go." She stops in front of me and looks me right in the face and says, "You ready?" Little gestures like that go a long way toward making someone like you. Life is an accumulation of little things.

When we leave the restaurant, she opens her hand to reveal a half-smoked joint and red Bic lighter. This, I assume, is what she went into the kitchen to get. She puts the joint in her mouth and is about to light it, then she stops and says, "Oh, I'm sorry."

She puts the joint in my mouth and lights it. I take a hit and say, "You can't smoke on the street in California."

She says, "Don't exhale or the cops will smell it."

"Wait," I say, trying to hold my breath and talk at the same time. "Really?"

"Really," she says. Then she takes a hit and blows a big cloud of smoke down the street.

After two more hits, the joint is less than an inch long. In a spontaneous act, she holds it out to a passing skateboarder. He grabs it reflexively, without slowing down, and as his wheels thump over the cracks in the sidewalk, he says a long drawn-out, "All right!" in a tone that suggests he's already stoned.

"How do you know my name?" I ask.

"Charlie showed me pictures of you," she says. "And he talked about you. Especially toward the end." Now she's looking at me with more interest, perhaps trying to see if the things Charlie said fit the person she is looking at.

"When was the last time you saw him?" I ask.

"About two weeks before he died. Right before he left for Colombia."

"Where was he?"

"Here."

"Celia said he left three weeks before he died."

"That's when he left Celia," she says.

"What did Charlie tell you about me?"

"Oh, just a lot of old stories. He said he trusted you to figure things out and do the right thing." Then she gives me a quick glance and adds, "Or the wrong thing."

"How did you know him?"

"Aren't we full of questions!"

"Well, I'm just curious, you know. I saw this photo of you and—"

She stops short and says, "What photo?"

"Of you walking by a red Impala."

She stands there thinking for a moment, then shakes her head and says, "Charlie never took photos of me. He didn't want there to be any digital evidence of our relationship."

"Oh, yeah. That."

"What?" Cali says, and she's studying me as though this is important.

"He used to say," and I realize that this is the first time I'm repeating to another person the words he said to me so many times, "he used to say that you don't put the really important things online. Those stay in the real world, where computers can't find them."

We start walking again, and Cali says, "Oh, was I so important? I thought he just didn't want Celia to know about me. Poor Celia! I would have stayed away from him if I had known."

"Poor Celia tolerated his escapades for years. She kept choosing to take him back. There is no *poor Celia*."

"That doesn't excuse what I did," she says. "How was the memorial service?"

"As expected. People telling stories and getting drunk."

"You don't sound very moved."

"To be honest, I didn't feel very close to him. We hadn't talked in four years. I don't mean to sound callous or anything, but I said goodbye to him a long time ago."

I can see as I say this that her mind is on something else. Or it might just be drifting from the pot, which, I'm starting to notice, has a nice easy ramp-up.

After a few seconds of silence, she says, "What photo of me did you see again?"

"The one with the red Impala."

She's quiet, thinking as we walk, and I can't help but admire that lovely face. As we approach the intersection, I see a spark of recognition in her eyes. She gives me a curious look and says, "My back was to the camera."

"Yeah."

"So how did you—"

"I couldn't stop thinking about you..." I stop mid-sentence because that didn't come out the way I intended. She's going to think I'm a stalker, when I'm really just lonely and obsessive. There's a fine line between the two, but I'm pretty sure I'm on the right side of it.

She says, "Yeah, I kept thinking about *you* after Charlie showed me that photo."

"What photo?"

"You're wearing jeans and a light blue t-shirt and you're standing in a park. The leaves on the trees have that moist shine, like the fog has just lifted. And you have like..." She smiles. "You have the sweetest smile."

"That can't be me."

I have no idea what photo she's talking about.

She stops and gives me a little tap on the chest, a little backhand flick with the tips of her fingers, and she says, "Smile!"

"I can't just smile on command," I say. "That's not my disposition."

Then she smiles at me, and I can't help but smile back.

"See," she says. "You looked just like that."

We're entering the crosswalk now, and the pot makes me feel like I'm floating a little. Cali is a step in front of me as a car turns across our path. Without thinking, I pull her gently by the belt away from the car, back toward me. We're walking hip to hip now, and she makes no effort to reopen the distance between us.

Her face is right at my shoulder when she turns and says, "So how did you connect me to the woman in the photo?"

"You were wearing the same earring."

"What?"

"In the photo and in one of Charlie's drawings."

She blushes a deep red, and says "Oh God!" She half-stifles a laugh and grabs my arm, leaning on me for a couple of steps.

We've gone a few blocks now, and I suddenly realize, "The BART station is the other way."

"I know," Cali says. "I wanted to check out some paintings my friend put up. Do you mind?"

"No. That's fine." I look back down the street and notice three small trees, like the ones from the photo. I look for the barber's pole, and then, as if she's reading my mind, Cali says, "It wasn't here. He wouldn't have taken that picture so close to where I work."

I give her a curious look, and she says, "I know, 'cause it looks just like this, right?"

I'm still looking at her funny when she says, as if to lay the matter to rest once and for all, "It was in Sacramento."

After another block, we reach the little coffee shop where her friend's paintings are on display. The interior is a pristine white: white tile floor, white counter, white tables, and white walls hung with half a dozen amateur paintings. Cali says hi to the barista and orders a lemon soda. She offers me the first sip, which I need because my mouth is dry.

That pot we smoked was Sativa, not the brain-crushing Indica that usually debilitates me. I know this because a) I'm still functioning, and b) I can follow a line of thought for more than five seconds. I'm standing by a white marble-top table with the air-conditioning blowing down on me, staring at an abstract acrylic painting of two angry squares. Why is the orange square so aggressive? Why does it oppress the yellow square beneath it? Does it sense the yellow square's resentment?

Cali is watching me. "You like that one?" she asks.

"I don't like abstract art."

"Then why were you staring at it for so long?"

"I was trying to figure out what I hate about it."

Cali laughs. "You think you don't like abstract art, but you still respond to it."

Somehow, her pointing out my own traits to me makes me think of Charlie's remark that day in the park four years ago. "You're just as devious as me." And then I think of Jamie's recurrent complaint that I'm not in touch with my feelings, and a comment she made a few weeks ago. "You're sleepwalking through life."

Other people think they can see in me things I can't see in myself. Maybe this is true of all of us, to some extent. Maybe we're all transparent to others in ways we're not aware of.

My mind starts swinging around to the big questions again. How *should* I live? *Why am I here?*

And then I hear Jamie's voice, "Why do you ask yourself questions that have no answer? Do something useful and put the dishes away." That voice irks me, but it still has the power to stifle my thoughts. At least, when I'm not stoned.

But now that I am stoned, my thoughts wander. How long have I been standing here thinking about whatever I was just thinking about? I don't know. But I'm pretty sure I've been staring at Cali the whole time. And I'm pretty sure she can feel it and doesn't mind. She's looking at a watercolor painting of a salmon. Her face in profile looks younger than it does from the front. I wonder what's going through her mind. What's so special about that fish?

A truck rumbles by outside, shaking the floor of the coffee shop, and my thoughts shift all at once. I'm suddenly aware that I'm thousands of miles from the past four years of crushing boredom. I'm in a strange place that a month ago, a week ago, an hour ago, I never would have guessed I'd be in. And beside me is the woman who, until just yesterday, I didn't know I was looking for. And somehow, it all feels natural and right.

impala

How did I get here? I have an uncanny feeling that all of this is happening on purpose. As though the extraordinary events of the past ten days have awakened some part of me that understands exactly which way to go at every turn. As if a map of these events was written into me long ago, waiting to be discovered, and time at last is unfolding all the cues that tell me which route to follow through a world I have not yet seen but have always known.

Cali turns to me at last and says, "Do you ever wonder how the salmon and the swallows and the Monarch butterflies find their way to the same exact spot year after year?"

"What?"

"It's not something they have to figure out. It's just built into them, you know?"

"What?"

"Which makes me wonder. Do they have a whole subconscious map of the world inside them? So they know the layout of it all before they've even seen it? Or are they just somehow in tune with the universe's time-line, so like, they intuitively understand all the cues and know exactly where and when to turn?"

"Oh my God!"

"What?"

I grab her by the shoulders and kiss her on the mouth. "I fucking love you!"

She's startled. Her back is straight and tense, her shoulders are up, and she has this look on her face like, *Where the hell did that come from?* I might have drooled on her a little, because she's wiping her mouth.

I let go of her and say, "Sorry. It made sense when I did it."

Her posture relaxes, and she laughs a little before she says, "Wait. Do that again."

This time she's ready for my kiss. Her mouth is cool and sweet.

andrew diamond

3

ON THE TRAIN TO Oakland, we sit in the sideways-facing seats by the door, turned toward each other so our knees are touching. She tells me she should have graduated from Berkeley two years ago. She studies art and psychology and math, and has more interests than focus. Which makes me wonder exactly how much pot she smokes.

I tell her about Richmond and work. She traces the scratches on my face and says, "Did you get in a fight with your girlfriend?"

"Umm…excuse me?" Does she think Jamie and I hit each other?

She laughs and says, "You're so serious! I was just trying to find out if you had a girlfriend."

"I used to. She dumped me for a BMW named Rod."

From the train, we walk to a block of single-story industrial brick buildings. We enter through the back of what used to be a furniture store. The late afternoon sun pours in through the windows of the roll-up garage doors, where the furniture was once unloaded, and spills across the dark wood floor of the interior. A cooler light comes in through the big display windows at the eastern end of the building, sixty feet away.

This place looks like a hookah bar or an opium den, and it smells like marijuana. The ceiling is high, with exposed wood beams, and the walls are hung with paintings and drawings, in the abounding, haphazard style of a nineteenth-century art studio. The floor in the middle of the vast room is covered by worn oriental rugs and scuffed Moroccan furniture with richly colored arabesques, beside which hang faded Chinese tapestries of red and gold. This abundance of extravagant beauty moldering in neglect reminds me of whole neighborhoods of San Francisco.

There's a cot by the door, and beside it are a mini fridge and a hot plate. Cali introduces me to Jim, the pot-bellied, bohemian man of fifty or so who sleeps in that little bed and has paint in his untrimmed whiskers.

Jim says hello. He looks like he just woke up.

"Take a look around," he says, with a wave toward nothing in particular. Then he pulls a gallon Ziploc bag of weed from under the cot. I assume this is what Cali came to pick up.

While she and Jim pull buds from the bag, I wander to the far end of the room, to the big four-poster bed with the missing post. It's the one Cali was sitting on in the drawing I saw back at Celia's.

I remember when Charlie and I found this bed in pieces on the street. It was in front of an apartment house not far from here, beside the carelessly piled belongings of its evicted owner, who, rumor had it, was dying in a public hospital. The rumor was repeated with grave sympathy by the scavengers as they adopted the man's possessions one by one from the heap.

In the end, the bed was still there, because it was too heavy for anyone to carry. Whoever brought it down to the street had dismantled it first. They carefully unscrewed the brackets that held the frame and posts together, but when they got to the last post, they either lost patience or came across a screw they couldn't remove, so they broke the post off from the frame. I remember Charlie saying what a shame that was.

We were drunk, and a cold mist was starting to fall. Charlie flagged down two guys in a pickup truck and gave them twenty dollars to haul the bed to what he called "the arts center." He said he was going to fix it up and put a proper mattress on it. I helped him load it onto the truck and then watched him drive off, sitting precariously atop the unstable pile of wood, waving his beer bottle.

And now here it is again after all these years. Apparently this was the place. Funny, the little things we remember. I guess Charlie put it all back together, except for the broken post. The one post that now remains at the foot of the bed is carved with all manner of graffiti. Maybe that's new, or maybe it was like that when we found it. I don't remember.

The corner of the frame where the missing post was broken off is still splintered. Charlie took the broken post and attached four feet to the bottom of it, and four hooks to the top. One day he showed up at my apartment and gave it to me to use as a coat rack. The funny thing is, I actually used it. I even brought it with me when I moved across country.

andrew diamond

Right now it's sitting in Jamie's apartment, next to the door, with her raincoat and her spring sweaters hanging on it.

As I stroll back to Cali, I look at the artwork that lines the walls and notice that the bed and the furniture and the tapestries in the room appear in many of the paintings. Some of the Moroccan pieces are ornate enough to be the subject of their own compositions. But more often, they're in the background of a still life or a nude.

Cali is sitting on the little bed with Jim, rolling a joint. There's a nude of her hanging on the wall across from the bed. It's an oil painting. She's standing, leaning her hip against a black-lacquered Chinese wardrobe inlaid with gold and coral. Her hips are slightly forward, her shoulders slightly back, in a casual, almost careless pose. Whoever painted this either didn't have the same talent as Charlie or didn't have the same love for his subject. Still, her beauty comes through.

The smell of pot and rolling paper wafts up from behind me, and I turn to see Cali in the bright stream of light that pours in through the windows. She blushes as she watches me look at the painting of her. The whites of her eyes are a little red from the smoke, and the greens look a little greener. She smiles and offers me a hit.

I look her up and down, trying to match her to the woman in the painting. I know I'm being horribly rude, but how many times in your life do you turn from a beautiful painting to find the woman herself smiling quietly beside you? I know she can see what I'm thinking because it's right there on my reddening face. She has this calm, slightly amused smile, and she says, "Everything check out okay?"

Then she laughs and gently pushes my shoulder, turning me back toward the painting, which I continue to examine as I take a puff of the joint.

She goes back to the bed and sits with Jim, and they talk.

"Charlie spent many nights in this building," Jim says.

That's interesting. I used to wonder where he went sometimes. He probably slept in dozens of random places like this.

"I watched him go downhill," Jim says as I bring the joint back to the two of them. "All that drinking, and the paranoia started showing in his eyes. Shame he didn't stick to his art. He had the talent. And it probably wouldn't have got him killed."

"Yeah, but who can make a living drawing and painting?" Cali says as she takes the joint from me.

"Some people can," Jim says. Cali takes a hit and passes him the joint. He gives a little wave toward the walls. "What about these other guys?"

"What about them?" Cali asks.

"You think they painted you as well as Charlie did?"

Cali shrugs. "It's not what I think. It's whether they painted what they felt and meant."

Jim hands me the joint and says to Cali, "Charlie did you right. He took the time, and he had the passion. You can feel it in his work."

Cali turns her now unsmiling face toward the sunlit windows, and I feel a sudden emptiness as she withdraws, as if the sea has just gone quiet.

"Charlie had a lot of passion for a lot of things," she says unhappily. "When you have his interest and he takes his time with you, you're the center of the universe. And then when he's done, you're nothing."

Her words fill me with jealousy, resentment, and longing. The power of these feelings is out of proportion to the simple statements that evoked them. Maybe I'm feeling what she's feeling. Or maybe the pot is playing tricks on me.

I hand the joint back to Jim and he says with a smile, "Charlie once spent a week here, sitting on that bed, knitting her a sweater. Did you know Charlie could knit?"

"No," I say.

"He wasn't very good it," Cali says, and nods toward the white sweater on the bed. She is smiling, and I'm surprised at her sudden recovery, how quickly she goes from unhappy to okay.

I look at the sweater. It's the one she was wearing in the photo. The knitting is uneven, and the yarn is flecked with red, green, blue, and black. An amateur job with inexplicable aesthetics.

Jim asks Cali if she can fill in on Thursday evening for a model who

andrew diamond

can't make it. She shakes her head and says, "I won't be here. And I don't want to model anymore anyway."

Jim puts the joint in the ashtray. "Where you going?"

Cali looks at me and says, "I don't know. Can I have some of that for the road?"

As Jim puts a few fresh buds into a little baggie for her, she says to me, "You want to go into the city?"

"Sure."

I still have that cash in my backpack, and I want to see Wisp.

4

ON THE TRAIN BACK to San Francisco, I tell Cali about getting jumped by Mario and Donkey Kong. And then I ramble on, stoned, about the Impala ad and the self-deleting photo, the encryption key, the server in Russia and the Apache web logs. I tell her about the Russians in the alley, and the first interview with Jack Hayes.

Normally, I'm not such a blabbermouth. But I'm stoned, and she's actually listening to everything I say. I'm so used to Jamie shutting me down, I forgot how good it feels to be heard.

Maybe I've gone on too long. Her eyes are starting to glaze over as we approach 16th and Mission. Poor Cali. What the hell does she care about Apache logs? As the train rolls to a stop, I say, "Thanks for listening." I give her a little kiss on the cheek, and when that smile blossoms on her face, I get that feeling again, like the sun has come out just for me.

It's getting dark, and the Mission is kind of sketchy this time of evening. I take Cali's hand on the walk to Wisp's. I want to protect her.

We arrive at Wisp's four-unit building just as a woman is walking out. The entrance and the street-level windows are protected by bars, and dirty grey paint is peeling from the wood façade. I catch the door before it closes, and we go up to the second floor and knock. This time, he's home.

When he opens the door, he looks at me without surprise and says, "Hey man," like I just returned from a trip around the corner. Wisp doesn't get out much, so maybe he has no sense of time. He's pale and skinny, like the yellow-white grass you find flattened beneath the kiddie pool at the end of summer.

He's wearing a black t-shirt with a cartoon skateboarder whose eyes are popping out, and his long blonde hair hangs straight down past his narrow shoulders. He's shockingly thin, but he's always looked like this. Like the next good breeze might blow him away.

"You look like shit," I say.

"Thanks. Your friend is pretty."

"Isn't she?"

"She cool?"

He's asking if she's trustworthy, and I realize all of a sudden I haven't bothered to ask myself that question. Is she? I don't know. But I want her to come in, so I play the little game we all play in our head now and then to convince ourselves that we're not technically lying or speaking out of ignorance. I tell myself she seems pretty damn cool and at ease to me. So, yeah. "She's cool," I say.

Wisp opens the door and invites us in.

The apartment is lit by the glow of two computer monitors. Wisp's real passion, aside from stealing, is hacking hardware. The whole place is cluttered with motherboards, credit card readers, old mobile phones, keyboards, hard drives, bar code scanners, police radio scanners, and a thousand things I can't identify.

We talk for a minute about old times, then Wisp cuts it short and says, "So why are you here?"

I remind myself that he's not used to having people around, and he doesn't know how to talk to them.

"I need some ID. And some credit cards wouldn't hurt."

"You on the run from something?"

"Maybe."

Wisp keeps an eye on Cali as she looks around the apartment.

"Why didn't you go to Charlie's memorial?" I ask.

"Why would I?"

"See your old friends."

"That's exactly why I didn't go. With all the shit swirling around since Twilight went offline, I don't want to be associated with Charlie in any way. Was the FBI there taking photos?"

"I don't know. Maybe they were outside."

"I pictured the whole thing like DEF CON. You know—Spot the Fed?"

I shrug.

"Where'd you pick her up?" Wisp asks, with a nod toward Cali.

"Why don't you ask her," I say. "Instead of talking about her like she can't hear you."

Wisp turns to Cali and says, "Where'd he pick you up?"

"In a bar," Cali says as she examines a credit card skimmer.

"Nice," says Wisp. "You don't want your fingerprints on that."

Cali puts the skimmer down and Wisp says, "How about a few credit cards with some matching IDs. That'll let you move around without leaving a trail."

"Sounds good."

"You need a passport?"

"Probably."

"Come over here."

He clears a pile of junk from an old chair and then stands on it and hangs a white sheet from the ceiling. I sit in front of the sheet and he takes my photo. Then he brings the image into Photoshop and changes my hair and eyes to dark brown. Cali stands beside him and watches the transformation.

"Do you have any of the new EMV credit cards, with the chip embedded on the front?" I ask.

He shakes his head. "I can't fake those yet. I can give you some of the older kind, with just the magnetic stripe. They still work most places."

"That's fine." I look again at the doctored photo of me and ask, "How am I supposed to get my eyes brown?"

Cali says, "Contacts."

Wisp opens a spreadsheet full of names, addresses, and credit card numbers. He picks three names and creates licenses from Washington, Nevada, and Kansas. While they're printing out, he takes a blank credit card from a box and puts it into a machine that looks like a card reader. "This encodes the data onto the magnetic stripe," he says. Another machine embosses the number on the front and prints the three-digit security code on the back.

He makes three credit cards in a matter of minutes, then laminates the licenses. Then he checks them against the spreadsheet before handing them to me.

I look over the cards briefly, then take out my wallet, which I like to keep light and slim, and jam them all inside. The wallet is a little too fat now, which makes it hard to close.

"The passport's going to be expensive," Wisp says. "How much cash do you have?"

"Five thousand. Actually, a little less."

"Keep a couple hundred and give me the rest."

I put my wallet down and rummage through my backpack for the envelope of cash. There's forty-eight hundred dollars inside. I count it, just to be sure, while Cali looks through my wallet.

"Nice license photo," she says. "You look like you're sixteen."

I pull two hundreds from the envelope, then hand the rest to Wisp. "Forty-six hundred? I can send more later if you need it."

"Forty-six hundred is cool."

I ask Cali to put the two hundreds into my wallet, but she's examining a business card and doesn't seem to hear me. So I put the cash in my pocket and ask if I can use the bathroom. Wisp just points toward the hall without saying anything.

As I'm leaving the room, Cali says, "Make the passport in this name." And then Wisp lets out a little laugh. I've never heard that guy laugh before.

Judging from Wisp's bathroom, his life seems to have gone a little sideways since I last saw him. I don't remember it ever being this filthy.

When I return to the main room, Wisp is stooped over an open printer and Cali looks bored.

"What the hell do you do with all your money?" I ask Wisp.

He closes up the printer and says, "Right now, I'm paying off this guy who's extorting me."

"That sucks."

"It's gonna suck for him real soon," Wisp says as the printer starts to whir.

We hang out for a few more minutes while Wisp finishes preparing the passport. He tells us about the difficulty of hacking the new EMV cards. If he can get the chips right, he says, he stands to make a lot of money.

When we leave, Wisp stuffs a couple of cards into the passport and hands it to me. I put it in my backpack without examining it. Except I notice that it's red.

andrew diamond

5

On the street, Cali holds onto my arm and says, "Your friend needs to work on his manners."

"Did he offend you?"

"No. But I feel kind of sorry for him."

We walk up toward Hayes Valley and stop in a bar for a burger and a beer. I like how casual Cali is in her jeans with a pint of beer in her hand. I ask if she paints, and she says she thinks about it more than she actually does it.

"In my head," she says, "I'm a brilliant painter. In reality, I'm not. So I don't do it often. What's the point of disillusioning myself? How about you?"

"I write code. That's about as creative as I get."

"Do you have a passion for it? Charlie said all the good developers do."

I haven't asked myself this question in a while, and the certainty of my answer surprises me. "No. I used to. But it's hard to get excited about projects that have no real point in the end. I mean, my code is probably helping someone earn a lot of money. But that's it. It doesn't actually *mean* anything."

"But you keep doing it."

"Yeah, well. I have to pay the bills. And as long as my mind is engaged...You know, I'm the kind of person, if you put a problem in front of me and say, 'Solve this,' that's all I need to keep busy."

She nods and says, "You have trouble letting go of things."

"What?"

"Like if someone gives you a problem, you can't rest until you figure it out."

"Did Charlie tell you that?"

"Yeah, but I can also see it in you."

I don't know how she can see that. I think back through our day together, trying to remember what I did that would make her think that.

She looks amused as she watches me think. Finally, she says, "On the train, Russ. When you were telling me about all your troubles. It's just the way you tell a story."

What is she talking about? How *do* I tell a story? And how does she keep reading my mind?

"You dwell on the details," she says with a smile. "Most people let the little things slide. They just give you the gist of what happened."

For a few seconds, I'm self-conscious. Is this something I need to change?

When the burgers come, I find I'm hungrier than I thought. And she seems to be too. We eat without talking.

After the bartender clears our plates, Cali says, "Are you staying in the city?"

"I'm not really staying anywhere. I'm supposed to be back in Richmond."

Her eyes are no longer half-closed like when she's stoned, but I can see she's tired.

"Do you want to go home?" I ask.

"Can we get a hotel?"

I can't tell you how those words lift my heart. And I know things are really going my way, because as soon as we leave the bar, there's an empty cab sitting by the curb. A cab! In San Francisco! The whole reason Uber exists is because you can't get a taxi in this town.

We're quiet, for the most part, as the cab makes its way up Van Ness and turns onto California. I put my hand on her thigh as she looks out the window, watching the lights of the city glide by. I can see she's thinking again. Just before we reach the hotel, she says, "When Jack Hayes turned the computer to you and asked about the ad, was the other cop in the room?"

This is not what I imagined she was thinking about.

"No."

Five minutes later, I'm testing out one of Wisp's new credit cards at the front desk of a pretty swank hotel on the eastern slope of Nob Hill. We get a room on the top floor with a view of the city. In the elevator, I pin Cali in the corner and kiss her. Her hands are on my shoulders. She touches with her fingertips, then squeezes as her hands slide down my arms and then around my back.

Fingertips, squeeze. Fingertips, squeeze. Taste, eat. Taste. Eat.

Our room is huge, and Cali spends the first few minutes just walking around. The view looks north toward Coit Tower and Alcatraz. Cali takes off her shoes at the window, then walks to the bed, where she sits and removes the silver bracelets from her wrist one by one, placing them softly on the nightstand. She unties her hair, lowers her hands softly into her lap, and watches me.

When I walk to the bed and sit beside her, she looks down at her feet. She's much more shy than I expected. I turn her toward me and kiss her mouth. Then I draw back and see a look of uncertainty in her eyes. I'm about to ask if she really wants to do this when she pulls me in for another kiss. Maybe that's her way of saying yes, or maybe she just wants to stop me from asking.

I don't know why her shyness turns me on so much, but it does. I'm ready to strip off all her clothes and push her down right now, but she's so demure I feel any touch might be a violation. How can this be the same woman who had her hands all over me in the elevator just a few minutes ago?

I whisper in her ear, "You know, I liked you from the moment I saw you."

I kiss her neck, and she says, "When you saw me naked in the drawings, or in real life?"

"Both."

She pushes me gently away, and when I look at her face to see what's wrong, she seems conflicted. She sees I don't know what to do, so she takes my hand and puts it up beneath her shirt, on the soft part of her side between her ribs and hip. I lean in and kiss her again. She's warmer now. But when I move my hand up to her breast, she starts, as if she weren't expecting it. I'm about to stop and suggest we just watch a movie, but then she reaches back and unhooks her bra, looking straight at me as she does it. In her eyes I see shyness yielding to determination, and I don't quite know what to make of that. Is she a virgin? She couldn't be.

She leaves every move to me. As I kiss her and undress her, I feel her apprehension rise and fall like the tides. Each time we approach her wall, she responds to my playful little kisses with a smile, and her tensing body relaxes. I look her in the eye as her shirt comes off, her bra, her pants. Why does she keep going if she's so scared? I've never felt anything so powerfully seductive as watching her defenses fall.

But, except for her deep breathing, I can't tell if she's really turned on. She's hardly touched me, and I'm starting to wonder if, when we get down to it, she's just going to lie there and wait for me to finish.

She watches me undress, and then I'm on the bed beside her. She's on her back, raising her hips as I slide the underwear down her thighs. The look of complete trust and openness in her eyes catches me off guard, and I start, just as she did when I touched her breast.

Then it hits me all at once that *I'm* the one who's not ready for this. That this is not a hook-up, or the semi-drunk routine of first-date sex I've always known. Her vulnerability has opened up a tenderness in me that I wasn't prepared to feel. She is entirely present. Entirely unguarded. Her heart is right there for the taking. And all of a sudden, so is mine.

She sees the confusion in my face as I struggle with this ambush of emotion, and our roles reverse. Now I'm the one worried about taking the next step, and she is wild with desire. She pulls me in. And in a minute, we're the man and woman from the elevator. I can't get close enough to her, can't be deep enough inside her. And her hands taste every part of me.

* * *

A while later, we're lying side by side beneath the sheets, me on my back, she on her side, her soft breast pressed against my ribs. I look at the ceiling and she watches my face as I think about the mess I'm in with Mario and the Russians and Jack Hayes. This whole situation feels much more complicated now.

She must be reading my thoughts again, because she says, "Why are you doing this, Russ? Do you really want to find whatever Charlie left for you?"

I think this through for a few seconds, and finally I say, "Part of me can't let go of it because I want to find out what's at the end of this string Charlie left for me. I just have to get there. You know, because I'm—"

"Obsessive?"

"Yeah. And part of me just doesn't want those damn Colombians to get it first. They beat the crap out of me for no reason, so I don't want them to get jack shit."

Cali starts laughing quietly.

"And same with the fucking Russians. I was quiet when they told me to be quiet, and when the guy asked for my password, I gave it to him. I even complimented their car. I mean, how much more polite can a victim be? And then the guy cracks me on the head with his gun. So those two are on my shit list. And don't even get me started on Jack Hayes. I hate that motherfucker!"

She's laughing harder now, silently shaking the bed.

"What's so funny?" I ask.

It takes her a few seconds to stop laughing, and then she says, "Just how pissed you are about the FBI guy. Because you didn't like the way he looked at you."

"He's a dick!"

She laughs and says, "You and your delicate little ego. Charlie said nothing pisses you off more than people being rude to you."

"He said that?"

"You can't stand being slighted."

"Or beaten, or pistol-whipped, or glared at by some dickhead cop. You know, I had my life pretty well together before those guys came along and fucked it all up. I had no worries. None."

"Mmm," she says, nuzzling into my chest. "You had a job you didn't care about and a girlfriend you didn't love."

"Exactly. There was no *thing* hanging over my head, like there is now. Nothing to be anxious or nervous about."

"Oh, that's never true," Cali says. "Unless your mind is completely blank."

"Whatever. I just resent having to worry about a bunch of assholes who want to kill me."

"They're not going to kill you, Russ," Cali says in a sleepy voice.

"How do you know that?"

"Because if they wanted to, they would have done it already."

"Well why haven't they?"

She lifts her head from my chest and looks me in the face and says, "Think about it, Russ. Why haven't they?"

She watches as I think it through, and finally I say, "I don't know."

She lays her head back on my chest and says, "They couldn't make sense of the photo, but you could. Charlie's twisted mind is an encryption algorithm they've never seen before. And you're the only one who can figure it out. They can't get rid of you because you *are* the encryption key."

She's right. Everything she says is right. Everything she does is right. And she is warm and beautiful and smart. And I'm falling. And I'm scared, because this is all too much at once. Why now? Why did I have to meet her now, when I might be about to lose everything?

I think she's asleep, but I can't stop myself from asking. "What do you mean, I could make sense of the photo?"

She says, "You're the only one who's found me so far." She takes a couple of deep, quiet breaths, and the last thing she says before she drifts to sleep is, "Remind me tomorrow, I have something for you."

6

DAYLIGHT WAKES ME AT eight or nine or ten a.m. Time doesn't matter today. Cali sits at the table by the window in her underwear and shirt, looking out over the city. With her head turned away from me, I can just see the round edge of her cheek, as it was in the photo. She watches the light rise over the city. There is a shine on everything, and the world looks new in the clear Northern California air.

There's a faint odor of marijuana in the room, and I wonder how long she's been awake. She turns slowly and looks at me and smiles. Her big green eyes are half-closed, like a contented cat.

She gets up and walks to the side of the bed and undresses, and for a moment she just stands there, not shy at all. She climbs beneath the covers and kisses my cheek and starts rubbing the inside of my thigh. Her kisses are playful, and so is her touch.

In a few minutes, we're making love again...or, not really making love. We're having sex. Last night was a surprise emotional encounter. Today, we're just having fun, and I feel like I'm with a different person. This is the woman I saw at the bar yesterday: cool and entirely at ease with herself. She started this, and she's on top.

She reaches beneath my hip and starts to roll to her side, pulling me with her. We turn in unison, and we actually make the transition. Now she's on her back and I'm on top. That was so smooth, I want to give her a high-five.

She holds my gaze for a moment, and with just the slightest touch to my stomach, she tells me to slow down. She grabs her legs, pulls her knees up toward her shoulders and holds them there. Then she gives me this funny little look like, "I'll see you in a few minutes," and she turns her head to the side.

Her eyes are open, but they don't seem to focus on anything. She's just quietly absorbing every sensation. Her breaths are long and deep, and she holds them for a second before letting them out. Watching her face in profile, this purring sphinx luxuriating in her own sensuality, I see a purely physical being every bit as seductive as the emotional one that opened up to me last night.

Her breath is getting shorter and more urgent. She lets go of her legs, and her hips pick up speed. She's getting closer. I can feel it. I'm close too. I really don't want to let her down, but I just can't hold it. Everything goes at once with blinding intensity. And that's what pushes her over the top.

It takes me a while to catch my breath, and in the aftermath, still dazed, I say aloud, "Oh my God!"

She lets out a little laugh and says, "Yeah!" And for a long time, neither of us can move.

* * *

We order breakfast in, steak and eggs, and shower while we wait for the food. We're as hungry now as we were at the bar last night. I haven't felt this kind of appetite in months.

Afterward, as we finish off the coffee at the little table by the window, scattered with silverware and empty dishes, I look out over the hills of the city and wonder why I ever left this place. Cali says she wants to go back to her apartment in Berkeley for a change of clothes.

"It's kind of a step down from this place," she says. "And it's messy."

When I turn to look at her, she says, "It sucks to have to leave here, don't you think? Do you ever dream about just leaving your whole life behind and living out of fancy hotels?"

"The first part, yeah. Not so much the hotels. A simple beach would do."

I picture the sand and palms of Costa Rica, and maybe she sees on my face that I'm actually thinking about what she said, because she gets a playful look, like she wants to razz me, and she says, "You'd get bored of the beach."

"How do you know?"

"Everyone does. Why do you think the people who live there drink so much?"

"Wouldn't you get bored of fancy hotels?"

She shakes her head. "If I got bored of one, I'd just go somewhere else. That's the part that appeals to me. Not being pampered. Being free." She takes the last sip of coffee from her little white cup and says, "At work, I fantasize about running away to Rio."

"Brazil?"

"Yeah. It keeps me sane. Pretending that someday I'll just walk away from all those demanding, ungrateful customers and never have to answer to anyone again."

"The problem with that kind of fantasy," I say, "is that as long as it keeps giving you comfort, it'll keep you stuck in the life you're trying to get out of."

"I know."

"If you want to make it happen, you have to do something about it."

"I know."

"So what's your plan?"

She sighs and looks out the window.

"See," I say. "You're just like me. All fantasy and no plan."

* * *

When we check out, I'm shocked at the bill, and I'm sure Barney Kohl of Sequim, Washington, will be too. Poor guy. I wonder how Wisp got his credit card number. Oh, well. He won't be liable for charges over fifty dollars. And I'm pretty sure twenty-four hundred dollars isn't going to kill Wells Fargo.

We walk slowly down Powell Street toward the BART station on Market. A few blocks from the hotel, I ask Cali the question that's been on my mind since breakfast. "Why did you ask me that question in the cab last night? About Jack Hayes?"

Cali says, "I think he's working with the Russians."

This stops me in my tracks. She stops two steps past me, then turns and gives me a funny look and says, "What?"

"How exactly did you figure that out?"

"What you said on the train yesterday about the Apache server logs."

"Yeah?" I say, encouraging her to elaborate. "What about that?"

"The web logs said the photo of the Impala was accessed only once."

"Go on." We start walking again.

"That once had to be you. *You* were the only one who accessed it. And then it was deleted, right? You said you checked the server and the file was gone."

"Yeah..."

"So then the only copy of the image was on your laptop, right?"

"Right." She's walking through the same line of thought I had as I left the FBI building in Richmond after that first interview.

"Then the Russians take your laptop, so they have the only copy of the photo, right? And then, a couple of days later, Jack Hayes has the photo on *his* laptop. Which means he either took it from the Russians or they gave it to him."

I love this woman.

"And the fact that he waited until the other agent was out of the room before confronting you with it," she says. "That's a tip-off. He's doing this on his own, and his partner doesn't know about it."

I think back to how Hayes picked up my phone and felt how warm it was. How when I asked if we were done, he said, "I am. Are you?"

Finally I say, "No, I don't think his partner knows. But I'm pretty sure Hayes let me steal the photo from him. The Russians were sitting outside my apartment snooping on my Wi-Fi that night. Jack Hayes must have told them I got the photo back. They're waiting for me to figure out all the clues, so they can come in at the end and swipe the prize."

We walk in silence for another block, and then I say, "You know, I fucked up."

"How?"

"When I was leaving the FBI building, I told Hayes that one of the Russians said hello. So he knows I'm on to him."

"Why would you do that?" Cali asks.

"I wanted to incriminate him in front of the other agent. Or humiliate him. Or just be an asshole. I don't know."

"But why?"

My hands tighten into fists at the thought of that arrogant bastard. "Because I hate that fucking guy! Seriously! I've never met anyone who can piss me off so much just sitting there."

"Jeez, Russ. Learn to control your feelings."

"I've been controlling my feelings for four fucking years. I'm sick of being Mister Nice Guy. Fuck him. Fuck everyone, for that matter."

"Oooo-kaaaaay," Cali says slowly. "Do we need a little time out to calm down?"

"Don't fuck with me."

She smiles playfully and says, "But you make it so fun!"

We're a block from the BART station when my phone rings. It's Cred calling.

"That's funny," I say, as I stare at the phone. "I turned this thing off yesterday at the airport."

Cali says, "I put my number in there while you were in the bathroom. So you can call me."

"You...Fuck! You could have written it on a piece of paper!"

She winces at my anger. "What's your problem?"

"You don't turn my fucking phone on! The FBI can track me and give my location to the Russians!"

She puts her hand to her mouth and says, "Oh shit. I'm sorry, Russ. I fucked up."

I answer on the fifth ring and an unfamiliar voice says in a thick Spanish accent, "Hello? Ah, Rusell?" It's a man's voice, but it's high and thin. The voice of a small man, perhaps. Someone in the background is breathing hard and moaning in distress.

"Who is this?"

"Is your friend," says the man, "Bill. Say hello, Bill."

The desperate gasping in the background gets closer to the phone. Someone exhales sharply into the mike, and I have to pull my ear away for a second. Then comes Cred's frantic, breaking voice. "Russ, do you know where the server is? Do you have the key?"

"What? Cred? I don't—"

"You don't what?" says the Spanish voice again. "You don't have key?"

"No!" I say. "I don't have the key!"

Cali is watching me now with fear in her eyes.

"You know where is vault?"

"No!"

"And you friend, Bill? He don't know either?"

I hear Cred yelp in response to a thudding blow. They're hitting him with something heavy.

"Cred has no part in this," I say. "He doesn't know anything! Leave him alone!"

I can hear Cred's raspy, gurgling breath. They must have moved the phone back to him. "Russ," he says in a weak voice, "give them what they want. Please!"

"I don't have it, Cred."

The other voice comes back on the line and says, "You friend no use to us." Then he says to someone else, "*Vaya pues! Mátale!*" Go ahead. Kill him.

I hear three thumping blows, and then silence. I stand there, a block off Market, straining to hear the other end of the line above the noise of traffic. Cali is still staring at me, wide-eyed with terror.

Finally, the man on the other end says, "Ah...Russell?"

"What?"

"You have more friend?"

"What?"

"All you friend in danger, Russell. Until we get the key, you friend no safe." Then he says, "You have girlfriend, Russell?"

I turn the phone over, pull off the back cover, and remove the battery. Then I say to Cali angrily, "Why did you turn this on? What the fuck is wrong with you?" As if what Mario and his gorilla just did was her fault.

She just stands there, paralyzed, and I can't tell if she's heard me or not. Finally she says in a meek, regretful voice, "I'm sorry, Russ."

"Let's get out of here."

andrew diamond

As we head into the BART station, I keep hearing Cred's raspy gurgling, and I picture that big bald ape beating him with a crow bar or a baseball bat. I remember the blow he delivered to the back of my leg and imagine that landing on Cred's skull. Three of those would kill anyone.

But what if he's still alive? Should I call 911? I don't even know where he is. Should I call Jack Hayes? I know he's an asshole, but if he's working with the Russians, he's probably against the Colombians. Right now, I just want them all dead.

And why did Mario ask if I had a girlfriend? Of all the things to say right now! Does he know about Cali? Or is he talking about Jamie? Or was it just a shot in the dark to intimidate me? Whatever it was, it worked.

We walk to the far end of the platform before I realize where I am. I'm so lost in thought I forget Cali is with me until I stop and she bumps into me. She's quiet and unhappy.

This is all so wrong. Let them come after me if they want. But Cred had nothing to do with this. And what if they really do come after Cali? I can't even think about that. And I can't bear the look of pain on her face right now.

"I'm sorry," I say as the Oakland train rolls into the station. "This isn't your fault."

She seems to be steeling herself, summoning up some inner strength, and then she says, "Actually, Russ—"

Before she can finish, I see two familiar faces at the far end of the station. The Russians. She sees me react and she says, "What?"

They see me too, but we're at the opposite end of the platform, and the train doors have just opened.

"Shit!" I say.

"What?" Cali asks, as I pull her roughly by the arm into the train.

"The Russians." I peek my head through the door and look down the platform just in time to see them dash onto the train five cars back. The doors chime, then close halfway, then open again.

"So I finally get to meet them?" Cali says with a hint of gallows humor.

"They don't know about you," I say. "And I don't want them to. Get out!" I push her out just as the doors start to slide shut for the second time. But in my panic, I push too hard. She bangs against the edge of the closing door and stumbles back onto the platform before landing on her butt. The doors slide open again.

"What the fuck, Russ?" She's up on her feet and lunging toward the door. I'm surprised at how quickly she can move.

I shove her back as the doors start to close again. "Get away from me!" I say. "I don't want you to get hurt." I catch a glimpse of the Russians darting out of one car and into the next as I duck back inside the doors. They've moved a little closer to the front of the train.

"Russ, you stupid fucking fuck! You don't know what you're doing!"

The last two words are muffled because the doors shut as she says them. As the train rolls away, she stares at me angrily. I want her to go back to her life. I want her to be safe. But I don't want to be away from her. In my desire to protect her, I've just assaulted her. That first push would have knocked down a football player.

The anger in her eyes is an expression I haven't seen before. That easy-going manner of hers made me think she was immune to this kind of emotion. But there it is.

As the train lurches forward, the anger on her face melts into hurt. I can't stand to see her look like that. The car with the Russians will pass her in a couple of seconds. I want her to turn around, so they don't see her face. Please don't let them see you!

"Turn around!" I say. And I twirl my finger as if I'm stirring an upside-down drink.

She's several feet back on the platform now, with a puzzled, slightly insulted look. She didn't understand the gesture. What did she think I said? People sometimes twirl their finger like that when they say a sarcastic "Whoop-de-doo!" I hope she doesn't think I'm making fun of her.

Please take care of yourself, Cali.

andrew diamond

7

THE TRAIN RUMBLES TOWARD Montgomery Street and I'm in the front car, with no place to run as the Russians make their way forward from car to car. I can see the lights of the next stop just ahead, and the train is beginning to slow.

This station should be bustling this time of day, and I should be able to lose myself in the crowd. Except it isn't, and I can't, because it's Sunday. I have a moment of panic when we roll into the near-empty station. I stand by the door with my hand on the metal post, waiting to take off like Usain Bolt when the doors open.

The dour-faced Yuri and his tall, athletic friend are coming through the door at the far end of the car. Between them and me is the length of the car, and at the middle door, a woman with a stroller and a man listening to an iPod.

The train comes to a halt and then...nothing. Yuri and his friend have almost reached the center of the car, where the man and woman wait to exit. I pound on the doors. "Come on! Come on! Come on!"

When they open, I bolt, full speed ahead toward the escalator. Don't look back! That'll slow you half a step, and that could be all the difference. I hear the woman scream, and then a male voice. "Motherfucker!" That must be the guy with the iPod. A baby wails. Did one of the Russians knock over the stroller? I hear a scuffle.

I go up the escalator, hop the turnstile, head up to the street, and run toward the Galleria, hoping the sidewalks will be crowded with tourists. My throat and chest are burning as I round the corner at Kearny and head up the hill.

They say when your life is on the line you get a burst of adrenaline that gives you superpowers. I got that burst and spent it all getting out of the station. Now I'm starting to drag. Should I keep running? Or try to fade into the crowd? Without thinking it through, I merge into the stream of pedestrians in the crosswalk, slowing to match their pace.

Looking back for the first time since I left the train, I see Yuri rounding the corner one block behind me. Good thing my enemies sent a smoker out to chase me. I can see him heaving all the way from here. His friend is just now catching up to him. I'm guessing he got tied up in the scuffle back there on the train.

Both men slow to a walk and scan the street. Do they see me? I don't know. I'm walking in stride with the other pedestrians now, looking at the pavement, watching my feet go. One, two. One, two. One, two.

As soon as I'm past the edge of the first building, out of their view, I take off again, running as fast as I can. I go two blocks west, but I'm going uphill. My throat and lungs burn, and I'm getting a stitch in my side.

In high school, when the coach tried to recruit me onto the cross-country team, I ran a mile in under six minutes. And I hated every step of it. The coach kept pleading with me to give it some time. "You have a gift," he said. "Most people aren't physiologically capable of running a six-minute mile." But I just didn't like it. I was thirteen years younger then, and fifteen pounds lighter, and right now I'm feeling every bit of the extra weight and years.

I turn left, just so I can head downhill. I keep the same pace, but it's easier now. At the next intersection, I instinctively look left, back toward the Galleria where the Russians lost me. And *shit!* There they are, just half a block away!

While I was running uphill and turning and coming back down, they just walked straight up Geary street. They're rested, and I'm almost spent. When they spot me, they break into a run. The tall one is much faster than Yuri. I start to sprint, but I can't go much farther.

As I approach the end of the block, four women are exiting Macy's. I push right through them, past the Chanel counter and turn left. I duck behind a cosmetics counter and try to catch my breath.

The taller Russian was only a few seconds behind me. He must be in the store by now, but I don't want to risk standing up or peeking around the counter. There's some kind of ruckus at the other end of the store, down by men's fragrances. When I look that way, I see the tall Russian dashing toward the source of the noise.

"Thank God," I whisper. The exit is just a few steps from where I'm hiding. Again, I keep my head bowed and my eyes on the floor as I walk quickly toward the door. If he turns, I don't want my head above the crowd, and I don't want him to see me running.

Just as I'm passing through the door, I think *Shit! You forgot about Yu—* He grabs my shirt with both hands, and he has an unpleasant smile on his face. *What's wrong with you, Russ? You knew he'd be lagging behind the athletic one. What were you thinking?*

My mistake fills me with a surge of anger, and as he pulls me toward him, I crouch and then lunge upward so that the crown of my head catches him under the chin. He staggers backward onto the sidewalk, still holding my shirt. He lands on his back, pulling me down on top of him, and my forehead hits his face with enough force to flatten his nose and pound the back of his skull into the pavement. His grasp relaxes all at once, and as he lies there looking up at the sky glassy-eyed, I take off again. I run down Stockton, around the corner onto Market, and back into the BART station.

The airport train is just rolling in as I reach the platform. I guess I'm going back to Richmond.

8

On Monday morning, I get to work at 9:30. Apparently, I'm supposed to be in a meeting that's just starting. Brad, Ethan, and Karim are in Ethan's office talking about the developers they interviewed up in DC. Karim hands me four paper résumés with printed code samples attached.

"Two of the candidates failed the code challenge," Karim says. "These four did well, but this guy Travis might have a personality problem, and Cindy doesn't really have a personality. She's a non-communicator. I don't know if we can work with her."

I look at the résumés and say, "So Nelson and Alex passed the code test and you think they'll fit in with..."

That's about as much conversation as I can muster today. I don't care about Nelson or Alex or anyone else in this room right now. I keep hearing Cred's plea. "Give them what they want. Please!" And the three thudding blows and the silence at the other end of the line.

Then I think of Cali in the hotel, and the shyness in her eyes, Cali smashing into the door of the train and falling backwards onto the platform. And Mario, that little beast! "You have more friend? You have girlfriend, Russell?" I'll kill him if he goes near her. I'll kill them both!

But what can I do from here? They could be knocking at her door right now. Maybe she's already dead.

That thought makes my heart pound with grief. My chest is tight, and it's getting hard to breathe. I'm in a cold sweat. I'm losing it. I don't know what to do. I don't know...

Who am I supposed to tell about this? The FBI? If Jack Hayes is the special agent in charge, anything I say will get back to him. And what the hell is he going to do for me?

Do I tell the local cops? "Yeah, some guy ripped off a bunch of people in an online black market and left me the proceeds after he got murdered. Can you get that crooked fed off my case so I can just live in peace?"

What if I just turn myself in? I *could* do that.

But for what? I haven't done anything. They'll tell me to go home, and I'll be right back where I am now, waiting helplessly for the next beating. Or worse. And besides, Hayes wants the key to the server, and I don't have it.

Mario and Donkey Kong are psychopaths, but what about the Russians? They're pretty businesslike. This is just a job for them. If they're working with Hayes, it has to be a marriage of convenience. He feeds them information they can't otherwise get, like the GPS data that Verizon picks up from my phone. And they can do things an FBI agent can't do, like beat me up and take my computer and then not have it show up in the agency's evidence lockers.

What if I gave *the Russians* the key? Mario and Donkey Kong would probably kill me.

But these speculations are pointless, because I don't even have the key. I have nothing to bargain with and no way out of this mess. I keep thinking of what Cali said. "You *are* the encryption key." All that's left for me to do is lead my enemies to their pot of gold, so they can kill me.

I hate you, Charlie Taylor. I fucking hate you.

My only hope right now is a clean escape. I'll take a bus to another city and fly from there with the passport Wisp made. I'll go to Costa Rica, where I'll be just another expat, living with the surfers. Hell, I'll do freelance jobs on Upwork if I have to. No one will know who I am.

I close my eyes and the vision of the sand, the palms, the broad blue horizon puts me at ease. I'll leave tonight. Maybe this afternoon. Maybe even now.

When I open my eyes again, Brad, Ethan, and Karim are all staring at me.

"You okay?" Brad asks.

A silver SUV rolls up in the alley, just outside the window behind Ethan's desk. One monstrous arm hangs over the edge of the driver's door as the vehicle comes to a stop. As I stare at the driver's ugly head, that hairless egg standing pointy-side up with rolls of fat behind the ears, my coworkers turn to see what's out there. Donkey Kong is wearing cheap black-rimmed sunglasses with reflective lenses and making kissy faces at me.

"Who's that?" Karim asks.

"Someone who's going to be dead in a few hours," I say. Because it's not just his ugly face and what he did to Cred. It's four stifling years of life on the straight and narrow. Four years of pent-up frustration. You stupid fucking ape. You have no idea what you're getting into.

9

I MUST HAVE LOOKED PRETTY agitated when I left the office. And I'm sorry I had to hit Trish and Brad, but why the fuck did they try to block the exit?

The clerk in the gun store is just as unhelpful as my coworkers, but he's going to be harder to hit, because he's behind the counter. He puts the Ruger twenty-two back into the glass case and he's locking it up.

"God dammit," I say. "I don't want a little pussy twenty-two."

"And you're not getting one," he says.

"I need something that'll take a guy's head off with one shot. 'Cause this is a big-ass motherfucker I'm going to kill, and he has a friend. Do you have those hollow-tip bullets?"

The guy behind the counter waves to another clerk, who comes over and puts his hand on my shoulder and says, "You're gonna have to leave, pal." He's a strong guy, a little chubby, with close-cropped hair, a mustache, and a camouflage shirt.

"I just need a gun, okay? This is a gun shop, right?"

The two gentlemen escort me out to the parking lot, and the chubby guy says, "What's the matter with you, buddy? You in some kind of trouble?"

"I'm in all kinds of trouble."

"You own a gun?"

"No. That's why I'm here."

"You own any weapons of any kind? A knife? A crossbow?"

"No. Those wouldn't do me any good. This guy's too big to fight."

We chat for a couple of minutes out there in front of the store, and he seems pretty nice. I mean, he seems like he actually cares about what I'm saying. He keeps asking me questions, and he listens to my answers. He's got his hand on my shoulder the whole time.

"You owe someone money?"

"No," I say.

"He owe you money?"

"No."

The hand on my shoulder. It's not for reassurance. He's holding me here.

"Is this about a woman?"

I think of Cali, and what Donkey Kong did to Cred, and I say, "If he touches her, I'll fucking kill him. I'll rip his head off with my bare hands and throw it in the sewer."

A police car comes roaring into the lot with its flashers on. It skids to a stop in front of us and a cop jumps out with a club in his hand.

"What do we got here?" he says to the clerk.

The clerk finally lets go of my shoulder. "This guy came in for a gun. He's talking about shooting someone. I think his lady's mixed up with another man."

"Where's your girlfriend?" the cop says.

Is he asking about Jamie, or Cali?

"One's in New York," I say. "The other's in California."

The cop asks which one of them is seeing someone else.

"Jamie. The one in New York."

He wants to know if I'll be traveling up there. I tell him no.

"Is Jamie coming down here?"

"Not for another week or so."

"Who was it you wanted to shoot?"

"Donkey Kong. Mario too."

The cop nods his head and looks me up and down.

"What about your other girl? The one in California?"

I tell him I'm never going to see her again. And then I just start crying.

The cop asks me if I want to sit down. I sit on the back bumper of his car, and the clerk brings me an orange soda.

"Can I see your ID?" the cop says.

"Sure." I open my wallet and find four licenses. For a moment, I'm confused. They all have my picture.

I finally hand him my real license, and he says, "Russell Fitzpatrick? You live here in Richmond, huh?"

He checks his computer and says, "No priors." Then he asks where I work. He calls the office and, from what I hear, it sounds like Brad tells him I left there in a huff. They talk for a minute and the cop says, "That so?" Then he makes another call. I can't hear what he's saying, but he's keeping an eye on me as I drink my soda.

After a minute, he hangs up and he says, "You feeling any better?"

"A little," I say.

"You want to go for a ride?"

"Where to?"

"The hospital."

As we leave the parking lot, the cop says, "So it's been ten days since you got the concussion?"

"Yeah. I forgot about that."

"Had a lot of headaches?"

"Yeah." I actually don't recall if my head has been hurting more than usual. But figuratively, yes, I've had a lot of headaches these last ten days.

"Mood swings?"

"Crazy mood swings," I say.

The cop nods. "Irritable and short-tempered too, huh? You remember Dr. Drescher?"

"The neurologist?"

"He wants to check up on you."

The cop sits with me in the ER waiting room, and I nod off.

Dr. Drescher wants to keep me overnight for observation. That's fine with me. I need a little rest.

10

AFTER A LUNCH OF grilled cheese and green beans, I spend the afternoon watching TV and drifting in and out of sleep. One of Dr. Drescher's interns comes by to check my vision and reflexes. He says I'm A-OK. When he asks what set me off, I say very calmly and thoughtfully, "I just didn't like what I saw in the alley. I don't want to talk about it, because it might get me all worked up again."

The intern smiles and says I'm thinking more clearly now, and the psychiatrist will come see me this evening.

He's right about one thing. My thinking is crystal clear, and I know exactly what to do.

The shift changes at 5:00 p.m., and at 5:30 I get a visit from the new nurse. When she asks if I need anything, I rattle off the list: a juicer, a pair of those yellow rubber gloves that the cleaning lady wears, some black cloth tape, the wooden Japanese sword I saw in the thrift shop a couple of weeks ago, a decent helmet, and—I know this last one is expensive, but we have to be serious about our safety—one of those padded leather outfits that the motorcycle racers wear.

She makes a note on my chart and asks if I'd like to watch TV. No. I've been watching Mexican soap operas all afternoon, and I'm bored as hell. But my Spanish is pretty good.

At 6:45, I walk out. If someone was supposed to be watching me, they fucked up. The thrift store closes at 7:00, so I go there first. They still have the sword. Jamie wanted it for her birthday, which is in three weeks. She can have it when I'm done.

CVS has the juicer and gloves, but there's no motorcycle shop within walking distance. There is a used sporting-goods store, and they have the black cloth tape. The kind you wrap around the handle of a hockey stick. That gives me an idea. I should wrap the USB stick too. Nice and thick. So I get a second roll.

I also get two of those padded chest protectors that the catchers wear in baseball, along with the catcher's knee and shin guards. And a football helmet. That ought to do me. It's 8:00 p.m. and I should eat, but I have work on my mind.

I head over to Jamie's place and pick up the mail. The painters removed the doorknob and lock from the door of the apartment across the hall. The whole place smells of paint, the floor inside is covered with a tarp, and the windows are covered in a thin plastic film framed by blue masking tape.

I unlock Jamie's door, put the mail on the table, and set up the juicer. This is going to take an hour or so. Should I turn my phone on, in case anyone needs to find me? Sure. Why not?

I take off the rubber gloves and turn on the phone. As soon as it boots up, I see three texts from Cali.

Miss you.
Sorry I yelled.
Russ?

Cali Rey. She put her name and number into my contact list, and her name is Cali Rey. Somehow, that makes me like her even more.

Why is she texting me? *She's doing it because she feels just like you do, Russ.* But she was safe. No one knew she existed. And now there's a record of her contacting you. She just gave herself away, and they'll be after her. Oh, Cali. I wanted to keep you out of all this. I pushed you away just to keep you safe! And now you've gone and exposed yourself.

They can't get her if you kill them, Russ. Get back to work.

I push the thought of her aside and find Jamie's little USB stick on the table by her books. I wrap it in black tape. Then I tape the sword handle nice and thick. Now the gloves. Then the juicer. That takes the most time.

Now get dressed. First, the catcher's padding. One in front and one in back. That still leaves a hole over my ribs, but it does cover my crotch. And these shin guards are much stronger than the ones soccer players wear. They even cover my kneecaps.

I put the little USB stick, wrapped in a fat cocoon of wet cloth tape, into Jamie's underwear drawer. It's starting to get dark, so I turn on the lights. If Mario is out on the street, that will tip him off. Oh, and I should close the curtains at least part way, so the neighbors won't have to watch me get beat up. Don't close them all the way though. Mario needs to see a sliver of light coming through, so he'll know I'm here.

Mario and his gorilla are still cruising around in that SUV. I'm sure of it. They know where I live, where I work, and where Jamie lives. Maybe they're looping by all three places, trying to find me. I sit on the edge of the bed, with the wooden sword between my knees, contemplating this possibility. But after a minute, my mind starts drifting to other things.

Does Cali really miss me? Where is she now? Why couldn't we have stayed in that hotel forever? If I had had time to think things through, I would have asked her to run away with me. I already had the passport. Why did the Russians have to come and ruin everything?

I'm starting to nod off when I hear a gentle knock on the door. I wonder if it's the Russians. Donkey Kong would certainly knock harder. I can't get a good view through the peephole with this football helmet on, but it looks like there's a little guy and a big guy out there. Which is a good thing, because I just remembered that the Russians carry guns and this whole plan wouldn't work at all on them.

When I open the door, Donkey Kong steps right around Mario and I catch the puzzled look on his face as he reaches to grab my collar. I'm holding the wooden sword by the wrong end when I bring the handle down with a sharp crack in the center of his forehead. He blinks, a trickle of blood appears, and I drop the sword.

Donkey Kong picks it up by the handle and is about to swing at my head when he stops himself. He takes a swing at my throat and the wooden blade nicks me as I pull away. Mario shuts the door and Donkey Kong pins me sideways against the wall. His left hand is pushing so hard against the side of my neck that I'm starting to see stars. He delivers three quick, hard blows to my right thigh, and my body goes limp. But I can't fall down, because he's holding me up.

He turns me around so I'm facing the wall, wraps one big hand around the back of my neck and pushes me forward with the strength of an elephant. The facemask of the football helmet is pressing into the wall and tilting my head back at a sharp, painful angle. I know he's look-

andrew diamond

ing for another soft spot to hit, and I can hear Mario dumping out the drawers of Jamie's desk.

He says in his little voice, "Where the key is, Russell?"

Donkey Kong gives me a chop on the calf with the sword, followed by another just above the back of the knee. When I yell, Mario says, "Shhh! You bother the neighbors."

He turns on the radio—Steely Dan, "My Old School"—and when Donkey Kong yanks me away from the wall, I catch a glimpse of Mario dumping out Jamie's jewelry box. Donkey Kong sticks out his leg and pushes me over it. I land on the floor on all fours, and he brings the sword down four times on my back. I can feel the blows right through the padding, and I yell again.

Mario, now heading for the kitchen, tells Donkey Kong in Spanish to put something in my mouth. There's nothing handy, so Mario tosses him a dishrag. Donkey Kong tries to shove the rag into my mouth, but he can't get his fat hand up inside the facemask. He starts trying to rip the helmet off by the mask, wrenching my head in seven directions at once.

I unsnap the chinstrap to keep my neck from breaking, and he pulls the helmet off. He pushes me onto the bed and stuffs the dishrag into my mouth. While he looks for a place to hit me, he's got my face pinned down with his left hand, which is so big it covers my mouth and nose. I can't breathe. I hear Mario dumping out the kitchen drawers.

I curl up in a ball, knees up like a dead bug, so the padding covers everything but my arms and head. Donkey Kong takes a couple of half-hearted swats at my knees and shins before I really start to struggle. His giant hand and that filthy rag are suffocating me, and I'm going to black out.

Mario says something, and the gorilla lets go of my face and pulls the rag out of my mouth. I stare at the ceiling for a couple of seconds, gasping and seeing stars.

"Eh?" Mario says. "You no good housekeeper? You flowers all die!" He's holding one of the empty flowerpots from the windowsill, digging through the soil. "You hide the key in here? USB stick maybe?"

impala   143

"No." I say, and Donkey Kong gives me a whack in the center of the forehead, in the same spot where I hit him a few minutes ago. Now I'm a little delirious. I don't know what's happening. His giant hand wraps around my throat and then…

Did I black out? The apartment is trashed. And Mario's on the other side of the room all of a sudden. He's going through Jamie's dresser drawers.

Maybe I did black out, because Donkey Kong was sitting down, and now he's standing up like he's suddenly back on duty. He's raising the sword. I curl up again, but I'm on my side now, and when the sword comes down on my thigh, it doesn't really hurt that bad. Is my body starting to shut out the pain? Or is Donkey Kong losing his power? He looks sick. His face is pale and sweaty, and he's a little shaky. He switches the sword to his left hand.

Mario is opening the drawer to the left of Jamie's underwear as Donkey Kong raises his arm for another blow. I say, "You're getting warmer, Mario." The little guy turns and looks at me, and he has a funny expression on his face. He holds up his hand to Donkey Kong, palm forward, like a traffic cop signaling him to stop.

Donkey Kong lowers the sword and takes a seat on the bed. He wipes his sweaty face with the cloth-wrapped sword handle. The idiot!

Mario leans down toward me with a puzzled look and says, "How do you know my name?"

"The key," I say, "is in the underwear drawer. The one you were about to open."

Mario straightens up and looks at his gorilla, who is sweating and struggling for breath. He smiles and says in Spanish, "I told you. You drank too much rum last night. You're not ready for work." Mario gives him a little pat on the back as he goes over to the dresser, where he digs through the underwear drawer until he finds the wet black wad of cloth tape.

"It's in here?" he asks.

"It's in there," I say.

Mario gives me an uncertain look and then begins to pick at the tape. Donkey Kong shakes his right arm out twice, then puts the sword back in his right hand and shakes his left arm. Mario sees this out of the corner of his eye as he peels back a layer of tape, and he asks in Spanish, "Did you wear yourself out?"

In a raspy voice, Donkey Kong says, "My arm is numb."

Mario says, "Use the other one."

"It's tingling."

Charlie was right. I am just as devious as him. As Donkey Kong's breathing grows more difficult, I start to breathe easier. I know it's only a matter of time. Aconite absorbs straight through the skin. First you feel the tingling, then the numbness. And if you've been in contact with it long enough, the neurotoxin will stop your breathing. The black cloth tape on the sword handle and the tape Mario is trying to pick off the USB stick are soaked in the liquid I juiced from the leaves, stems, and roots of Jamie's flowers. She calls them monkshood. I call them wolfsbane. Tom-ay-to, tom-ah-to. Some things we just never could agree on.

Mario has started to shake his hands and is sweating when Donkey Kong slumps off the side of the bed and goes face-first onto the floor. The big guy took a while to go. Mario is much smaller, and he's had both hands all over that tape for a few minutes now. Mario rubs his eyes and lets out a slow breath. He looks at his fallen friend and says to me, "Hey, what you put..." He leans against the dresser and examines the wad of cloth tape in his hand. "What you put in here?" He looks queasy and unsteady.

"Shh," I say. "Go to sleep."

Beneath that big mustache of his, all I can see is his bottom lip. It's turning blue. When he slumps to the floor, I get up off the bed and start cleaning up the contaminated items. All of Jamie's underwear goes into a black garbage bag, along with the juicer and the sword and the wad of tape that just fell out of Mario's hand. He's on his side on the floor by the dresser, still breathing a little bit. His glazed, reddening eyes follow me in a delayed, half-conscious way.

I fill a second garbage bag with the helmet and the baseball pads.

My whole body hurts, and the apartment is trashed. The contents of the shelves and drawers are strewn across the floor. The coat rack is knocked over, and in the middle of it all are two soon-to-be-dead bodies. I should clean those up. Jamie hates it when I leave stuff lying around.

I drag them into the empty apartment across the hall. First Mario, then the gorilla, which takes a lot of work. Funny how he looks like a big sleeping baby. I put Mario on top of him, and then wrap the ape's giant arm around him, like a teddy bear. Good night, you two.

Back in Jamie's place, I turn off the lights and open the curtains. There's not much of a moon tonight, but the street lamps send plenty of light into the second-story windows as the end of Coldplay's "High Speed" streams through the speakers.

I GO OUT THROUGH THE back door and toss the black garbage bags into a dumpster a block away. I was thinking about taking them farther, but why bother covering my tracks? It's not like I'm going to stick around here. What do I have left in this town anyway?

The only thing I still care about is...My phone chimes, and wouldn't you know it? We're always on the same wavelength.

Cali: I miss you.

I might as well respond. She's already established the digital link between us.

Russ: Miss you too.
Cali: Why'd you leave?
Russ: To keep you out of trouble.
Cali: I have a surprise for you.
Russ: Somehow that makes me uncomfortable.

When I reach my block, I scan the street in front of my building. I see plenty of parked cars, but no little black Honda. The street is dead. At the building entrance, my phone chimes again.

Cali: Do you really miss me?

I stop on the old wood floor inside the front door and type.

Russ: Very much. But you shouldn't have texted me. You're giving yourself away.

I miss her face, her voice, the sound of her bracelets, the feel of her body, her laugh, and her scent. As I start up the stairs, there's nothing in the world I want more than to be with her somewhere far from all this trouble.

Then I get another text.

Cali: Can't wait to see you!

Does love make us perceive what we want to perceive? Or is it just desire that does that? Because I can almost feel her next to me as I climb the stairs. I can smell her scent. Or else it's one of the neighbors smoking pot.

I stop at the landing and type a response.

Russ: will call in a few.

Should I send that message? Should I call her? What's the point of torturing myself with something I can't have? I just killed two people to try to get out of a mess I'm not fully out of yet. I consider erasing the message and just typing *No*.

As I climb the last few steps, this ordeal begins to feel like an unbearable weight. I still can't see the way out, and the dark currents are pulling me down. The voice inside my head says, *Maybe the Russians will be waiting in your apartment. Maybe they'll spare you the trouble of running.* In a way, I hope they *are* in there. Let them put a bullet through my head and end all this.

And then I think again of Cali. It's a painful, bittersweet thought. *You showed me what I was missing. But no one said I'd get to keep you.* No one said life would be fair.

If I do call her, what will I say? Goodbye?

I send the text.

As I exit the stairway to the second floor, I see someone knocking on my door down the hall. She's wearing a backpack, a long green skirt, and a white blouse. Her phone chimes as my text arrives, and her bracelets clink as she turns the little screen to her eyes. The door opens in front of her, and when she looks up with an expectant smile, they pull her in and slam it shut.

andrew diamond

12

"CALI!"

Did she hear me before they got her?

I try to sprint toward my door, and wind up half running, half hobbling. Those blows to my thighs and calves really took their toll.

I bang on the apartment door, shouting Cali's name until the tall athletic Russian answers with a gun in my face. He has his finger up in front of his lips. *Shhh!* I forgot, these guys like quiet. He waves me in with his left hand, keeping the gun pointed at my head. Then he shuts the door and scowls and flicks the gun up twice, motioning me to put my hands up. I raise them to my ears and keep them there.

Yuri is holding Cali near the foot of the bed. They're both standing, and he has her arm twisted up behind her, just like he did to me back in the alley. His other hand covers her mouth. Her eyes are wide and her nostrils flare in panic above his chunky, nicotine-stained fingers.

Yuri grunts something to his friend, and the guy with the gun nudges me over toward him. Yuri's hand comes off of Cali's mouth and transforms into a fist that flattens my nose with shocking speed and power. The blow sends me stumbling backwards into the dresser, but I stay on my feet.

Yuri smiles and points to his own swollen nose. It looks like I might have broken it when my head smashed into his face on the sidewalk in San Francisco the other day. Hot blood is gushing onto my shirt.

The tall Russian tells me to sit down in the swivel chair by my desk and to keep my hands on my head. I do as he says. He keeps the gun on me as he picks up a roll of duct tape from the dresser. They've come prepared.

Yuri wraps the tape around Cali's mouth, leaving a little slit so she can breathe. As he tapes her wrists behind her back, I scan the apartment. The clothing from my dresser is on the floor, all neatly folded. Some other items that were in the dresser, including a dead Android phone, an old digital camera, and an old wallet, are arranged neatly on top.

These guys are so much more methodical than Mario and his ape. I wonder where they trained. Maybe they were cops, and this is what Russian law enforcement officers do when they retire.

I notice they closed the curtains. They've also removed all the sheets and pillowcases from the bed and left them on the floor, beside the contents of my night table drawer. The mattress is askew. They've already been under there. I can hear someone else in the kitchen, going through the drawers.

Once Cali is taped up, Yuri leaves her sitting on the floor, with her knees drawn up and her back against the bed. He stands in front of me and smiles again. Then his face turns mean, and I know another punch is coming. I try to turn away, but it catches me on the cheek and snaps my head around. Now I'm dizzy.

Yuri hollered right when the blow landed. I think he hurt his hand. The other guy is saying something to him in a hushed, angry tone. Probably telling him to shut up.

Yuri stuffs a sock in my mouth and wraps tape over it, but he does a sloppy job. I can still breathe a little through my mouth, which is a good thing, because I can't get any air through my nose after that punch he landed.

He tapes my wrists to the arms of the swivel chair and starts spinning me around. Every three or four turns, I get a punch in the face from Yuri's left hand. He's not very good with his left. Not against a moving target anyway. Most of the blows are glancing, but even the little ones hurt.

"Where is key?" asks the big Russian.

How am I supposed to answer that with my mouth taped shut? "Mmmph!"

"You have answer? Untape him!"

Yuri protests, and the tall guy says again, "Where is key? Photograph key is fake."

"Mmmph," I say again. I'm not actually saying anything. I'm just making noises, hoping to get the tall one to stop Yuri from beating me. And I'm starting to panic because I can't get enough air. The panic makes

andrew diamond

me breathe harder, and that makes things worse.

As I spin, I see Cali on the floor, then the curtained window, the desk, the door to the kitchen, the front door, then the big fist coming at me. My head snaps back again, and the next thing I see is the desk. Two desks. And then Jack Hayes coming though the kitchen door saying, "Nothing in there."

The apartment is getting dimmer. I can't keep my head up, but I feel the little jerk each time Yuri gives the chair another spin.

Cali is half crying, half yelling through her tape. I can't lift my head up high enough to see her anymore.

"Does he have the key?" Jack asks.

"Don't know," says the Russian.

"Have you searched him?"

"Not yet."

"What about the girl?"

My chair stops spinning. Jack Hayes' hands are on my forearms and he's leaning over me. "Where's the key, Russ?" I can't lift my head to look at him, but I can hear Cali crying. The room is spinning. I'm about to black out.

Jack gives my chair a forceful shove. It rolls back and slams against the edge of the desk, jolting my head. I'm starting to panic even more. I can't get enough air no matter how hard I try. My heart is racing, and my lungs hurt. The room keeps getting darker, and the sounds are getting farther away.

From somewhere in the distance, I hear Hayes say, "Is it in the girl?"

I lift my head up with my last bit of strength. He's standing over her. They both go spinning by, left to right, left to right, over and over again. I don't think my chair is moving anymore. But everything else seems to be. He grabs her under the arm and pulls her roughly up onto the bed. He reaches up her skirt and pulls her underwear down as she tries to clamp her legs shut.

"Check the girl, Yuri. I don't like getting my hands dirty."

My head slumps again as Yuri turns toward Cali. I try to stand up, but I'm too weak and dizzy. I wind up on my side on the floor, listening to Cali's muffled screams.

I can see her from the corner of my eye. Yuri is about to grab her when the other Russian pulls him back.

"Take off tape," he says.

Yuri tries to argue, but the tall one brushes him aside and removes the tape himself.

As soon as it's off, she gasps, "*I* have the key! *I* have it! Stop hurting him!" I close my eyes and listen to her sob.

The three men are standing around her in a semicircle at the foot of the bed. I'm trying to breathe as slowly and deeply as I can, but my heart is racing.

"Untie my hands," Cali says. "Will you let us go if we give you the key? Will you?"

"Give us the key," Jack says.

Yuri removes the tape from her wrists, and I can just see her, in the space between the two Russians, as she pulls up the big turquoise stone on the wide silver bracelet. It's on a hinge, and she removes from beneath it a micro-SD card, no bigger than a woman's fingernail. She hands it to Jack, and there is an air of quiet calm in the room.

Hayes examines the little chip for a moment and then walks into the kitchen. He returns with a black shoulder bag from which he removes a laptop. He puts it on the dresser, then fishes through the pockets of the bag for something. The big Russian hands his pistol to Yuri, who pulls a silencer from his jacket pocket and slowly starts screwing it onto the end of the gun.

The big Russian walks over to Jack Hayes and watches him fit the micro-SD card into a standard SD adapter. Hayes slides that into his computer, and the two of them study the screen while he types. Then the big Russian points and says, "Is key. RSA."

"Yeah, but where's the server?"

The Russian points again. "Text file."

Hayes clicks the track pad, and the Russian says, "You see? Is IP address."

"All right," says Hayes. "Let's see if this works."

He begins to type. Yuri has finished attaching the silencer, and Cali watches him with wide eyes. I keep my eyes on her now. Her face might be the last thing I ever see. She must feel that I'm watching her. I say her name silently in my mind. *Cali.* She turns to me, and her eyes are full of fear.

And then Jack Hayes says an excited, "Ah!"

He turns the screen to the big Russian, who reads aloud from the screen. "Root at vault." That's the command prompt you would see after a successful login.

Without looking up, Jack Hayes says, "Put that down, Yuri."

Yuri points the pistol at Cali's forehead and says, "Nyet!"

"I'll take care of these two," Hayes says.

The big Russian turns and gives Yuri a nod. Then he takes a step to the side, and the atmosphere in the room changes all at once as Yuri turns the gun toward Hayes. But the big Russian's movement must have tipped Hayes off, because just as Yuri pulls the trigger, Hayes ducks down and to the side. The bullet rips through the apartment door near where Hayes' head had been.

Hayes is upright again in a split second, and he pulls the big Russian toward him as Yuri fires a second shot. The big Russian yells as the bullet grazes his shoulder, putting a hole and a splatter of blood on the wall.

Yuri rushes toward Hayes to get a closer shot, but the big Russian is off balance, and Hayes is able to push him backward into Yuri. The two Russians end up on the floor, Yuri and his gun pinned beneath the bigger guy. Hayes grabs his computer and bolts through the front door, pulling it shut on the way out. The big Russian is up first, then Yuri, and the two of them run after Hayes. The big Russian lets out a yelp when his shoulder hits the doorframe. Yuri pushes past him and heads down the hall.

A few seconds later, from down on the street I hear the roar of a car engine and screeching tires. Then muffled gunshots and Yuri yelling in Russian. The other Russian yells back. Car doors open and close, another engine roars, and the Russians' car takes off.

Cali is sobbing and hyperventilating as she untapes me from the fallen chair. She helps me up off the floor without a word, and when I'm on my feet, she grabs her bag and runs out the door.

"Cali?"

I try to run after her, but my muscles are too sore and I'm weak from lack of oxygen.

I open the stairway door just in time to hear the rear door of the building close.

"Cali?"

I hobble down the stairs as fast as I can. In the alley I look left, and she's not there. I look right, and I see she's almost made it to the street.

"Cali!"

She stops at the end of the alley. One more step, and she would be in the street, beneath the light. I don't know who I'm afraid of now, but I don't want her to be exposed and visible. I run, hop, hobble down to her, and she doesn't turn to me until I'm just a step away.

I wrap my arms around her. She presses her head into my chest, and her whole body is shaking.

Or is that me?

andrew diamond

13

WE START WALKING SLOWLY toward Jamie's. Cali is leaning on me, and I keep saying, "Shhh," until she says, "Stop shushing me. I'm not saying anything."

"But you're scared and you're breathing fast."

"No, that's you."

It is me.

We walk in silence for two blocks and my senses are on high alert. When the crickets rub their legs together, I hear the rasp at the beginning of the chirp like a violinist's bow on the strings. Cali is calm. She watches the fireflies.

"Where are we going?" she says.

"Jamie's. We need her car keys."

Cali looks at me, and I say, "I don't want to take my car. If Hayes got away, he's going to come looking for us."

"Right," she says. "You think the Russians got him?"

"I don't know," I say. "What does it matter? If he gets away, he has the key, and maybe a lot of money. Maybe he disappears and retires."

"Or maybe he kills us first," Cali says. "And if he didn't get away…"

"Then it's game over. The Russians kill him, and they have their loot. They go home, and we're free."

"What about the Colombians?"

I stop for a second, startled, and Cali says, "What?"

"I forgot about them."

"You think they'll come after us? For giving the key to someone else?"

"No."

"How can you be so sure?" She examines my face for a second, and her nostrils flare in surprise. "Did you…" She checks my face again. "Russ, what did you do?"

"They won't be bothering us," I say.

She grips my hand a little tighter and says, "Then it's not over. We're fugitives."

"I am."

"We are," she says. "I'm with you."

I can't move too fast, so it takes us a while to get to Jamie's. When we get into the air-conditioning, Cali puts her sweater on. I open the apartment door and feel a moment of terror at the sight of that mess. Cali scans the apartment, hugging herself like she's cold, and she whispers, "Are they here?"

"Across the hall," I say. And I see a little shiver run through her.

When she goes into the bathroom, I start looking for Jamie's car keys. They're somewhere on the floor with everything else. I start digging though the clothes, and in a few seconds I find the long, jagged Ford key. I hold it up just to be sure.

Cali is standing by the door with her arms crossed.

"You ready to go?" I ask.

"Can we clean you up a little? You look awful."

I touch my nose and instantly regret it. It's hot and swollen. I must have blood all over my face.

We go into the bathroom, and Cali wipes my face down with toilet paper soaked in hydrogen peroxide. I like her touch, even when it hurts.

"Why did you come here?" I ask.

"I wanted to give you the key, so you could walk away from all of this. I told you I had something for you. Remember?"

"You could have emailed it."

"But I missed you too. I don't just…" She hesitates for a moment, "…do what we did and not feel anything."

"Well, I'm glad we're on the same page there. What did you think I'd do with the key?"

"I don't know. Get out of this mess somehow. You could have given it to the FBI guy and bought yourself some protection."

"I could never trust that guy."

"Or you could have just run. Fifteen million dollars would have taken you a long way."

"Fifteen million dollars?"

"The blood on your chin is all crusty." Cali tosses the bloody wad of tissue into the toilet and prepares another. "You need to shave," she says, and she picks little bits of toilet paper out of my whiskers with her left hand and scrubs at the blood on my chin with her right.

"Fifteen million dollars?"

"At least," she says. "Charlie said he wasn't going to make his move until there was fifteen million in escrow. The only problem was—does this hurt?" She presses her fingertips lightly against my left cheekbone.

"Ow! Yes!"

"That might be broken, the way it's swollen."

"The only problem was what?" I ask.

She kisses me on the mouth.

"What was the problem?"

"The problem was that he talked the South Americans into doing a bunch of big transactions. And he let those go through. Then they did another round, and he let those through. So they started to trust him. Someone else was watching, and they put through some big transactions at about the same time. I guess those were the Russians. He was holding a lot of money from both of them."

She throws another wet wad of tissue into the toilet and picks the remnants from my whiskers.

"With those big transactions pending, and the usual money that flowed through escrow, he must have hit his fifteen million."

"Was that when he was down in Colombia? What was he doing there?"

She hesitates for a second, then says, "Something went wrong. He told me if I didn't hear from him, I should wait for you, and you would know what to do."

"Wait, you didn't answer the question. What was he doing in Colombia?"

Cali steps back and looks me over. "God, look at you! You could have been killed. Fucking Charlie, with his stupid plans!"

"It's not all his fault. You seem to have played along."

She gives me a guilty look, like a kid caught stealing, and she's about to say something, but she stops and says, "Let's not fight, okay?"

"Who's fighting?" I ask. "I just want to know…"

She shakes her head and says in a breaking voice, "I never should have gotten into this."

"Oh, I understand that feeling."

"Charlie has a way of getting people to do things they wouldn't normally do."

"Cred used to say the same thing."

"He asks you to make one little promise, and you have no idea what you're signing up for."

"Ha! You can say that again."

She takes a deep breath, and in a steadier voice she says, "It was like that with modeling too."

"What was like that?"

"The way he lures you in and tells you how beautiful you are, and, *Come on Cali, just take that off. Let your beauty shine. You're beautiful, Cali. You're beautiful!*"

"You are."

"I'm modest. And I'm shy."

"You're that too."

"But he could still make me do what he wanted me to do."

"You're not the only one."

"I know." She's quiet for a few seconds, just looking at the floor. Then she says, "What are you going to do? You're kind of fucked."

"I don't know. Run away somewhere? With you?"

She smiles her big broad smile, and I pull her toward me for a kiss. When we leave the bathroom, I ask if she has a passport.

She just stands there by the apartment door, staring at the fallen coat rack on the floor.

"Because we should probably leave the country," I say.

Still, she just stands there, staring down and breathing slowly.

"Cali," I say.

When she turns to look at me, her eyes are wide, like an owl's.

"Russ!" There's something ominous in her tone.

andrew diamond

"Wait," I say. "Where *is* my passport?"

I left my backpack in the kitchen when I came in with the juicer and the rubber gloves. The passport Wisp made me is in there. I go into the kitchen, but I don't see it. Where did I put it? Oh yeah. On top of the dish cabinet because I knew Mario was too short to see up there. I knew he'd be doing the searching while Donkey Kong did the beating.

When I return to the main room, Cali is setting the coat rack upright.

"Do you have a passport?" I ask again.

Her index finger traces the graffiti carved alongside the spiral pattern of the wooden post.

I hunch my shoulders to put my arms through the straps of the backpack, and in that moment as I look down, I see a strand of yarn hanging from the bottom of her sweater. I take it between my fingers and examine the marks near the end. This is a thin, firm yarn that doesn't stretch.

"Russ…" Cali says again. Her voice has a hollow tone, like she's struggling to recover from some surprise.

Three inches from the end of the white strand are the four colors that repeat in little irregular flecks throughout the sweater. Red, blue, green, and black, in that order, dabbed on with permanent marker. And it hits me all at once.

When I look up, Cali is staring into my face, and I can feel the energy running through her. I know she understands. Her hand is on the coat rack. She knows! God, I love this woman. I love her! I just want to hear her say it.

"That wasn't the key," she says.

"No," I say. "It wasn't."

"The markings carved into the coat rack…" Cali trails off because she sees that I get it too.

For giving us this blissful moment of oneness, I don't hate you anymore, Charlie. This is worth everything you put me through.

"Say it," I say.

"They're exactly the same as the markings carved into the post on the bed in Oakland."

"Yes…" I'm smiling.

"And the sweater," she says. She lifts the thread that has begun to unravel and looks at the colored markings.

This is the barber's pole. The final clue from the photo. It's one of the oldest encryption devices in the world. When the Spartans used it to pass messages in battle twenty-five centuries ago, they called it a scytale. They would wrap a leather strap around a wooden baton, and write a message on the leather from left to right. When they reached the end of the baton, they would rotate it and continue the message on a second line, and then a third, and so on. When they unwound the leather from the stick, the letters would all be out of order.

It was a simple transposition cipher. If the enemy captured the messenger, they couldn't make sense of the jumbled markings on the leather strap. But if the recipient was another Spartan, all he needed to decode the message was a baton of the same diameter, which had been arranged before the battle. He'd wind the leather strap around it, and the letters would all be in order again.

Charlie's version of the scytale is a little more complex. Someone carved words around the spiral grooves of the coat rack. It looks like simple graffiti swirling from bottom to top. Charlie lined up the colored markings at the end of the yarn with a screw at the bottom of the coat rack, and then wound the yarn through the spiral grooves until he reached a letter he wanted to encode. He put a mark on the yarn at that point, and continued winding upward until he reached the next letter he wanted to record. Then he'd put another mark on the yarn there. When he reached the top of the groove, he'd start again at the bottom.

The colors at the end of the yarn—red, blue, green and black— probably describe the order in which to decode the message. First all the red marks, then the blues, the greens, and then the blacks.

This is right in line with Charlie's paranoid philosophy: keep the most important information out of the digital realm. Don't leave the key on a server or even an SD card. Keep it where no computer will ever find it.

andrew diamond

"Where is your passport?" I ask.

"In California."

"Okay," I say. "Let's get out of here. And turn your phone off."

We take our backpacks, the coat rack, and the sweater and head to Jamie's car.

14

THE COAT RACK STICKS out the window when we lay it across the back seat of Jamie's little Ford, so we have to drive with the back window slightly open.

The events of the evening have left us both quiet but alert. Before we leave town, we stop at three bank machines, and I withdraw the three hundred dollar limit from each. It's good to have some cash when you're on the run.

We take the interstate west. After ninety minutes or so, we've passed Charlottesville and are heading over the mountains of the Blue Ridge. As we descend the pass from Afton into the Shenandoah Valley, Cali at last begins to relax. I didn't realize until now how much I'd felt her tension.

Route 64 merges into 81, and we head south beneath the thickening clouds. The lights of Richmond are a world away. The highway here winds along a lush valley floor, between fields and pastures punctuated occasionally by lonely farmhouse lights.

It's past midnight, and I'm thinking about hotels. Which takes my mind back to the hotel in San Francisco. I know we won't find anything that fancy, but I at least want someplace quiet and comfortable, where we can close the door on the world, if only for a night.

We find a Courtyard Marriott near Lexington, where I-81 and I-64 split.

"Will this do?"

Cali smiles. "This will do."

We sit in the parking lot for a moment, watching the headlights go by on the dark country highway. What are people doing out here at this time of night? Are they all on the run like us?

I point back to the road and say, "Think we'll follow that all the way to the West Coast? To pick up your passport?"

She leans against me and takes my hand. "That would be a nice trip."

"Maybe stop and see the Grand Canyon along the way?"

"I've always wanted to go there."

andrew diamond

In the lobby, a young man of twenty-five or so tends the desk. He is slim and upright in his dark suit, and his pomaded black hair shines beneath the bright yellow light. He seems out of place here, all alone in the night, groomed as if he stepped out of a movie from the 1930s. He welcomes us with the smile he's been waiting to use all evening, and asks in an officious tone, "Are we checking in?"

"We are."

His eyes keep moving from my face to my shirt, and I remember the shirt is covered with blood.

He looks at his computer and says, "Would you like a king?"

"Yes, please."

"And your name?"

I pull a credit card from my wallet and I have to read the name as I hand it to him. He sees this and gives me a funny look.

"Terry Armstrong," I say.

He forces a smile. "ID?"

I look through the licenses Wisp made. I should have done this out in the car. Terry Armstrong is from Overland Park, Kansas. The version of me in the photo has brown eyes and dark brown hair, while my hair is still light brown and my eyes are blue. I hand him the ID, but I have a sinking feeling about this.

He swipes the credit card and stands there blinking at the screen for a moment. Then he examines the license and looks me over.

He smiles and says, "Pardon me for just a moment." Then he goes into a little office behind the counter and shuts the door. Cali goes around the end of the counter and listens. After half a minute, she sneaks back around, pointing to the exit.

In the car, as the first big raindrops splat against the windshield, she tells me that Terry Armstrong of Overland Park is a Marriott Rewards member. And he's a she. And her card was canceled after being reported stolen.

"Maybe we should go someplace that takes cash," I say.

"We wouldn't leave a trail," Cali says. "But we'll probably wind up in a dump."

"Maybe," I say. "But it's just for one night."

I think it hits us both at the same time. We have no home anymore, and no plan. This might be the first of many nights like this. Again, it's as if she's reading my mind when she says, "If we can get into the server and cash out some of what Charlie left, we can stay in nice places. The Ritz-Carlton or The Four Seasons."

When she smiles, I feel both the warmth of her heart and the desperation of her fantasy.

She puts her hand on my thigh as we head southwest on a small, dark country road in search of a cash motel. The rain is picking up, and thunder is rolling down from the mountains in the west.

After thirty minutes, we find our little dump. It's hard to see clearly through the heavy rain, and I decide maybe it's better that way.

I leave Cali in the car and head into the motel office. The shoulders of my shirt are soaked through by the time I get inside. The floor is a worn, dust-colored linoleum. The paneled ceiling above the dingy counter is yellow from decades of tobacco smoke, and the whole place smells like a stale ashtray. I don't want to be here, but how long can we keep driving? And where else is there to go?

I ring the bell and someone rises from a creaking chair on the other side of the brown door behind the counter. He comes out chewing a mouthful of something, rubbing his hands on an unbuttoned dirty brown shirt. Beneath the open button-down is a dingy white t-shirt.

He's thirty or so, with dark hair, and he hasn't shaved in a few days. Everything about him is greasy: his hair, his skin, his stained shirts, his whole demeanor. Before he says anything, before he even makes eye contact, he sizes me up. I don't like the look on his face.

"Looking for a room?"

"Just for the night."

"The whole night?"

"Yeah, the whole night."

He doesn't like the tone of my response, and I don't like him.

"You take cash?" I ask.

"Sixty bucks," he says. "Who you with?"

"What?"

"You got a girl with you?" He leans over the counter and looks out to the parking lot. The rain is tapering off, but he can't see my car because it's parked behind a black pickup.

"What's it to you?" I'm seriously ready to hit this guy. And I notice now there's someone in the pickup. The desk clerk just gave him a little nod.

He says, "Take it easy, pal." Not in a tone that says, *Take it easy, I didn't mean anything by it,* but more like, *Watch how you act, or I'll fuck you up.*

I slide three twenties onto the counter and he tosses a key. Not to me, but at me. It bounces off the counter onto the floor.

I pick it up and go back to the car. Cali doesn't look right. She's sitting with her face turned toward the driver seat, away from the black pickup.

"You okay?"

Her voice is high and anxious. "Are we staying here?"

"I got a room. Do you want to go somewhere else?"

"Let's just go in," she says. "That guy gives me the creeps."

When I look over, I see the man in the pickup staring into the screen of his phone, his big bearded face lit in blue behind the rain-spattered window.

We grab the coat rack and the backpacks and head into room nine. It's a sad little place with a lumpy bed and a scuffed night table beneath one of those spiral compact fluorescent bulbs. The red carpet is stained with coffee and I don't know what else. Piss? Puke? It looks like they've done their best to clean it. There's no TV, and the two chairs and the little round table don't match.

We're tired from the long drive, but we're not sleepy. We're both still on edge after what happened in Richmond. Perhaps to distract us from the depressing room and this whole depressing situation, Cali says, "You want to start decoding the key?"

"Sure."

I stand the coat rack next to the bed, and Cali starts to un-knit her sweater. There's a tiny screw at the bottom of the rack, just above the feet that Charlie attached. When Cali has a few feet of yarn ready, I line up the screw with the four colors at the end of the string and start winding up through the carved swirl pattern. The first red mark lines up with a capital A. The next one lines up with a lowercase q.

I read the letters out to Cali as I go, and she writes them in a neat, clear hand on a sheet of paper. Every few minutes, we have to stop so she can un-knit more yarn. It's slow going. After an hour, we've managed to transcribe only a few dozen letters.

"You want to call it a night?" I say.

Cali nods and goes into the bathroom. When she returns, I'm taking off my pants.

"My God, Russ!"

"What?"

"Look at you!"

My legs are purple and red and my left thigh is swollen. When I look up again, Cali is studying my face with a look of pity.

"It's not that bad," I say. Actually, it is. I've been pretending for hours now that I'm okay because I don't want her to be more unhappy than she already is. But she can read me. She knows.

I climb into bed in my shirt and underwear while Cali takes off her skirt and bra.

"How do you take that off without removing your shirt?"

"I just do," she says. And I can tell from her tone she's done. She wants this day to be over. She wants it all to be over.

When she gets under the covers, she doesn't mention the rough sheets, or the moldy smell of the blanket. She pulls up close to me and puts her head on my chest. Her hip is pressing my thigh, and it hurts, but I don't say anything. We just lay there, listening to the couple in the next room thump the bed against the wall as the mattress springs groan in a sordid rhythm. They've been at it for a long time.

"I wonder if she's getting sore," Cali says.

Ever since I pushed her off that train in San Francisco, all I've wanted is to have her back. Now here we are, in the most unsexy situation imaginable. I'd rather us be apart, if this is the kind of unhappy life I'd be pulling her into. I'd rather know she's sleeping soundly someplace far away than have her here next to me, being dragged through this.

* * *

I must have fallen asleep, because Cali's head is not on my chest anymore, and I don't remember her moving. There are two men in the next room now, and it sounds like they're going to fight. Cali is sitting on the edge of the bed, listening quietly.

The door in the next room opens, and the two men go outside. Actually, it sounds like one of them threw the other one out. Now they're fighting.

No. It's not a fight. It's a beating. One of them curses as he delivers the blows. The other pleads for him to stop. Then it's quiet for a minute. A car starts and drives away.

The man goes back into the room next door and says, "How much you get?"

A woman answers, but I can't hear the amount.

He says, "Give it to me." Then it sounds like he hits her.

The door opens and the man leaves. He starts his truck. The knocking diesel engine roars out of the lot, and Cali goes into the bathroom and runs the water. She might be crying in there. I don't know. I can't help her. I'm too tired.

When I wake again, it's still dark, except for the bit of light coming from behind the half-closed bathroom door. Cali sits in the sliver of light, in one of the chairs by the round table, unraveling the sweater. Without looking up from her work, she whispers, "Go back to sleep, Russ." I don't know how she knows I'm awake.

15

IN THE MORNING, SUNLIGHT streams through the crack in the curtains, and Cali sits by the table with paper and pen, the coat rack, and a heap of unraveled yarn.

"What time is it?" I ask.

"Eight." She holds up the paper and smiles. When I try to sit up, I feel the pain everywhere, but especially in my legs and head.

Cali says, "Take it easy, Russ."

She's written out sixteen lines of the key, with sixty-four characters per line, exactly how an RSA key is formatted when it's written to a file. I wonder how she knows this, but I don't ask. I take the yarn and start winding. We're all the way up to the black markings. The last set.

I read out the characters as I wind the yarn around the staff: 9, capital S, small p, forward slash...

At last, we reach the equal sign, which marks the end of the key. There's still some yarn left, and a few markings, so we continue deciphering. Four numbers, separated by dots. This must be the IP address of the server. After that comes some text I don't understand:

dbxc4.freenode.net-xyz1-mrgreene-greene-eggs-and-spam-$4.63

"What the hell is that?"

Cali shrugs. "Something for you to figure out." She's exhausted.

"You want to get some breakfast?"

"Yeah. And coffee would be good."

There's a Waffle House about five miles down the road. We passed it on the way in last night. We lock the room and go.

I actually feel a little better, even though last night's sleep wasn't the most comfortable. The sun is bright, and the air is clean and crisp.

When the wooded road opens out to the lush fields and the rolling hills of the wide green Shenandoah, I feel a little smile rising for the first time since...I can't remember when. But when I look over at Cali, I see we're not in sync. She stares dully out the window.

"Did you sleep at all?"

She shakes her head.

"Too tired to talk?"

She doesn't respond.

Even three cups of coffee at the Waffle House can't rouse her, and she eats her pancakes slowly, as if she has to force them down. The sight of her looking so woeful takes my appetite away, and I end up eating nothing.

"You should lay down," I tell her.

"Can we go back?"

"Yeah."

On the drive back to the motel, I try to think of things to cheer her up. But I know she just needs sleep. And time. And a little peace of mind. She will nap, I hope, and I will work on getting us out of this mess.

16

CALI COLLAPSES ON THE bed as soon as we return. I sit at the little round table and pick up the yarn and start winding it around the coat rack, verifying Cali's work from the night before, letter by letter. When I get to line three, I hear the rumbling diesel engine from last night. Through the space in the curtains, I can see the blue and white Ford logo on the black grille of the pickup.

The man gets out and knocks on the door of the next room. He chats with the woman inside, then goes back out and sits in his truck. Cali is awake and listening too.

"You shouldn't have had three cups of coffee," I say.

"Russ," she whispers.

"What?"

"Come here."

I know what she wants. I undo my belt on the way over and stop to close the curtains. When I reach the bed, she has her arms out to receive me.

The scent of her skin and her warm, moist breath in my ear draw me in. But my legs are bruised and I can't move too well.

She runs her hands gently down my back. "Does that hurt?"

"No."

When she touches my ribs, I wince, and she moves her hands up to my shoulders.

She keeps shifting beside me, trying to make me comfortable, and every time she moves, the lumpy bedsprings pop and groan.

Then we hear the woman in the next room welcome her new guest.

"Fifty," she says.

I don't know what they're doing, but I can guess. He's loud. She's not. This time the bed isn't banging against the wall.

So much for our little idyll.

We get up and spend the next two hours winding the yarn and double-checking Cali's deciphered text. Everything looks good.

"Nice work," I tell her. "That's a lot of text to get through without any errors."

"I checked everything twice before I wrote it down," she says with a yawn. "And Charlie was smart enough to pick yarn that doesn't stretch."

"What's that stuff made of anyway?"

"Hell if I know."

There's a knock on the door, and the two of us exchange glances.

"Just answer it," Cali whispers.

"What if it's a cop?"

She shrugs. "Then we're busted."

"Wait, did we commit a crime?"

"You did. The Colombians, remember?"

Shit.

I go to the door and put my hand on the knob. There's no peephole. I stop and take a deep breath and then open it up.

It's the motel manager, still wearing the same filthy clothes from last night. He says, "It's past noon. If you're planning on staying, you gotta pay."

I peek out at the guy in the black Ford pickup. He's just sitting there behind the wheel looking at his phone. He looks like a biker. Big guy with long curly hair and a full beard and a body that's halfway between muscular and fat. It looks like he cut the sleeves off his black Harley shirt himself. He took off a little too much. I can see his sideboob through the armhole.

He glances up at me with an unfriendly look, and we have one of those awkward moments where our eyes lock and neither one of us can look away. I finally force myself to turn around and say to Cali, "You ready to go?"

"Where are we going?"

"I don't know."

She shakes her head. "I want to take a shower first. Wash this place off me." Then, as if startled by her own words, she glances up at the manager to see if she's offended him. If she did, he's not showing it.

I ask if we can stay another hour or two.

"You gotta pay," says the manager.

"How about twenty bucks for two more hours?"

"You got cash?"

My cash is in the backpack. "I'll bring it by in a few minutes."

"You know where I am," he says.

I open my backpack while Cali gets into the shower. I still have a change of clothes in there from my trip to San Francisco. I take off my bloody t-shirt and put on a clean one. I also have eight hundred and forty dollars. I take a twenty out of the stack, then spend a minute examining the letters Cali wrote out on the little slip of paper. I like her handwriting.

I put the paper into my pocket as I slip on my shoes. The shower stops.

"You okay in there?"

"There's no hot water," Cali says. "And no soap."

"I'll be back in a minute."

When I step outside, Harley Sideboob is escorting an unhappy-looking middle-aged man from the room next door to a white Lincoln Continental.

"I wasn't done," the man protests.

"Twenty minutes, fuckhead. Ain't my problem if you can't finish."

Harley opens the door of the Lincoln and shoves the man inside. Then he turns and catches my eye. Again, I have to force myself to look away.

The office is at the far end of the motel, six doors down. I go in but no one's there. Another car pulls into the lot. Two young skinny guys get out and talk to Harley.

"Hello!" I take a peek behind the counter. "Anyone here?"

The door behind the counter is not quite closed. I give it a nudge and it opens up. Behind it is a messy office with an old metal desk and an ancient television. There's another door beyond the desk. Someone is peeing back there.

I go back around the counter just in time to hear the toilet flush, and then I hear the greasy clerk sit down at his desk and sniffle.

"Anyone here?" I say again.

The chair squeaks as he stands up. He comes out to the counter, and I slide him a twenty. He doesn't pick it up, or even look at it.

"There's your money," I say.

He eyes me for a few seconds and kind of nods, like he's come to a decision, and he says, "That car stolen?"

"Excuse me?"

"Is that your car out in the lot? The blue one?"

"Yeah. Actually, no."

"Well, which is it?"

"It's my girlfriend's car." I guess that's kind of true. It's Jamie's.

"The one you got there in the room?"

"What's it to you?"

"What's it to me? Maybe I don't like having criminals in my establishment."

"Then get the hooker out of the room next to us! And tell her nasty-ass pimp to get out of here too."

"You watch that mouth of yours, mister. You come limping in here in the middle of the night with your face all busted up asking if you can pay cash. You got blood on your shirt, and a fine-looking girl, and a piece of furniture sticking outta your car."

"So?"

"So what's the story there, pal? You wanna tell me? Or how 'bout I call the cops and get 'em to run your plates? Maybe someone's looking for you."

He glances for just a second toward Harley's truck. I suddenly remember the door to the room doesn't lock automatically when you shut it.

"Shit!"

I can hear the manager laughing as I run out of the office. Harley's truck is empty and I can see the door to our room is open just a crack.

When I burst through it a few seconds later, Harley is sitting on the bed next to Cali, counting the cash from my backpack. At least she's dressed. It takes me half a second to see all this before someone catches me around the neck from behind. He loses his grip as I spin around and swing blindly with all my strength. I catch the guy on the jaw with a leaping, spinning blow. There's so much force in that punch, it shakes my bones all the way up to my shoulder.

The guy's head snaps to the left, and he falls face-first onto the carpet by the door. Then someone else grabs me from behind. His arm is around my neck and he's pushing something cold and hard into my kidney and laughing as he struggles to control me.

"He has a gun!" Cali shouts.

Harley Sideboob backhands her with a closed fist and splits her lip. She punches him in the mouth, and he smashes her in the cheek with his giant elbow. Cali puts her hand over her cheek, and she has this angry look like she's going to hit him again. When I try to move, the guy with the gun starts choking me.

"You got over eight hundred bucks here," Harley says. "How far you planning to run?"

I struggle against the guy who's choking me, who's having a hard time keeping me still. I start thinking about what they might do to Cali if they shoot me, and I stop.

"Ain't never seen Billy knocked out before," says the guy behind me. He's breathing hard. "You a boxer?" He presses the gun into my back and says, "Don't answer, or I'll shoot you."

"Fella like you could use the protection of the law," says Harley as he stuffs the cash into his pocket. "You with all your money, and her." He turns to Cali. "This is some top-shelf pussy right here, ain't it, Chuck-O?"

"Ain't no fifty-dollar trick," Chuck-O says.

I start squirming again, ready to explode. Chuck-O is having a lot of trouble holding on to me, and I can tell he's getting scared. I'm scared too, because what's rising in me is a blind animal rage that I haven't felt since I was a kid. He can feel it in me. I know he can. I twist and squirm and back him toward the table, toward the coat rack, stepping on his feet, and ramming the back of my head into his face to annoy him.

"Cut that shit out," he says. "Before I shoot your fucking ass!"

His voice is starting to break with panic. If I push him any further, he'll snap. But he's going to have to empty that whole gun on me to get me to stop fighting.

"Don't shoot him yet," says Harley. "I want to show him how to do a girl right."

Chuck-O brings his gun hand up to my shoulder because his one-arm chokehold is slipping. He's trying to use both arms to get me in a sleeper hold. I feel the side of the gun bumping against the back of my head as he struggles to control me.

I give him a hard elbow to the gut, loosening his grip just enough for me to slip out and lunge for the coat rack. When I pick it up, Harley screams, "Shoot him, you faggot!"

Harley is halfway standing when I jab the coat rack into his face. One of the hooks goes into his eye, and he yelps like a dog and falls back onto the bed. Chuck-O yells too as I yank the coat rack back, jabbing the foot of it into his soft belly. As I spin around to take a swing at him, the gun goes off and Cali screams. Chuck-O has a look of horror on his face, and doesn't see the big piece of wood that's about to connect with the side of his head.

The first blow stuns him, but he's still on his feet. I hear Cali run by behind me, muffling a scream. I hit Chuck-O two more times in the face. Two hard, home-run blows. He crumples to the floor, and I hope the motherfucker is dead.

When I turn to the bed, I see what horrified him. The bullet that missed me went right into Harley's throat. He's slumped over sideways, gushing blood.

But where is Cali?

I have to find her. Where's my backpack? It's still on the bed by Harley, and thankfully he hasn't bled on it yet. I grab it and run outside. Cali is running down the road, and the manager is on his way out of the office.

I hop in the little Ford and back up. Then I aim the car at the motel manager and floor it. Which doesn't do a whole lot in an old Ford Focus. He jumps out of the way, and I go after Cali.

She's running blind, heaving and sobbing, and when I pull up beside her, I see there's blood all over her face. Splatter from the bullet that went into Harley's throat. I roll down the window and yell to her but she doesn't hear me.

I stop the car and chase after her. When I grab her, she doesn't know who I am, and she fights. I wrap my arms around her waist and carry her to the passenger door. She's thrashing wildly and hitting me. I can't believe how strong she is. If I'd known she'd be this crazy, I'd have opened the passenger door first.

She starts calling frantically, "Russ! Russ!"

"What? I'm right here!"

"Russ!"

"I'm holding you!"

"Help me!"

"Cali, get in the car."

She finally goes limp with exhaustion, and I get her into the passenger seat.

We drive...I don't know, maybe south. Maybe west. We're on a country road, heading toward the mountains. It's a long, long way to California, and poor Cali is exhausted and shuddering.

Please Lord, let her sleep.

17

BY THE TIME WE pull into the little country gas station, the tank is nearly empty. I don't know how far we've gone. Maybe fifty miles. Maybe sixty. Cali is awake. Her eyes are glazed, and she hasn't spoken since I put her in the car.

"Cali? Baby?"

I tried to wipe the blood from her face as we drove, but I didn't get all of it. The blood on her neck is streaked with tears. Her lower lip is swollen and split open, and there's a shiny purple welt below her eye from Harley's elbow.

"Cali?"

"Hmm?"

"I'm going to get some gas."

She nods absently.

"We're almost out of gas."

She looks at me, but I can see she isn't really listening.

"Do you want to come into the station with me?"

She shakes her head slowly.

"I'll be right in there," I say, and she gives a little nod as I point to the tiny country store.

This place looks like it was built back in the 1940s, when the little two-lane road we've been driving on was probably the main thorough-fare of whatever rural county we're in. The old pumps, with their black mechanical meters, must be from the '80s. They don't have credit card readers built in, just a sign that says, "Pay inside first."

A pudgy, middle-aged man in jeans and a polo shirt holds the shop door open for me on his way out. He must belong to the minivan at the other pump. As I go in, I turn for a second to look at Cali. She's sitting upright now, staring straight ahead.

The store is musty inside. The fat old man on the stool behind the counter smokes a cigarette, and a fan blows the smoke toward the door.

"Help ya?"

"I want to fill up that little Ford out there."

"Ford?" The man leans forward and looks through the glass door toward the car. "How much does it take?"

"I don't know. Can I just give you forty and fill it up?"

"Sure, sure."

My wallet is empty. The cash was in the backpack. Now it's in Harley's pocket.

I let out a little sigh. "You take credit?"

"Course we take credit!"

"Okay, put forty on the card. And a Mountain Dew. And a bottle of water."

"Will do," he says. "But if the car don't take forty, I can't give you no change. Ain't no change on credit."

"Okay," I say, "but how am I supposed to know ahead of time how much gas it'll take?"

"Most people pump first, then pay."

"But the sign says to pay first."

"That's if you ain't from here."

"Well I ain't."

"So pay up," he says.

I give him the card, and he says, "Forty?"

"Yeah. Forty."

"If she don't take forty, and she won't, you can take the difference in food."

"Okay," I say.

I get a bottle of Mountain Dew and a bottle of water from the cooler while the old man swipes my card. On the fourth swipe, I start to get nervous. Is the card going to be declined? This is the last one I have. Terry Armstrong's was reported stolen, and I assume the credit card company has notified the guy in Sequim about the hotel we charged in San Francisco.

"Is uh…Is there something wrong with the card?"

The old man looks up at me. "The card? Hell, I don't know. I can't get no response."

I look out through the door and I see Cali talking to a plump middle-aged woman in stretch pants next to the mini van. Cali is wringing her hands and nodding. Now the man is replacing the nozzle on the gas pump, and he walks over to Cali and the other woman. He puts his hand on her shoulder. They are comforting her. Why? I don't like the look of this.

"System goes down now and then," says the old man at the register. "No telling when it'll come back up."

"Fuck the system!" I shout as I burst through the door.

At the pump, the man, the woman, and Cali turn their heads at once to look at me.

"Cali!" I shout. "What's going on?"

The woman slides the van door open and starts to push Cali inside. Only, she doesn't really have to push. Cali is climbing in on her own, squeezing past a little girl of seven or so.

"Cali!" I start running toward the van—limping quickly, I should say—and the man runs around to the driver side and starts the engine. The woman jumps in after Cali and starts to pull the sliding door shut. I get ahold of the handle just as the man hits the gas. The door slides all the way open as the van takes off, pulling me off my feet. The woman still has her hand on the inside handle, and she's pulled off balance. She comes tumbling out at my feet, and her husband slams on the brakes.

"Cali!" I yell. "What are you doing?"

The woman leaps to her feet and pushes me and says, "You leave her alone, you beast!" She hits me in the chest and says, "You monster!"

"Cali!"

She looks out at me with her swollen, bloody face and says through her sobs, "I'm sorry, Russ. I'm sorry."

"Don't apologize to him," the woman snaps. Now her husband flies at me with violent indignation. He shoves me backward with both hands and says, "If you ever hit that woman again, I will find you and I will kill you myself. What kind of a person does that to a woman? What kind of a person—" Then he gives me another shove, knocking me down with the immense strength that only rage can give a man.

The woman climbs into the van, and as the door slides shut, I hear Cali say, "I'm sorry, Russ. I just can't do this."

The man stands above me with his red face and flaring nostrils, guarding me until everyone is safely in. But he doesn't have to. She put her knife right through my heart, and I'm done. I have nothing left.

Does it show on my face, how much that hurt? It must. Because the man who just a second ago wanted to kill me is now looking down at me with pity.

18

TEN MINUTES AFTER THEY drive off, I'm sitting on the hood of the Ford. I'm really stuck now. I have no gas, no cash, no Cali, and no will to do anything.

I can keep running, I can surrender and get locked up, or I can die. And of those three options, the only one I can rule out right off the bat is getting locked up. Between the other two, it's a coin toss. And I don't even have a goddamn coin.

About all I have left is this car, and I need to ditch it, since it's the last thing anyone can use to trace me. If Jack Hayes and the FBI aren't looking for this little blue Focus, the cops at the motel probably are.

Besides the car, I have one stolen credit card—which I need to get back from that store clerk—a bunch of fake IDs, a slip of paper with a hand-written SSH key, and a USB stick with the Tails operating system. I also have a change of underwear and a passport. Somehow, those didn't get dumped out when Harley Sideboob was going through my backpack.

I'm ready to just start walking, only I'm so damn hungry, I know I won't last more than an hour. And there's nowhere to walk to from here anyway. I'll probably have to go ten miles just to reach another old gas station like this one.

I'm sitting on the hood of the Ford thinking about how fucked I am when an old grey Buick with open windows rolls up to the pump. The suspension on its sagging rear-end creaks as the bald tires crush the gravel. The harried, tired woman behind the wheel wears a white tank top that shows her thick arms and fat, powerful shoulders. She looks to be around thirty. She has dark eyes, a long, thin nose, and straight, dyed-yellow hair.

The man in the passenger seat is asleep. His head is tilted forward, with his chin on his chest and his mouth wide open. Two school-age kids are fighting in the back seat, and a toddler is crying.

The woman cuts the engine, turns around, and screams, "Y'all shut the fuck up before you wake the goddamn baby!" The school-age kids and the toddler shut up, and the baby starts wailing. Then the woman gives the man a sharp backhand smack to the stomach and says, "Get out and pump!"

He wakes with a start and wipes his mouth, then says with a slow drawl, "Woman!"

He's a few years younger than her, and their faces bear a strong resemblance, though hers is puffy while his is almost gaunt. She gives him a shove, and he opens the passenger door and gets out. He's a thin man, wearing a dirty black Kid Rock t-shirt, black work boots, and an old pair of paint-spattered jeans. His haggard face and bleary eyes tell me he's had a long night. Maybe a few long nights in a row. He looks like he'll fall right back to sleep as soon as he gets a chance to sit down.

"Hey!" the woman shouts. She leans across the front seat and waves a fifty-dollar bill through the open passenger door. "Fill it up!" she says.

The man takes the bill without a word and shuffles into the old station. He returns a minute later, puts the nozzle into the tank, locks the trigger open, and leans against the pump looking like he's going to doze off.

The woman yells, "Eddie!" and his eyes pop open. "Clean the windows, dammit!" The baby, who had quieted for a moment, starts crying again.

Eddie shakes his head and says, "Naw," then closes his eyes.

The woman throws her door open and it hits the pump, giving Eddie a start. She hauls her hefty body out of the car with the force of an angry rhino, and gives Eddie a shove. "How the hell'd you spend eight hundred dollars in one night?"

He replies slowly, "Now that's the eight-hundred-dollar question right there."

The woman shoves him again, harder this time, and he stumbles and falls.

"That's the last time I'm bailing you out," she says. "You can rot in jail for all I care."

The pump clicks and the gas stops. The woman looks at the display and says, "Thirty dollars? Eddie, I gave you a fifty!"

andrew diamond

Eddie sits up, but says nothing.

The woman puts the nozzle back into its cradle, replaces the gas cap, and yells, "You rot in hell, Eddie Dupree!"

She gets in the car, slams the door, and the rear wheels spray the back of Eddie's head with sand and gravel when she hits the accelerator.

Eddie sits there for a while looking hungover, then slowly gets up and walks into the station. He comes out a minute later with a case of Busch beer. He opens one up, takes a sip, and looks around the lot. His eyes stop on me, and he looks me up and down. He glances at my car, then back at me. The look on his face tells me the thoughts are slowly coalescing in his clouded brain. Perhaps he realizes that the car and I are connected.

He walks over and hands me the credit card I left in the station and says, "Man says that's yours. Say, bro. Can you give me a ride?"

"I could if I had gas."

He reaches into his pocket and pulls out the change from the beer. Four dollars and a few coins. He slaps it in my hand and says, "Will that get us thirty miles?"

"That'll do it," I say.

I pay the cashier and put two gallons in the tank. Eddie's already in the passenger seat, and as we pull out of the station, he tosses his empty beer can out the window and cracks open another one.

"Which way?" I say.

"Straight down this road for about twenty miles. I'll tell you where to turn."

"You have food at your house?"

Eddie thinks for a moment, then says, "I can't remember. But if you're hungry, have one of these." He hands me a Busch. I drink the whole thing in about thirty seconds, and it fills my stomach. Then I get a nice, warm, light-headed feeling.

I hand Eddie the empty can. He tosses it out the window, hands me another beer, and says, "I never feel right till after breakfast. What the hell happened to you?"

"I don't even know where to start."

"Yeah, I know that feeling. How about you start at now and work backwards? What were you doing before I showed up?"

I punch the steering wheel and then the mirror and the dashboard, and the car goes onto the grassy shoulder beside the road. The warm feeling is gone. "Fucking bitch! Goddamn fucking bitch!"

Eddie grabs the steering wheel and swerves the car back onto the road.

"Whoa! You sure you're okay to drive, buddy?"

"No. You ever have a woman put a knife in your heart?"

"I once had a guy stick one in my ribs."

"It hurts more when a woman does it."

He eyes me for a second and says, "You're in a bad way, pal."

"Yes I am."

"Finish up that beer. I'll give you another."

That sounds like a good idea.

I can't control my thoughts or my reactions to them. One minute, I'm thinking about wrapping this car around a tree and ending it all. Then my mind flashes back to Berkeley, to that first moment when Cali turned from the bar and smiled at me, and I start smiling. Before the smile even fades, I see her running down the road, spattered in blood, and I push the pedal to the floor, looking for something to crash into.

I look over at Eddie, who's sipping his beer. He looks surprisingly at ease.

I let off the gas and say, "Who was that in the car with you?"

"My sister."

Eddie tells me she just bailed him out of jail in Harrisonburg, which is a long drive north up Highway 81. He went up there with his friend Earl, for a night of drinking and gambling that ended in a fight, though he doesn't remember who was involved or what started it.

"Where you from, anyway?" Eddie asks.

"Richmond," I say.

"Now that's a fine town! I've had some good times in Richmond. Good times!"

In a few minutes, we reach his turn, which leads to a winding country road even narrower than the one we just turned off. Eddie's on his fourth beer now, staring quietly out at the thick woods along the roadside. We're heading southwest, toward the mountains and the Jefferson National Forest. After a couple of miles, we come to a long, broad clearing where every quarter mile or so we pass a single-story cinder-block house, or a trailer propped up on blocks.

"Hey, hey, slow down!" says Eddie.

As I slow the car, Eddie leans out the window and winds up to throw his half-empty beer can at the house we're approaching. It's a single-story ranch with a bay window, a well-kept lawn, and a paved driveway. When we reach the driveway, Eddie lets the can fly. It hits the side of the mailbox with a thud, and the mailbox door drops open as we pass.

"Damn!" says Eddie as he slides back into the car. "I was aiming for the house."

"Whose house is that?" I ask.

"Dick Woods. Sheriff's deputy. Guy's crooked as hell."

Eddie tells me he's an odd-jobber. He does some house painting and small-engine repair, but he makes most of his money selling Oxycontin and Oxycodone. Dick Woods chased him down a while ago, and Eddie's car went into a ditch. The cop searched it and found a coffee can filled with thirty-eight hundred dollars hidden in the trunk.

"He just took it," Eddie says. "Didn't arrest me or nothing. Told me to have a nice day, left me in the ditch, and went out and spent all my money. You have any idea how long it takes to earn thirty-eight hundred dollars selling pills?"

I tell him I had to deal with a crooked cop too.

"He take your money?"

"No. He took my photo. But I took it back."

"A photo?"

"Yeah. With a key in it. I mean, it was a photo of a car. And a girl."

"Same girl who stuck the knife in your heart?"

"Yeah. The same one."

"Shit, you would've been better off letting the cop keep that one."

"I probably would have."

Eddie points up the road and says, "Mine is the next house after that blue one. Right around the bend."

We pass a light-blue clapboard house—the first two-story house I've seen on this road—followed by fifty yards of unmowed grass and a stand of trees. Around the bend is a little white cinder-block house with a door in the middle and a window on either side. An old red Mustang is parked in the grass in front, next to a John Deere riding mower with a faded For Sale sign. I can see the scrapes along the front quarter panel of the Mustang, from when it ran into the ditch.

"Pull around back," Eddie says. "Park it in the grass."

I pull up behind the house, and as soon as I cut the engine, a huge weight of despair starts to smother me. Now that we've stopped moving, I can't pretend I'm heading to someplace better than the one I'm in. That's been my strategy all these years with Costa Rica. It's my Someday place, and when things get bad, I picture the beach and say to myself, *Don't worry. Someday you'll run down there and leave all your problems behind.*

But now I'm here in this backwoods dump, and I have no way out. I don't even have enough fuel to get back to that godforsaken gas station where Cali abandoned me.

Where is she now? Did they give her a bath and a change of clothes and a hot meal? Are they taking her to the airport, so she can get a comfortable flight home? I'm starting to get angry.

If I can't turn my mind to something positive, these thoughts will pull me under. But what is there to turn to out here? A house and a shed in a lonely patch of weeds beneath a greying sky.

Eddie says, "You okay, bro?"

I remind myself that I have the key. That's one good thing. I can get to the vault. Money will get me out of here, and I'll go somewhere beautiful and pass my days by the sea, in the warmth of the sun. This little thought, without substance or mass, is the last thing I have to hold on to. I keep inflating it until it becomes my life raft.

"Positive," I whisper. "Think positive."

"What's that?" Eddie says.

I want to tell him I will use the key to get the money and move on to a better place, but what comes out of my mouth is, "You have any liquor?"

Eddie smiles broadly, showing two broken teeth. "Fuck, yeah!"

19

EDDIE'S KITCHEN IS A depressing mess. Everything is a dingy off-white: the sagging linoleum floor, the laminate counter, the dish-cluttered sink, the aging fridge, and the filthy electric stove.

Eddie himself, however, is quite cheerful. He's an enthusiastic host, handing me a near-full bottle of Jim Beam as he sets about making peanut butter sandwiches. On the table in the corner of the kitchen, nestled in a pile of empty beer cans, is an old Hewlett Packard laptop. I know the exact model. It has a Core 2 Duo processor, one or two gigs of RAM, and a cheap plastic keyboard.

"That thing work?" I ask.

"Kinda."

"What do you mean *kinda*? Either it works or it doesn't."

"It'll boot up," Eddie says. "But don't try doing nothing with it. The whole thing's choked with porn and viruses, and there ain't no Internet here."

"No Internet?" I realize my tone makes me sound like a spoiled kid offended by the lack of amenities.

Eddie puts down the bag of chips he's been pouring into a bowl and says, "No, there ain't no Internet, okay? And there ain't no lattes either."

"Sorry, dude. I was just hoping to check something."

"It's all right, *dude*," Eddie says, mocking me. "Dr. Garrison has a satellite dish. You can get on his Wi-Fi from the shed." He brings the sandwiches and chips to the table and pours a shot of bourbon into a coffee cup.

"Who's Dr. Garrison?"

Eddie points toward the wall and says, "Next house over."

"You mind if I try the computer?"

"Go ahead," he says, drinking down the whiskey.

I boot the machine from the USB stick, and it's running my secure Tails OS. Eddie looks at the screen and says, "How'd you get it to look like that?"

I point to the USB stick. "Booted from here." Then I take the paper from my pocket, the one with the hand-written SSH key, and I start typing in the characters as I eat my sandwich. Twenty-four lines of sixty-four characters each. The last line is a few characters short and ends with an equal sign.

Eddie doesn't seem to mind that I'm focused on the screen. He just keeps talking. I get the feeling he doesn't have a lot of visitors, other than Earl, who drove him up to Harrisonburg the other night. Earl, he tells me, makes the ladies laugh and pees himself when he gets too drunk.

Eddie tells me more about his jobs: he mows lawns, paints sheds, plows snow, and fixes anything mechanical in and around Botetourt county, which, by the way, is pronounced Bot-a-tot around here. He drives to Roanoke, Lynchburg, Blacksburg, Christiansburg, Harrison-burg, Waynesboro, and Staunton because, he says, the rich folk throw things away instead of fixing them. For twenty minutes, I hear about all the things that can cause a perfectly good lawn mower to die, and how little time and money it takes to bring one back to life.

Now he's selling Oxycontin and Oxycodone again, trying to recoup the thirty-eight hundred dollars Dick Woods took from him. From his description of himself, Eddie is quite an entrepreneur, plowing a couple hundred bucks he earns from odd jobs into a couple of bottles of pills, then selling those and buying five more.

Back in the Bay Area, we call that bootstrapping. The start-ups that want to avoid selling out to the vulture capital pimps scrape their way to profitability by being frugal and working endless hours.

"I was halfway to getting my thirty-eight hundred back when Earl came over and we got drunk and took off on that road trip. See now, Earl ain't got no sense. He spends every penny he's got, every time we go to town. Me, I learned not to take all my money with me, because I do the same thing. Only way to save your money is to not have it with you. You want some Oxycontin?"

"No thanks." Actually, I wouldn't mind some because my head has not stopped aching since Yuri beat my face in back at the apartment. But it's hard for me focus right now, and the drug would probably make that worse. My vision is still a little blurry, although I'm not sure if it's from the concussion or the alcohol. I should lay off the beer.

"You want a shot of Jim Beam?" Eddie asks.

"Sure." The way he says it, it sounds pretty good. So much for what I *should* be doing.

Eddie takes little sips of whiskey while he talks, chasing them down with sips of beer. From what I gather, he's a loner when he's sober, but quite gregarious when he's drunk. I keep my primary goal in the back of my mind: I have to get out of here. And though I hate myself for it, my hacker's mind has been scanning the attack surface and taking notes on Eddie's vulnerabilities.

He has three weaknesses. He's lonely. He trusts me. And he's starting to get drunk.

I let him go on talking. The more he talks, the more he drinks, and the more he seems to like me. He's already given me some good information. I have an idea of what I can take from him, where I might find it, and how I can get to it without him stopping me. If I'm right, he has enough cash to get me at least halfway to my destination.

I'm typing in the last few characters of the SSH key and half-listening to Eddie's stories as I think through how I'll get his money. Charlie's words come back and sting me once again. "You're just as devious as I am."

I am.

"Only I embrace my inner deviant," Charlie said. "And you run from yours."

I do.

I'd really rather *not* be this person. But this is who I have to be to get out of the mess I'm in. And I'm drinking beer and whiskey because, if you have a conscience, it's hard to look someone in the face and act like their friend when you know you're going to betray them before the day is out. Betrayal hurts. Maybe more than anything. It sucks to be on either side of it.

I compare the letters on the screen to the ones on the page, one by one. When I'm satisfied that the SSH key is correct, I say, "How do I get onto the Wi-Fi?"

Eddie points toward the rear of the house and says, "The shed."

"You mind if we go out there for a little bit?"

Eddie grabs the whiskey bottle and a couple of beers and says, "I'll show you what I'm working on."

20

THE WEATHER-BEATEN WOODEN SHED that sits thirty yards off the southeast corner of the house is only a little smaller than the house itself. It's surrounded by push mowers, riding mowers, snow blowers, an aerator, three old motorcycles, and the frames and rusted parts of other items I can't identify. The shed has a doorway but no door. Inside is a high, pitched ceiling, and the smell of mildew, grease, and gasoline. The east and west walls have old-fashioned grille windows, dusty but unbroken. Two long orange extension cords run from the house, across the tall grass, and through the shed's doorway.

There's a fair bit of light in here from the windows, and when Eddie turns on the shop light that hangs from the rafters, the space is plenty bright for working. On the floor are three mowers in various stages of disassembly, along with a dehumidifier and two window air-conditioning units. There's a cluttered workbench along the south wall, piled with tools, machine parts, and old metal coffee cans full of screws and washers and nuts and bolts. There's also a little bench by the western window.

I take a seat on the bench and search for Wi-Fi networks. There's only one, *Garrison*, and the signal is weak but steady.

"It's wide open," I say. "No password? No encryption?"

"Doctor says anyone can use it. Sometimes you'll see a car pulled up in front of his house. Someone stopping to check their email or buy a part on eBay."

Eddie picks up a socket wrench from the workbench and starts to dismantle an air conditioner. He's telling me about each of the items in the shed, who he's fixing them for, and what's wrong with them. But I'm not really listening.

When I get the Wi-Fi connection, I request the Google home page through Tor. It takes a few seconds to load.

Then I take another look at the gibberish at the end of the handwritten key. There's an IP address, and then this:

dbxc4.freenode.net-xyz1-mrgreene-greene-eggs-and-spam-$4.63

The first item, dbxc4.freenode.net, is an IRC server. When I connect to that, the /LIST command tells me there's a channel called xyz1. I go in and look for Mr. Greene, but the channel is empty.

I think about the story Charlie told me about Sixx. How after he swiped all that money from the bank, he laundered it through a guy named Mr. Greene.

I type in the SSH command to connect to the IP address written on the slip of paper. Cali's handwriting is neat and crisp, and the sight of it sends a pang of longing through me.

I take a deep breath and hit Enter. Then I wait.

"What do you do for a living?" Eddie asks.

"Write software."

Eddie nods. "I figured. I can't look at a screen that long unless there's a movie on it. Or at least some pictures." He takes a sip of beer and asks, "You got kids?"

"No."

"A girlfriend?"

I just look at him.

He says, "Sorry. I forgot about that. Okay, how about politics? You a Democrat or a Republican?"

"Neither. They're all crooked."

Still no response from the server.

"What about God?" Eddie asks. "You believe in God?"

I read the message in the terminal window.

```
Connection timed out.
```

I run the SSH connection command again and say, "God? I don't know. I'm on the fence about that one."

"Lot of you science types are pretty adamant there ain't no God."

"Well, science didn't create this world, or any of the creatures in it. So who are we to say?"

He starts to get absorbed in his work with the air conditioner, stopping now and then for a sip of beer or whiskey. I keep trying my connection, and it keeps timing out.

"Does this Internet connection even work?" I ask.

"It's satellite," Eddie says, "so it's slow when the weather's bad."

I look out the window. It's cloudy, but the weather's not that bad. I finish my beer, and I see Eddie's done with his. I tell him I'm going back to the house to get some more.

"Get my sandwich while you're in there," Eddie says. "I forgot to eat it."

"Because you were talking."

"Yeah," he says cheerfully, "I can talk!"

I go into the house and find the bathroom, which is attached to the bedroom. There's dried piss all over the floor. While I'm in there, I think about where he might be hiding the Oxycontin he offered me earlier. I check the medicine cabinet, but it's not there. It's not under the sink either.

The bedroom floor is piled with clothes that I don't really want to dig through. There's a little night table next to the bed, but the only things in the drawer are a pistol and an old copy of Penthouse.

The top drawer of the dresser contains pants, shirts, socks, and underwear, all mixed together. And three large prescription bottles. I take two Oxycontin from one of the bottles and go into the kitchen. There's Eddie's sandwich on the table. I lift the bread and slip the pills into the peanut butter, then grab four beers from the fridge.

Back in the shed, I hand Eddie the sandwich and a beer. I notice we've gone through a good bit of whiskey. But I've only had one shot. He must have had six or more. And how many beers did he drink? Four in the car. And a few more since we got to the house.

Eddie tells me the compressor in the air-conditioner is shot. When he turns to pick up a screwdriver from the workbench, he almost loses his balance.

"Eat some food," I say. "It'll soak up the alcohol."

Eddie tries to cram half the sandwich into his mouth at once, and part of it sticks out as he lifts the compressor with both hands. I watch him for a minute, hoping he doesn't bite right into one of those pills. He eats like a dog, choking down big unchewed lumps. When he gets the compressor out, he shoves the rest of the sandwich in, then washes it down with beer as he examines a fresh cut on his hand.

I pick up the laptop and stare quietly for several seconds at the little flashing cursor in the black terminal window. The command prompt says:

```
root@vault#
```

That means I'm in. And I have full administrator privileges.

I don't have to look far for the prize. There's one file called coin. dat, right there in the root directory, and it's not encrypted. It's a big fat Bitcoin wallet. I look to see if sx is installed. That's a suite of tools that will let me manage Bitcoin transactions from the command line. It's there.

The first thing I do is check what's in the wallet. The *sx balance* command tells me this wallet contains 73207.61 Bitcoin. I feel a tingling spread from my loins down my legs, up through my stomach and chest to my arms. I'm so light-headed I could fall over.

I take a few deep breaths to steady myself, then I open a browser window and check the Bitcoin converter at preev.com. It takes a few seconds to load, and when it does, I learn that 73207.61 Bitcoin at the current exchange rate comes to just over $18,400,000.

And it looks like someone popped into the IRC channel while I was away. A certain Mr. Greene.

21

Mr. Greene and I have a little chat.

```
Genie: Mr. Greene?
MrGreene: What's for breakfast?
```

What's for breakfast? What the hell is that supposed to mean? I take another look at the gibberish at the end of the SSH key we transcribed.
dbxc4.freenode.net-xyz1-mrgreene-greene-eggs-and-spam-$4.63

```
Genie: greene eggs and spam
MrGreene: How much will that run me?
Genie: $4.63
MrGreene: Just a minute.
```

He sets up a private channel and invites me in.

```
MrGreene: Your answer to the question tells me who referred you.
Genie: And I am...?
MrGreene: Dumping coin out of Twilight's wallet.
Genie: Can you handle $100k?
MrGreene: Easy. I keep 50%.
Genie: 50%???
MrGreene: That's the deal. Take it or leave it.
Genie: Fine.
MrGreene: Send it out to these Bitcoin addresses in chunks of
$35k, $35k, $30k.
```

I copy down the three addresses.

```
Genie: When will I have the cash?
MrGreene: What country are you in?
Genie: US
MrGreene: Day after tomorrow. Where should I send it?
Genie: One sec.
```

I open up a browser window and go to Roomkey.com to look for hotels. I want to head south. The New Orleans train runs through Lynchburg, which is an hour or so from here. The Hilton in New Orleans looks

andrew diamond

nice. I take out my wallet and look at the one license I haven't yet used. Chester McGowan of Reno, Nevada. I'm pretty sure that's not a woman.

```
Genie: Chester McGowan c/o Hilton Hotel. 333 St Charles Ave, New
Orleans, LA 70130
MrGreene: If I have the coin within the next two hours, you'll
have your money Thursday AM.
Genie: Will kick off transaction now.
MrGreene: Keep this channel open. Check back in half hour.
Genie: Will do.
```

When I put the computer down, I see Eddie wavering on his feet over by the workbench, breathing long, loud breaths through his mouth. He's given up trying to fix the air-conditioner. The alcohol is catching up to him, and the pills will kick in soon.

"You want another beer?" I ask.

"Naw."

"You need a little rest? Sounds like you had a long night."

It takes him a few seconds to respond. "Little catnap might not hurt."

When we walk back to the house, I have to grab his arm twice to keep him from falling. Inside, he slumps onto the couch and is asleep in a few seconds.

22

IT'S ALMOST 7:00 P.M., and the clouds are getting heavy. Eddie mentioned he had earned back about half of the thirty-eight hundred dollars that Dick Woods stole. That's nineteen hundred. If he blew eight hundred in Harrisonburg, he should have a thousand or so hidden somewhere around here.

I can get a bed on the Amtrak Crescent for about three hundred. That train comes through Lynchburg at ten o'clock.

Now where would Eddie keep his money? The first place I check is the drawer where I found the pills. No money in there. But I did learn that not only does Eddie not separate his pants from his shirts, he also doesn't separate clean clothes from dirty.

There's no money in any of the other drawers either. I start digging though the clothes on the floor, and then I check under the mattress. Nothing.

I can't find anything in the bathroom, so I head to the kitchen. I open every cabinet and drawer as carefully as I can. The way Eddie puts things away, I'm worried about falling pots and pans waking him up.

I have no luck in the kitchen, except I do find the keys to his old Mustang on the counter by the stove.

There's some clutter by the back door, and I'm about to start searching through it when a phone rings. It's a little dark green flip phone on the floor by the couch. It must have fallen out of Eddie's pocket. I pick it up and turn it off so it doesn't wake him. Then I look under the couch. Nothing there.

It's been more than half an hour. I better go check in with Mr. Greene. As I cross the grass back to the shed, the rain begins. Inside, when I pick up the laptop, I see a message waiting.

MrGreene: All's well. 50k will be waiting in the Big Easy Thursday by 10AM.
Genie: Cool!
MrGreene: Pleasure doing business with you again.
Genie: Again?

```
MrGreene: Who else would Hatter hand the reins to?
Genie: Who do you think I am?
MrGreene: Threee, Fourr, Fivve...
Genie: Sixx? Sorry. No.
MrGreene: As if you'd admit it. Everyone's seen the photo.
Genie: What photo?
MrGreene: You and Hatter in a bar.
```

Shit. That was meant for one person. I should have taken it down.

```
Genie: Think what you want. Thanks again.
MrGreene: Next time is 60-40.
Genie: What?
MrGreene: You get 60, I get 40. I like to keep good clients.
Genie: Cool. Later.
```

I shut down the laptop and put the USB key in my pocket. The rain is picking up, beating loudly on the roof of the shed. I'm starting to have flashes of doubt about Eddie's cash. Maybe he keeps it buried somewhere. Maybe he spent it before he even went to Harrisonburg.

Then I remember him saying the cash the cop took from him was in a coffee can in his trunk. I haven't checked his car yet. On the way out of the shed, the pile of coffee cans on the end of the workbench catches my eye. It's a row of four, stacked three high.

I start lifting the cans one by one and pawing through the contents. They're full of unsorted fasteners: bolts that don't match the nuts, and washers that don't match anything. How does this guy get anything done?

Finally, I get to a can at the bottom of the stack that's very light. Beneath the lid are sheets of folded sandpaper. And below those, green! Nine hundred and twenty dollars.

I stuff the money into my pocket and put the cans back. The rain soaks through my shirt on the short walk back to the house. Eddie hasn't moved.

I feel bad about taking his money. And I'm about to take his car too. And maybe the rest of his beer. There's a whole six-pack left in the fridge. I pop one open and walk back to the little Ford behind the house and get my backpack. It's still got the passport. And the change of underwear. In

impala 199

case I suddenly run into Cali, and we just have to go to bed. I want to look nice. Fucking Cali! Fucking bitch! Why am I crying?

I put the backpack in the Mustang, then get the big stack of mail from the mailbox. It looks like Eddie hasn't collected it in a while.

I take it into the house and find a pen and paper and copy down Eddie's address. I turn his phone back on and write down his number.

I finish my beer and grab two more from the fridge. Then I hop in the Mustang and cross my fingers and turn the key. It starts right up. I should have known. With all his mechanical skill, he probably keeps this thing in top shape.

After a long dark drive through heavy rain, I arrive in Lynchburg with a little time to spare. I stop at a gas station and fill the tank. I don't want to leave Eddie high and dry. He was pretty hospitable.

The little station shop sells sweatshirts. Should I get a Virginia Tech hoodie or the one with the Confederate flag? Better pick the flag. People might be looking for me, and the Virginia Tech one might give them a general idea of where I got on the train. The Confederate flag, on the other hand, might make them a little more inclined to leave me alone.

I get the sweatshirt, mainly because I want the hood, and I buy a quart of Budweiser and drive down to the station. I park in the lot and drink half the beer. Then I put on my sweatshirt, pull up the hood, and go inside. I buy the expensive ticket, a bed in the sleeping car, for three hundred dollars. The train will be here in fifteen minutes. I go back to the car, keeping my face turned away from the surveillance cameras. I finish my beer, put Eddie's keys in the glove compartment, and walk onto the platform. I'm ready to collapse from exhaustion.

andrew diamond

23

It's past noon when I awake, and a vague memory from last night returns:

The train was swaying, and I was walking from the restroom back to my sleeper. Someone was in my bunk. I grabbed his shoulder and started shaking him.

"Hey man. Hey!"

I turned the lights on. When he opened his eyes, I could see he didn't like the Confederate sweatshirt. He was a black guy. Middle-aged, with a little grey around the temples.

"What's the matter with you?" he said.

"You're in my bed. Hey, do you have any aspirin? My head is killing me."

"Maybe you shouldn't drink so much."

"It's not that. I got beat up, and…I don't know. Maybe I did drink too much. Hey, you look familiar. Do I know you?"

"I look familiar because you woke me up an hour ago. I don't have any aspirin. Go back to your damn room!"

"Sorry, dude."

The train is slowing as we approach Birmingham, Alabama. The rays of the afternoon sun stab my brain as I watch the man from last night wheel his suitcase along the platform.

When we pull out of the station a few minutes later, I go to the dining car and get two sandwiches and a beer. The beer soothes my pounding head, so I get another. My body still aches from the beatings.

* * *

We arrive in New Orleans around 7:30 p.m. I wander out of the station and turn right, beneath the Pontchartrain Expressway. The first street I see is Calliope Street. Now I'm thinking of her again, and I'm going to start sinking if I can't distract myself.

I go back to the station and get a map, which shows me that the Hilton on St. Charles is within walking distance. I stroll by, just to get an idea of where the place is. I consider checking in, but I'm going to need that last credit card to rent a car. If I charge the hotel on it, the card might get canceled.

So I walk on for a while and finally park myself at a bar that serves oysters and crawfish and beer. I still have about six hundred in cash. I buy a few drinks and make some friends. They ask about the cuts and bruises on my face. I try to come up with a new story each time someone asks, just to keep myself amused.

The hours drift by and it's 2:00 a.m. The bar is closing. The manager points me down the street, toward the bars that are still open.

* * *

The next morning, I awake under a bridge, in the dirt between two heavy steel girders. The road overhead thumps every time a truck passes. I can tell by the slant of the light that it's early. The air is thick and humid, and it's already way too hot. I've sweated through my clothes, and my mouth is dry.

I don't remember where I went after the bar closed. Did I come straight here? And where is my backpack? I sit up and my head throbs. The backpack was beneath my shoulder, and now I have a kink in my neck from sleeping on it. I unzip the front pocket and peek inside. The passport is still there. I count the money in my pocket. Three hundred and twelve dollars.

After sitting for a while and listening to the thump-thump of the trucks passing overhead, I make my way out to the street. It's 7:30 a.m. I feel like shit. And I'm still drunk.

I go into Walgreens and buy some hair coloring and brown tinted contacts. Then, just down the street, I find a consignment shop. When it opens at 8:00, I buy a pair of jeans, a couple of t-shirts, some socks, and a suit that fits, with a little room to spare in the chest and shoulders. That comes to two hundred and twenty dollars.

andrew diamond

At 8:30, I find the bar I was in last night. It's already open. I order a beer and take it into the bathroom. I take off my shirt and wash up. Then I put the dye in my hair. The process turns out to be a lot messier than I expected, and the dye drips down my neck and face. The box says I have to leave it in for a while. Longer than it takes me to finish my beer.

So I go back to the bar and get another. The bartender doesn't seem to care that my light brown hair is now almost black, but he does tell me I have to wear a shirt.

I take my beer back to the bathroom, and start rubbing the dye through my whiskers. I don't have a lot of facial hair. My three-day's growth is what some other men have after just one day. But when I rub the dye in it, and it changes from blonde to black, it looks much thicker. In fact, the dark stubbly beard changes my appearance even more than the hair coloring.

After finishing the second beer, I rinse out what I can of the coloring, and I use my t-shirt to scrub the excess dye from my face and neck. Then I crouch under the hand dryer and comb my hair back with my fingers until it's mostly dry.

I wash my hands and put the contacts in, which turns out to be trickier than I thought. I've never worn contacts before, but I've watched other people put them in, and I swear it looked easy. It's a good thing there are six pairs in this pack, because I've already dropped two on the floor.

When I finally get them in, I take another look in the mirror. The lens in my left eye hurts, and it's off center. After a few blinks, it slides into place.

I take off my clothes and start putting on the suit. The guy who walks in while I'm in front of the sink in my underwear is obviously a career drunk. He doesn't give me a second look.

When I'm dressed, I study the photo on Chester McGowan's license. It's me with dark hair, just like I look now, only without the stubble. I find Chester McGowan's MasterCard in my wallet. Then I head out for the Hilton on St. Charles.

Along the way, my phone chimes, and a bolt of fear shoots through me. Why the hell is my phone on?

The screen shows a reminder for a work meeting starting in ten minutes in Ethan's office. Sorry. I'm going to miss that one.

I have a dim recollection of fiddling with the phone last night, somewhere on the street, after I left the bar. I missed Cali. I wanted to send her a message. I hope I didn't.

I check my texts. One message came in a little after 4:00 a.m. That must have been when I turned on the phone. It's from Cali. She says, "I will not betray you."

What the hell is that supposed to mean? I remember puzzling over this message last night. The timestamp on the message is 4:14 a.m. But my phone marks the time the message was received, not when it was sent. I turned the phone off before we left Richmond. Which means Cali could have sent this anytime between then and the minute I turned my phone back on.

A helpless rage grows within me, and I shout, "What the hell do you mean you won't betray me? Did you write that before you betrayed me, or after? You liar! You fucking whore!"

The people walking by look at me, and then look away. I'm the crazy person they don't want to become.

I should have ditched this phone back in Richmond. It's almost 10:00 now, which means Jack Hayes has had six hours to track me. Why hasn't anyone picked me up?

I check my settings. Location services are off. That means the phone isn't reporting its GPS data. Doesn't it? I don't even know. But it had to connect to a cell tower when it came on, and Verizon definitely gets that data. And they share it with law enforcement if the feds have a warrant. A cell tower in a city like this can't serve much more than one square mile. Jack Hayes must know I'm somewhere in downtown New Orleans.

Wait. I remember now. I turned the phone on right before I got to the bridge where I slept. And then I crawled up between the huge steel girders. Could a cell signal reach the tower from beneath all that steel? I don't know.

I'm getting close to the hotel now. There's a FedEx truck making its way down the street from the other direction. I consider throwing the phone into the sewer, but a minivan with nylon suitcases piled on top gives me another idea. It's slowing down for the red light. There's a family inside. The plates say Arkansas. As I walk past, I swing around to the back of the van and slide my phone into the side pocket of a soft red nylon bag strapped to the rear of the roof rack.

That should keep the feds busy, if they're still after me. They might not get the fine-grained GPS data, but they'll be able to see the phone connecting to the cell towers in a northbound line straight up Interstate 49 to Arkansas. Let them try to guess which car the phone is in.

I keep walking down St. Charles. The FedEx truck pulls up to the hotel just before I get there, and I watch the driver go in with a dolly full of packages. Half a minute later, I'm in the lobby. The driver stands beside the check-in desk, talking to the concierge.

I walk up and say, "You have a package for Chester McGowan?"

He sifts through the packages, and hands me a slim box from Panama. He scans the bar code, and I show him McGowan's ID and sign for it.

The customs slip on the front of the package says it contains books valued at eighty-nine US dollars. I go to the bathroom and tear open the box. A surge of panic shoots through me and then my heart sinks. There's nothing inside but two large hardcover books.

I open the cover of the first book, and see packets of hundred dollar bills, neatly stacked and bound. I stare, light-headed for a moment. The second book contains mostly fifties, with a few stacks of twenties. I fan through the bills. They're real! Thank you, Mr. Greene!

On the way out of the hotel, I dump the box and the book covers in a garbage can, then hop in a cab. First stop, FedEx. Then Hertz.

At FedEx, I pull out the slip of paper with Eddie's address. I stuff ten grand into an overnight envelope and give it to the clerk.

"Can I borrow your phone?"

I call Eddie.

"Yo." He sounds alert. I expected him to be hungover.

"Hey Eddie."

"Who's this?"

"Russ. From the other day. Your car's at the train station in Lynchburg."

"You little fuck!"

"Sorry for all the trouble. Keep an eye out for the FedEx truck tomorrow. You got ten grand coming your way. And thanks for all your help."

"Ten grand?"

I hang up and get back into the waiting cab.

* * *

When the woman at Hertz asks what kind of car I'd like, I tell her I want a full size. I stand two feet behind the counter because I'm sure I smell like alcohol.

"We have a Chevy Impala."

"Cherry red?"

"No sir. Black." She points to it on the lot. It looks like a cop car. "Would you like it?"

"That'll do. As long as it'll make it back up to Little Rock." I say this just to cover my tracks. Just on the off chance that some cop finds his way in here and asks about me. She'll say, *He mentioned he was headed to Little Rock.* Straight up highway 49, just like the minivan that's carrying my phone.

After a quick stop for a bottle of aspirin and some Mountain Dew, I'm on the road at 10:55, heading for the border at Laredo. For the first time in days, I have a glimmer of hope. I almost don't recognize myself in the rearview mirror. The dark hair and beard. The dark eyes. The smile. I'm actually smiling! I have a nice car, a ton of cash, and something to look forward to.

I'm driving at a steady ten miles an hour over the speed limit, trying to make it to the border as fast as I can without getting pulled over. Laredo is the last hurdle between me and Costa Rica.

At 11:10 a.m., it's one hundred and one degrees outside. According to the radio, I'm heading into record heat in south Texas.

24

THE TEXAS COUNTRYSIDE ROLLS by to a country and western soundtrack, and the drive is smooth and uneventful. Between songs, the DJs talk about the heat and the strain of all those air-conditioners on the power grid. The utilities are warning of potential outages, and public health officials are asking people to stay indoors.

After a stop for gas and food near Katy, I turn southwest onto Route 35 at San Antonio, and continue past Cotulla and Encinal. Texas goes from green to brown as you go west. I'm in the brown part now. I'm making good time, despite getting caught in some traffic around Houston. My main problem has been staying awake. I think I slept three hours last night, and my drunkenness turned into a full-on hangover right around noon.

I came close to nodding off a couple of times, and I swear I saw that minivan with the red suitcase on top when I was approaching Houston. But I've been a little delirious all day.

I stop one last time just outside Laredo to use the restroom and to get some fuel and Mountain Dew. The sun went down a little while ago, and it's still over a hundred degrees. The air here is drier than in New Orleans, but one hundred is hot no matter what the humidity.

The radio says that rolling brownouts throughout south Texas have shut off power to parts of Austin, Round Rock, and San Marcos. A spokesman from the electric company says it should be back on shortly, but the brownout will just roll into some other part of the state. They're having the same problems in Tamaulipas, Nueva Leon, Coahuila, and Chihuahua on the Mexican side.

As I pull out of the gas station, I see something that disturbs me very deeply. Four black SUVs heading south toward the border at high speed, with full escort from the Texas State Troopers.

I pull out behind them and drive below the speed limit, with a sick, sinking feeling in the pit of my stomach.

As I drive slower and slower, the cars come up fast in my rearview mirror, then swerve around me into the other lane and fly by. One of them makes my heart skip a beat. A grey Chrysler minivan, with a bunch of luggage strapped on top. It passes in the left lane, and I'm looking at the red nylon bag on the back of the roof. The one with my phone in it.

So now what? I can turn around and head back into the heart of the US, but I'll never feel at ease as a fugitive in this country. I need to think this through without panicking. *What do you know, Russ? What are the facts?*

The facts are—the feds and the state troopers just went roaring by because they're looking for me. They can see my phone connecting to a series of cell towers along this road, making a line for the border. But they don't know which car the phone is in, because the GPS is off. So if they want to find it, they're going to have to stop and check every vehicle.

It's still a few miles to the crossing. There's bound to be at least one more cell tower between here and there. If I can get up far enough ahead of the minivan, I'll be in range of that cell tower before my phone is. They wouldn't bother to stop any vehicles until they know the phone has entered the service area of that last cell tower, right? I mean, why start searching cars if they know the one they're after is still a few miles back, connected to the previous tower?

I hit the gas and pull into the left lane. In front of me is a Chevy pickup and I start tailgating him, trying to pressure him to move over and let me pass. I'm pretty sure that minivan is half a mile ahead of me by now. But the pickup won't move.

I reach into the front pocket of the backpack to make sure the passport is still there. I'm pretty sure I checked it this morning. But I was drunk when I woke up, and I don't trust my memory. The guy in the pickup finally gets the message and changes lanes. I gun past him just as my hand feels the passport. And something else beneath it.

I pull out a little black flip phone. Whose is this? Where did it come from? This is trouble! A flip phone connects to cell towers just like any other mobile phone. Which means someone could be tracking me down this road right now.

In a panic, I open the window and throw the phone out.

andrew diamond

And my very next thought is, *I shouldn't have done that.* I should have opened it and checked the number. That might give me an idea of where it came from. If it was a 540 area code, the phone could have belonged to Harley Sideboob or one of his friends. Maybe they dropped it in while they were searching my backpack. But that doesn't make sense. Harley had a smart phone. I saw him using it.

What about Eddie Dupree? Why would he bother putting a phone in my bag? And I saw his phone on the floor by the couch when I left. I don't think it was him.

Who else then? Cali? Why would she even have a flip phone, much less put one in my bag?

I'm coming up on the border, and traffic is slowing. According to the radio, power is back on in Austin, though they're having trouble in San Antonio, and there are still a number of outages on the Mexican side.

I continue forward toward the border because…because I don't have a plan B. I've had it in my head for so many years that I'd run off to Costa Rica one day. And the thought of turning around and having no plan at all—on top of having no home and no friends—that's too much for me right now.

I'm just a few blocks from the crossing now. As the traffic slows at Victoria Street, I try to calm myself with deep, slow breaths and soothing words. *Your eyes are dark, your hair is dark, and your beard is dark. You don't look like Russell Fitzpatrick. You're wearing a suit and your passport says you're someone else. They'll look at your papers and glance into the car and then wave you through. And that will be it.*

And then I say to myself: *The cops are here. The feds are here. They came specifically for you. They're not just going to let a guy traveling solo breeze through. Especially if he's the right age and height and has bruises all over his face.*

At Houston Street, I check my face in the rearview mirror. I gave it a good washing in the bar this morning, but there's still a little puffiness around my left eye. My nose is still swollen, but the bruises and scratches don't look quite as bad as when they were fresh. And besides, it's getting dark. If I can keep my head in the car when I pass through the check-point, maybe they won't notice.

But I can't quite convince myself. And I can't stop myself from driving forward either. I wonder if the salmon and the swallows and the Monarchs feel this mixture of compulsion and doubt during their arduous migrations.

The cars are backed up from the checkpoint to Farragut Street. As I roll into the back of the line, I see three of the black SUVs and the flashing lights of the police cruisers up ahead to the right. They've pulled the Chrysler minivan off the main road. The doors are open and the feds are pulling the passengers out in the glare of police spotlights.

Who's that running the show? Is it Jack Hayes? I can't tell. He's talking to one of the state troopers, his face pulsing red and blue in the flash of the cruiser's lights. Pulse. Pulse. Pulse. Pulse. That awful, remorseless face. My strained, remorseful heart.

As I roll slowly past, I see the fourth black SUV up ahead, in the left-most lane of the checkpoint, beside two Texas State patrol cars. Two federal agents, dressed in black, and two Texas State Troopers are talking to the Mexican border agents just in front of the checkpoint. The road fans out here, from two lanes to six. The Mexicans are waving the cars up one by one and checking the drivers' IDs. In the far left lane, they have a guy out of his car. His trunk is open, and the guys in black start digging through it.

I pick the checkpoint that's second from the right, and I can't change now because the lanes here are separated by yellow plastic posts. The cars ahead of me are moving through fairly quickly, each one stopping a few seconds for an ID check. By the time I get close to the front, one of the men in black—FBI or border patrol or whatever he is—has moved two lanes closer.

Now there's one last car in front of me. A new silver Nissan. The driver hands his ID through the window. The Mexican official passes it back to a man behind him who has some kind of scanner. I can't tell if the scanner guy is American or Mexican. Are they checking IDs against a database? Do Wisp's IDs have valid chips or bar codes? Will they even pass a scan?

Calm down, Russ. Act cool and no one will suspect you.

I pull the passport from the backpack, and two little cards drop out of it onto my lap.

The agents wave the Nissan forward, and I roll up to the front of the line. One agent puts up his hand, giving me a silent halt signal, then he turns to talk to the man behind him. They're speaking English. I consider for a second just gunning the engine and blasting right through. But then I imagine that little maneuver ending like Bonnie and Clyde.

I roll the window down, and as the hot dry air rushes into the car, I find myself looking directly into a surveillance camera. It's pointing right at my face, like a gun. For a second, I have this fear that the little green light next to the lens will turn red, like the laser on a pistol that pinpoints where the bullet will go. I imagine what Harley must have felt when that bullet ripped into his throat, and what Charlie might have felt when the slug pierced his skull and sent him over the cliff. How did my life come to this?

As the agent turns around, the little green light on the surveillance camera blinks off, and the streetlights and all the buildings go dark at once. Everything is black now, except for the headlights and taillights of the cars. The rolling brownouts have finally reached Laredo.

The second agent, the one with the little scanner, says "No network." There's a tinge of disgust in his voice.

Who am I? The agent is going to ask for my ID. He's going to ask my name while he waits for the power to come back. What's the name on this passport? I have to be able to answer him. I turn on the cabin light inside the car. And why is this passport red?

As I open it up, I think back to that night at Wisp's. When I went to the bathroom, Cali pulled a card from the wallet I left on the table, and I heard her say, "Make one with this name." And then Wisp laughed. I'd been carrying that card ever since our first unpleasant meeting out on East Parham Road in Richmond.

I am Jack Hayes, FBI Special Agent. I have the official red passport reserved for US diplomats and federal agents traveling on government business. The cards that just fell into my lap are Jack Hayes's business card and a bogus copy of his FBI ID with my photo on it.

Thank you, Wisp! And Cali, I love you! You are brilliant, brilliant, brilliant!

When the border agent turns to me again with his little flashlight and asks for my papers, I show him the official passport and the FBI ID, and I say, "Any word on Fitzpatrick?"

The agent examines the documents for a moment and then shines his light in my face. He returns the passport and ID and says, "Hasn't come though yet. And our system just went down."

"You know how I can get to police headquarters in Nuevo Laredo?"

That sounds like something Jack Hayes might ask, doesn't it?

He gives me directions and waves me through.

andrew diamond

25

I CONTINUE DRIVING ALL THE way to Monterrey, but I can't shake these nagging fears. What if that border agent mentions to someone that Jack Hayes passed through in a black Chevy Impala? How long will it take them to catch up with me? All my thoughts on this long dark road are constrained by fear. The fugitive's paranoia is his prison.

I drive around Monterrey until I find train tracks. A little after 3:00 a.m., I ditch the car half a mile from the tracks and start walking. Then I sit by the rails with my backpack. The fatigue of all the beatings, the worry and the loss, the drunken nights and hungover days, the strain of constantly having to think on my feet, of never knowing what's coming next... It all catches up with me, overwhelming even my anxiety and fear, and I fall asleep.

At some point before dawn, I awake to the sound of a long freight train rumbling by. Most of the cars are tankers and hoppers with no place to sit or lay down, but near the back are some boxcars. The cargo door on the second-to-last car is open. The train is moving slowly, so it's easy to get on. The boxcar is empty. I lie down in back and rest my head on my backpack.

For the next twelve hours, I drift in and out of sleep. The car is loud and uncomfortable, but I'm so exhausted, I don't think I could stay awake under any conditions.

When I do wake up, it's from thirst. I haven't had anything to drink since I finished that Mountain Dew, about an hour after I crossed the border. I'm also dehydrated from all the drinking I did in New Orleans. It's hot here, but not as bad as it was in Texas. It takes me a few seconds to notice the train isn't moving.

When I look outside, I find my boxcar is no longer attached to an engine. I'm in a little siding, near a city. A real city, with big buildings.

I walk toward the center of town, stopping on the way to eat some churros and drink a bottle of water. I'm in Ciudad Victoria. And there's a station not far from here with passenger trains.

* * *

By early evening, I'm in a comfortable reclining seat, heading toward Mexico City. With each passing mile, I feel the weight lifting from my shoulders. My trail by now must be cold, even to the most determined detectives. I have no phone to trace. No credit card transactions. No record of me anywhere since New Orleans. The last thing they might be able to trace to me is the rental car in Monterrey, and it could be days or weeks before they find that. Even then, they might not tie it to me. After all, the car was rented to one Chester McGowan, of Reno, Nevada.

As my mind relaxes, I start thinking about Costa Rica, and the little seaside town of Sámara on the Pacific Coast. The thought of the breeze and the sand and the waves soothes me. I have eighteen million dollars. I'll never have to work again. I close my eyes and wallow in imagination, sinking into a comfortable ease I haven't felt in weeks.

But somehow, the vision of my little paradise isn't whole anymore. Somehow, that peaceful place, full of beauty and far from the madding crowd, is no longer enough. Until I met Cali, I didn't realize how deeply I'd been craving the kind of connection I felt with her. I had been wasting away for years in an unfulfilling job, with a woman I couldn't talk to, with no plan for building a life I actually cared about. Cali was like cool water in the desert, awakening me all at once from my torpor.

I can't blame her for leaving, even though part of me still wants to. I keep replaying the scene at the gas station. Did she tell those people I beat her? Or did she just let them assume it? Maybe the story spun out of control, and she just went with it to escape from the situation. She was in shock.

But the fact that she would let someone believe I ever hurt her... That stings. I would never hurt her.

And what about *I will not betray you*? When did she write those words?

I have to stop thinking about her because I'm getting angry again. And beneath the anger is a deep pool of sadness that terrifies me. I can't go down there. It's too dark.

All these years, I've held on to Costa Rica as my secret escape. But now I fantasize about a reunion with Cali. I had her twice within my reach, and twice she slipped away, like a mirage taunting my thirsty soul. Somehow, someday, I'll make it back to California and find her again.

The train rolls into Mexico City. I make my way through the crowded station in a haze and find a little mom-and-pop hotel where I sleep fitfully for most of the next two days. In my dreams, Cali and I live in a little house by the roiling sea, where the waves are always threatening to consume us, and the Russians stalk menacingly around the periphery of our precarious bliss. I awake sweating, in darkness, and alone.

My headache never goes away, and my emotions swing wildly out of control. I go from hope to despair to rage and back ten times in an hour. I start to worry that the beating I took after the concussion has injured my brain. These are the symptoms, right? The ceaseless headache, the anger and volatility.

Part of me hopes this is a brain injury, because if it is, the symptoms might subside after a few weeks. Madness, which is what this feels like, might be incurable.

I tell myself that in Sámara I will find a doctor and I'll rest for weeks. My head will stop hurting, and I'll be sane again.

On the third day, still without real rest or peace of mind, I head to the airport and get a direct flight to Costa Rica. It's a three-hour trip. The magazines are boring, so I practice my Spanish with the old woman in the middle seat. She is poor and thin and cannot read. She rubs the beads of the rosary between her fingers and reassures me several times that the plane will not crash, because she has been good and God loves her.

26

THE CAB DRIVER OUTSIDE the San Jose airport smiles and shakes his head. "Sámara?" he says. "No. Too far."

I tell him I'll pay cash, but he says, "Too expensive. Is four, five, six hours. Then I have to drive back. And gas here. Not like *los Estados*. Is expensive."

I'm tired, and I'm sick of traveling. I want a quiet room and a comfortable bed. I want to feel warm sand beneath my feet, and sink into the lazy tide-driven rhythms of the seaside life.

"Six hundred dollars," I say, and I hand the cabbie six crisp bills. "That'll cover you there and back."

He hesitates for a moment, then takes the cash and smiles and opens the door for me.

Despite the beauty of this country, the incredible, lush, breathtaking dark-green beauty, I cannot stay awake. I doze off somewhere on the outskirts of San Jose, and though I'm jolted awake a few times by bumps and hard turns, I sleep through most of the drive.

We're just outside of Sámara when I finally wake up, and my body can't quite shake off the deep fatigue of the nap it didn't want to end.

The driver asks me where exactly I'm going, and I tell him to drop me off at the first place that serves alcohol. I feel like having a beer. As I rub my eyes, he says maybe I should look for a place to sleep.

Then I say, "No, wait. The Mar Azul. Take me there."

Wasn't that the name of the place?

The driver has to look it up on his phone. It's on the northern edge of town, along the sea, just a hundred yards or so from the water. After a few minutes, we pull into the little round drive. The hotel is a one-story building with a dozen or so rooms that open out onto a nice-looking pool. Beside the pool is a restaurant, open on three sides, with a small bar and a dozen or so tables beneath a pitched thatch roof. The far end of the bar, where the restrooms and the kitchen are, is the only part with real walls. A few of the tables spill out onto the pool deck. Beyond the pool, little bungalows are scattered among the palms. I ask the cabbie to wait until I find out if there's an open room.

There is. I tell the clerk to check me in for a week. I pay cash up front and he hands me two magnetic key cards.

Check me in for a week. I feel like I'm committing myself to an asylum.

The cabbie drives off with a friendly wave, and I walk past the pool to my room. The doors are all on the outside of the building, like an American motel. But this place is clean and well kept. The room has a simple terra-cotta tile floor, a bed, a dresser, a night table and lamp. I drop my backpack on the floor, kick off my shoes, and wash my face. Then I go out to the little poolside restaurant.

It's quiet here, and the pace is slow. The lazy fans that hang from the high thatch ceiling pull humid air up from the cool stone floor. A waiter sits at an empty table, absently flipping a little white towel as he looks out at the half-dozen vacationers lounging on the beach.

A hundred yards away, the sea is calm, and tropical birds call out to one another above the quiet washing of the waves. I ask the bartender for a beer, and she pours me an Imperial from the bottle. I drink half of it at once, then set the glass on the bar and watch the beads of condensation form.

The days since San Francisco are a blur. But two images stick out clearly in my mind: Cali's big green eyes, and the little green light on the surveillance camera at the border.

I keep thinking about Charlie's old assertion, that if several things happen at once, and nothing comes of it, it's just a coincidence. But when a confluence of unlikely events produces some meaningful outcome, it's not a coincidence. It was meant to happen.

Charlie meant that in a limited sense. As a hacker, he would engineer "coincidences" to produce meaningful outcomes, like Sixx kicking the system administrator's computer under the train. That was the coincidence he needed to complete his hack.

But I'm thinking about Charlie's theory in a broader sense. We live in a world of DNA, where lifeless molecules blindly assemble themselves into living, conscious beings. Is it really just the outcome of billions of years of coincidence that every plant and every insect, every bird in the sky, and every fish in the sea, and you and I, and everyone we will ever know, were written into the matter of the universe? That we had only to wait till our time came round, and we would open our eyes, and the light would come pouring in? Was it all just chance?

And what about all the hardship and suffering we endure in this life? Is it all just pointless and random? Or are we players in some higher order that is as far beyond our comprehension as life and consciousness are beyond the comprehension of the inert minerals from which they're built?

There *has* to be some meaning to it all. *There has to be.* Cali found me at a time in my life when my soul was thirsty and I was finally ready to hold onto something. And she wounded me to the core. But for all my bitterness, I want her back.

As I lift my beer from the bar, I hear the clink of her bracelets behind me. She wasn't lying! She wouldn't betray me. She is true, and my heart soars.

But as I turn to look at her, I hear the ice tinkling in his glass, and the hair on the back of my neck stands on end at the sound of his voice. Charlie says, "Russ, my man! Sorry to dump all that in your lap, but things got a little too hot, and I had to disappear."

There are no coincidences.

Who was tracking me with that flip phone as I drove through South Texas? And the little green light on the camera at the border—why did it turn off right when I looked into it? Why did the power go out just at that moment?

Well…who used to hack into people's laptops and turn on the little green light next to the video camera? Who spent time as an FBI informant, learning to hack the power grid, and then bragged that he could take it down in half an hour? I picture him watching my progress down Interstate 35, his fingers poised over the keyboard, waiting for just the right moment to make the world go dark.

He knew I'd come here, like the salmon and the swallows and the

Monarchs that always find their way to the appointed place. He's the only one who ever knew.

In Cali's wide green eyes, I see the joy she feels at my return, the shame she feels for abandoning me, and a plea for forgiveness. But his arm is draped across her shoulder in a casual display of ownership, and as quickly as it rose, my heart falls for miles and miles and miles, into the dark downward currents from which nothing escapes.

There is no Someday anymore. I have reached my long-awaited paradise, this blackest pit of hopelessness, and there's nowhere left to run. I can't escape him, and she is his.

This is hell.

I am in hell.

27

CHARLIE SLAPS ME ON the back and says, "Let's have a shot!"

I'd take a shot of heroin right now. Or cyanide.

Charlie shakes my shoulder and says, "Cheer up, dude! You got the key. You got the money. And you made it!"

Cali stands silently by his side, her head and shoulders slightly bowed, her eyes fixed on me. She's trying to draw me into contact, which I refuse. I can't look at her face, so I look down. Her hands are clasped in front of her, just below the waist. Her posture reminds me of our first night together in San Francisco, when she sat on the side of the bed with her hands in her lap. Shy, open, hopeful, waiting. The memory makes my heart ache.

"All right, Charlie," I say, as I turn toward the bartender. "Let's drink some tequila. And tell your girlfriend to fuck off."

"That's the spirit," Charlie says as he takes the stool next to me. "Cali, go find something to do."

I hold up two fingers to the bartender, who's washing glasses at the other end of the bar. She smiles and makes the same gesture back to me and says playfully, "What's this? Is victory? Or peace?"

"Two shots of Patron," I say.

"Just bring the bottle," Charlie says.

Cali is still standing there behind me. I can feel her.

The bartender pours two shots and leaves the bottle in front of us. Charlie raises his glass and says, "To retirement!"

I leave my glass on the bar and stare angrily at the liquor bottles by the cash register. Charlie holds his glass in the air for a second, then puts it down. He flicks my shoulder and says, "What's up?"

I half turn toward Cali, but I still can't look at her. Now Charlie gets it. He turns to her and says, "Go on. This is guy talk. I'll catch up with you later."

For a couple of seconds, there's only the sound of the waves and the birds and the breeze. Then I hear her turn and walk away. Or maybe I just feel it. My emotions are churning so violently right now, I can't really tell what's going on with my senses.

Before she's even out of earshot, Charlie says, "You fuck her?"

I'm going to kill him. I don't know why he can't sense it, but I'm filled with nitroglycerin, and one more word will set me off.

As he raises the glass to his lips, he says, "She's incredibly warm, isn't she?"

All at once, I'm on my feet, twisting as I throw a left toward Charlie's mouth. His reflexes are quick though. He's up off his stool as fast as I am, and he jerks his head back to avoid the blow. My fist grazes his hand and knocks the shot glass up into the ceiling fan. The momentum of the swing carries me off my feet, and I wind up on my hands and knees on the floor. The gash on the knuckle of my left middle finger is oozing blood.

I get to my feet as quickly as I can and lunge at him with another wild blow. The smile on his face as he dodges my punch fills me with rage. He really thinks this is funny. Before I can swing again, the waiter is behind me with his arm around my throat. When he rams his knee into the back of my knee, my leg buckles, and I start to go down. He tightens his chokehold and pulls me toward the restrooms at the far end of the bar.

"*Que pasa?*" he says angrily. I'm looking at Charlie, whose head I want to smash against the bar. The waiter wrenches me around so I'm facing the bathroom doors, and he says in English, "What's your problem? Huh?" He sounds offended, and as he tightens his arm around my throat, he says, "You have woman problem?"

I'm going to black out if he doesn't let go. Just as my legs are about to give way, he loosens his hold and pushes me back against a bar stool. He says, "This is resort. You relax. This no fight club. You want to fight, get out!"

He stands there watching me as I turn toward the pool. The chokehold took all the energy out of me, and now the sight of sunlight and blue water and palms begins to soothe my lingering anger.

After a few seconds, the waiter says, "You good?" I stare at him blankly for a moment, and he says, "Okay," and he goes back to his table.

I turn my attention back to the pool, where a giant black sea bird has just landed beside the deck chairs. His feathers have a purple sheen in the bright afternoon sun as he turns his head from side to side and blinks. He looks lost and out of place. Or maybe that's me. I don't know.

There's something hypnotic about the swaying of the palms in the gentle breeze. They move to their own rhythm, while the waves behind me measure out time like a lazy metronome.

After a long period of calm and quiet, I notice the bird is gone. A young woman in a white bikini and sunhat reclines with a magazine by the pool. She is slim, with long bronze legs. When did she appear? Or the fat bald man with the hairy chest climbing out of the pool? Where have I been the last few minutes?

I look down the bar. Charlie is still sitting there in front of the tequila bottle. When he sees me turn, he stands and lifts the glasses and walks toward me, pushing the bottle down the bar as he approaches.

He takes the stool next to me and pours two shots and says, "Sorry about that, dude." He hands me a glass. "She really got to you, huh?"

He raises his glass and waits for me, but I don't pick mine up. He shrugs and drinks his down and says, "There's no kind of whipped like pussy-whipped."

"Shut up, Charlie."

"I'm just saying."

"Shut up."

"All right, man. You want a beer?"

"Yeah."

Charlie gives the bartender a wave and she brings a bottle of Imperial and a glass.

"I need some money," Charlie says.

"I'm not giving you that fucking key."

"I'm not asking for the key. I just need some cash."

I pour my beer and take a sip.

"Cali says you two ran into some pretty hardcore shit."

andrew diamond

"You almost got us killed," I say.

"Sorry, man. I had no idea things would turn out like that. But I knew something was wrong as soon as Cali got here. She was really rattled."

My stomach starts to churn again.

"What did she tell you?"

"She said some Russians were going to shoot you. And two other guys wound up dead."

"What else?" What else rattled Cali? Was any of it me? Did I mean anything to her at all?

"She said after Richmond, things got really bad."

"But what else?" I'm trying not to sound too desperate.

"She won't talk about it. Whatever it was really upset her."

"What won't she talk about?" I'm pleading now. "Me? She won't talk about me?"

"Jesus, Russ! Get a hold of yourself."

He pushes the glass of tequila toward me, and I take it.

28

NOW IT'S DARK, AND I can't remember which room is mine. Charlie is in the bushes. Stupid drunk, fell the fuck over and couldn't get up.

Which room? Try the key in every door. The one that opens is yours. But wait, where is the key? In my...Where are my pockets?

Okay, USB stick. That's the wrong key. Ooh, I have cash! And more cash in the back pocket. Cash all over the fucking ground. And...What's this? A credit card? No, that's the key. The room at the end, remember? The clerk gave me two cards.

This door...The slot is too small. Why do they make it so fucking hard to get this little plastic card in that tiny little slot? How do they expect old people to do this? Blind people? Drunk people? Fuckers!

Pinch the slot and hold it still. Hold it, then slide the card in with the other hand, right? Right? Fucking card! What's wrong with this country?

Oh, here come the sweats. My skin's getting prickly. Here come the spins!

Ohhhhhhhhhhhhhhhhhh that's a lot of puke.

* * *

Where am I?

Whose bed is this?

I try to sit up, but, *Oh, fuck!* How much did I drink?

And where's my shirt? *Shh! Shut up, Russ! Do you hear that? Some-one's in the bathroom!*

A silhouette emerges from the bathroom and glides silently across the floor.

Go back to sleep, Russ. You're in no condition to fight.

29

THE ROOM IS LIT with soft sunlight when I awake. Then the unease creeps over me. My shirt. Where did it go? And how did I get in here last night? I don't remember coming through the door. The last thing I remember, I couldn't get the key in the lock. And I was vomiting like a fire hose.

I have to get out of here. The sight of Cali will drive me mad, and Charlie is evil and useless. I have the key, and they have nothing, so fuck them!

But…but I don't have the key. It's not in my pocket. I sit up and my head is pounding. What did you do, Russ? You didn't give him the key, did you?

No. No, it was in my pocket last night when I came to the room, remember? I was looking for the room key. Yeah. I went through my pockets, and there was money all over the ground. Shit! Did I drop it?

I get up and stagger outside. It's only a hundred feet from my door to the bar, but there's nothing on the ground. No cash. No USB stick. Nothing. I walk the route three times there and three times back. Nothing in the pool. No money blown into the bushes. Just…just nothing.

Now I'm really screwed.

I go back to my door and it's covered with puke. The key card is still in my back pocket. Just one. And a few hundred bucks.

I go inside and strip the bed, but there's nothing there. I check the floors, the dresser, the night table, my backpack. But no USB stick anywhere. My other key card is gone, and so is all the cash that was in the backpack.

Wait. There was someone in here last night. Or was that just a dream? Wasn't there someone in the bathroom?

I check the bathroom. The white washcloth is covered with blood. I check the gash on my left knuckle. It's clean. I don't remember doing that. And my shirt, stained with puke, has been rinsed. It's hanging from the shower curtain rod. I don't remember that either.

Did I hide the USB stick when I was in here cleaning? I check under the sink, in the shower, behind the toilet, in the toilet. It's not here.

30

ON ANY OTHER DAY, a hangover like this would keep me in bed. But I'm too agitated. All I can think is, I have to have some measure of control. I have to get back to normal. To a place where I can think.

In the mirror, I look pale and queasy. The stubble on my chin is dark at the ends and light at the roots.

I'm going to buy a razor and some shaving cream. I'll get a toothbrush and some toothpaste and scrub the bitter remnants of the vomit from my mouth. That's a start.

And then what? Then what, Russ?

I don't know.

* * *

I follow the little seaside road south into town, replaying the events of yesterday. I could have walked away from Charlie after the first drink, or the second. Or I could have left as soon as he appeared.

Instead, I sat there getting wasted with a person I wish I'd never met.

When I told him about the coverage of his death online, he had a dozen questions. Then he asked who was at the memorial service, and what they said.

When I mentioned Celia, he waved her off and said, "I was done with her a long time ago." That part made me angry, and though I didn't say anything, he could see it. I think he tucked it away in his mind as a point to come back to.

Later, after he had two or three more shots in him, he said, "I should really send her some money. It's the decent thing to do, don't you think? Poor girl, up there in San Fran all alone, with rent and bills. A hundred grand would tide her over for a year. Long enough for her to get back on her feet."

"I'll send her some money," I said.

"But I want to send it," Charlie said. "I'm the one who did her wrong. It would mean a lot more, coming from me."

"Bullshit, Charlie. She'll never see a penny of anything I give you."

He could see I wasn't going to concede this point, so he changed directions and said, "Okay, we can work that out later. How about a little beer money? For me. Just, like, ten grand?"

There was something pathetic about seeing the mastermind of this whole operation begging for beer money from his victim.

I said, "Why don't you tell me about Colombia? What the hell happened there?"

He said no one knew he was going, except Cali and Celia. He let them believe he was going to arrange a business deal, but the whole thing was a setup. He went there specifically to disappear. I kept asking him what happened, but he wouldn't give me a straight answer.

He was biting his nails too. The only time I ever saw him bite his nails in the past was when he was stuck on a really hard hacking problem. But there at the bar, I noticed that all his nails were chewed down to the quick.

I noticed a few other things too. His skin looked unhealthy—dry, sunburned, and bug-bitten. His speech began to slur after just a few drinks, and I remembered what Celia had said about him not being able to hold his liquor anymore. But his eyes struck me most. They seemed to recede as he drank, as if they were descending into their sockets; and as it got dark, the lights of the bar glinting from his sunken pupils made him look unhinged.

All he would say about Columbia was that he was really drunk *that night*. So drunk that he forgot to take his laptop out of the car before it went over the hillside.

"And then I was locked out," he said. "Completely fucking locked out of Twilight, the vault, everything."

He poured a couple of shots and pushed a glass toward me. He drank his, but I left mine on the bar.

"I went on a little bender after that," he said. "Just drinking and drifting north. I couldn't reach my servers, so I couldn't stop the dead man's switch. When I got to Panama, I called Cali at work. I guess it was the day before the memorial service."

"What? You called her?"

"Fuck, yeah! I wanted to know where the hell you were. She said you hadn't showed up yet."

"So she knew you were alive?"

"Not until I called. I told her to come down here. Bring me a laptop and that sweater."

"No..." I shook my head. "No. That can't be. She was on *my* side." I felt like I was choking on my words, and I think my voice was breaking a little at that point.

"Russ, you stupid fuck! Turn off your emotions for a minute and think about this rationally. How long after you met her did she sleep with you?"

How long was it? Six hours? Eight?

"And how many women want to go to bed with you as soon as they meet you, Mr. Charming? Hello-o!"

"There've been a few," I said defensively.

"Yeah, wasted girls you brought home from parties in college. How drunk was Cali when you screwed her?"

I tried to keep a lid on my emotions, but my throat and chest kept getting tighter. Charlie could see this was getting to me. He nudged my shot glass a little closer, and as soon as I drank it, he poured me another.

"Dude," he said. "She thought she had the encryption key on that little SD card. I bet she was logging into that fake server with that fake key, trying to make sense of the bogus files I left there. She wanted all that money for herself. I would never trust her with the real key. Or any woman. That's why I left it for you."

The alcohol was starting to blur my thoughts. I tried to picture Cali typing the SSH command to open an encrypted connection to a remote server.

"She couldn't do it," I said. "She just...No!"

"You just don't want to believe it," Charlie said. "I told her to put the flip phone in your backpack, so I could keep tabs on you, in case you

impala   229

figured out the puzzle. You want to explain how else that phone got in there?"

Charlie was smiling when he said that, because he knew he had me. And then I remembered Cali unwinding the yarn in that motel room, decoding the key, and how she wrote out the letters on the page—exactly sixty-four characters per line. Exactly the correct format for an RSA key. She knew what she was doing.

The alcohol started giving me a heavy, toxic feeling.

"If you want her back, you can have her," Charlie said. "She can follow orders, but she's fucking worthless when things go wrong. Can't keep her cool. Can't tell a fucking lie to save her life. Everything she feels is right there on her face, plain as fucking day. Cali, with her little school-girl conscience! That's the kind of woman you leave at home."

If I wasn't so tired at that point, I would have hit him. The thought of him with Cali disgusts me. Especially now, in the light of day, when I'm already sick with a hangover. I stop to puke in front of a little tienda, bracing myself against the wall. The great heaving surge from my guts makes my eyeballs hurt.

* * *

On my way back to the hotel, I realize I should have bought a pair of sunglasses. But I don't want to turn around now. I have toothpaste and a toothbrush and mouthwash in a bag, along with a razor and shaving cream, deodorant, sunscreen, and a pair of white swim trunks with a blue stripe down the side.

Just up ahead, I see Cali sitting on a driftwood log on the beach side of the road. She wears white soccer shorts and a blue V-neck shirt with red around the collar and the ends of the sleeves. Her feet are bare, and there's something in her hand, but I'm too far away to see what it is. My first instinct is to run and hug her. Then my stomach starts to churn, and I stop, thinking I might throw up again.

Why is she just sitting there? And why is she looking inland, instead of out to sea? There's nothing in front of her but the little hotel across the street. She's lost in thought, but what is she thinking?

andrew diamond

A yellow DHL truck rolls up to the hotel in front of Cali. She perks up. When the truck leaves, she crosses the street and goes inside. A minute later, she comes out with a large envelope. She lifts her shirt and tucks the envelope into her shorts, then pulls her shirt down over it. The thing in her hand is a phone. She flips it open and walks quickly as she dials. She's agitated, and now so am I. I follow her, but she's going so fast, it's hard for me to catch up.

She has the phone to her ear, but I'm too far behind to hear what she's saying. I'm not even sure she's talking. I trot up closer, holding my plastic bag under my arm, so it won't make any noise.

I'm twenty feet behind her when she says, "He got here yesterday." Her voice is higher than usual. She's tense. "Last night," she says. Then she listens and says, "Tomorrow. It'll be here tomorrow." Her pace slows as she listens and nods. "Okay," she says. "But what time? I need to know what time."

Even from this far behind, I can feel the anxiety running through her.

She stops to listen, and I keep walking. I'm two steps behind her when she begins to turn. "No," she says, "it just drove by, and it's like, what? Eleven?" When she sees me, she jumps.

Part of me wants to soothe her. Part of me wants to ask what the hell she's up to. And part of me wants to punish her. She sees all this at a glance, in that moment when her eyes lock onto mine, and she says angrily, "Not now, Russ." Then she turns and runs across the street, with one hand holding the phone to her ear and the other pressing the envelope under her shirt.

As I watch her walk away along the beach, and the anger, and the love, and the hate go roiling through me, the one thing that affects me above all else…the one thing…is how gracefully she moves.

31

At 4:00 P.M., I'm finishing a burger at the bar. After returning from town, I cleaned up, had a hot shower, and fell asleep. My hangover was mostly gone after the nap, but I'm still feeling slow. I don't think I'll be drinking again any time soon.

After eating, I pick up a towel from my room and head down to the beach for a swim. The waves are gentle and the water is warm. I'd stay in, but the burger has me feeling sleepy. So I stretch out in the sand and doze off.

When I awake, I hear her voice a little ways behind me. She says, "A beer might take the edge off." Charlie, sounding sick, replies, "Get me one, will you?" I turn to get a glimpse of them. He looks like a frail old man in that folding beach chair, while his lovely young nurse wraps a towel around his bony shoulders.

The sun is going down over the water. I go in for another swim, heading north, parallel to the beach. When I turn onto my back, I see Cali walking toward the towel and shirt I left in the sand. She stoops for a moment and lifts the shirt. Then she puts it down and walks back to Charlie. Against the white of her shorts, I can see the bright red card she holds in her hand.

She stops in front of Charlie and drops it in his lap. My key card. She gave him my key card.

But how could she have done that? The card is still here, in the back pocket of my swim trunks.

I start heading back, doing the breaststroke with my head above water, so I can keep an eye on them. But this is too slow. I swim to shore and walk, watching them the whole time. They know it too.

When I get back, I say, "How you doing, Charlie?"

He takes a sip of his beer and says, "Getting better."

"You look like shit."

He drains off the last of his beer, throws the bottle in the sand, and says, "I'm going back to the bungalow."

Cali says, "Goddammit, Charlie!" And she goes and picks up his beer bottle, just like I once did.

Charlie says, "Why don't you two stay and talk? Seems like you have some issues to work out."

"Why don't I walk you back to your bungalow, Charlie? Two old friends can have a nice little chat, without some little tart getting between them."

I can see this stings her.

"Stay and talk to your girlfriend," Charlie says. He sounds tired and worn. His hand is in the pocket of his shorts, absently fingering the key card.

"She's your girlfriend, now," I say. "I'm sure you can give her everything I used to give her, and do it just as well."

Charlie turns and walks away. I glance at Cali before I follow him. She's wounded, like a doe with an arrow in its side. It hurts me to hurt her, but I'm not done. The hunter in me wants to track her down and finish her off. But there's no need to rush. In this quiet little beach town, we have all the time in the world.

I follow Charlie back to the bungalow. He sits heavily on the bed and says with a sigh, "What do you want, Russ?"

"What do *you* want, Charlie?"

"I want you to get the fuck out of here."

"Okay, Charlie."

I know he's watching me as I head back toward the beach. I know he's standing there in the doorway with my key card in his pocket, watching to make sure I'm gone.

This is what I want. Cali, all alone.

32

CALI WATCHES ME RETURN. I see her silhouette against the twilight on the horizon. She hasn't moved from where I left her.

When I get close, she turns and walks toward the water. I follow patiently. I will take my time at this. When she put the knife in my heart, she did it all at once, without warning. I want to do it slowly. And I want her to feel the fear of it coming.

At the water, she heads north along the shoreline. I follow, narrowing the distance a little with each step. Her arms are folded across her chest, and I can feel her tension. Let her be scared. Let her feel every ounce of pain I felt when she abandoned me. Let that untrue heart of hers reap its reward.

I close in as she approaches a stand of palms that juts out toward the water. I'm four steps behind her now. What will I do when I catch her? Three steps. Her skin is moist with sweat. Two steps. And then…The swaying of her hips in the moonlight. Her grace…Her grace undoes me.

She turns and backs against one of the palms, and the skin that was glowing just a moment ago is covered with goose bumps. She puts her hands behind the small of her back and leans on them, pressing her palms into the tree. I can feel her fear. I can feel her cowering like a spent fighter, backed against the ropes, in dread of the coming punishment.

She says, "Go ahead, Russ."

"Go ahead and what?"

"Hurt me. That's what you want. Isn't it?"

Her eyes are fixed on me. She is passive. Waiting. She will let me do anything to her now.

The scent of her hair brings back our night in San Francisco. I can feel the softness of her skin before I touch it. I can hear the beating of her heart. And when I kiss her, I can taste that the madness in her is every bit as strong as the madness in me.

In a moment, I have her pinned down in the sand, my forearm across her collarbone, as I pull off her shorts. When they reach her ankles, she kicks them away. And when I'm inside her, I know I'm being too rough, but I can't stop myself. Every time I go forward, she lets out a little cry that could be pleasure or could be pain. I'm so blinded by desire, anger, love, confusion, and fear, I don't know what she's feeling.

She doesn't try to get away. She thwarts me instead, moving back as I move forward, and forward as I move back, deliberately breaking the rhythm. I can't control her. She's way too strong. Way too fierce. And just as we're starting to get back in sync, she slides her right hand up past my left cheek and over the top of my head. She grabs a fistful of hair above my right ear and starts wrenching my head down toward my left shoulder. She's so damn strong, I have to move where she's pulling me to keep from breaking my neck. At the same time, she's pushing my right shoulder up, so I'm twisting at the waist. I start leaning so far to my left that my shoulder is almost in the sand. And just as she has me off balance, she extends her left leg and swings it hard over my hip, flipping us both in a smooth, easy motion.

Now the moon and stars are glinting through her swaying hair as it hangs down in my face. She sweeps it back with her right hand while she steadies herself with her left on my shoulder. Then she lets out a little laugh that startles me. Like this is a game. How could she laugh, after what I was just doing to her? Can't she feel how out of control I am? Why isn't she scared? I am.

We got separated somewhere in the process of her little wrestling move, but she puts us back together and her hot breath fills my ear as she whispers, "Not so hard, Russ!" She bites the back of my ear hard enough to make me yell, and we start again. Nice and slow.

* * *

The waves are lapping at our feet as we stare at the stars. For a long time, neither of us speaks. Then she says, "I'm sorry about what happened in Virginia."

"You were terrified," I say. "And you hadn't slept. Everyone has their breaking point."

"No, I mean all of it. It was all my fault."

"No it wasn't."

"Oh, but it was."

She gets up and walks into the sea.

I watch her bathe in the moonlight, and I wade in to join her. She has a slightly pained expression.

"You Okay?" I ask.

"I got sand in me."

"Did Charlie send you out here to distract me? So he could search my room?"

"That was the plan," she says.

"He won't find the key."

"I know."

She goes back to shore and puts her clothes on. When I join her on the beach a minute later, she says, "You know why I never finished college, Russ?"

"Why?"

"I don't know. I was an A student. But there's this part of me that, every time life starts getting too comfortable, I want to sabotage it. I have this fear that I'll become complacent. That I'll wake up one day in a house in the suburbs, all fat and pampered, and not know who I am, or how I got there, or how to get out."

"It's funny hearing your own thoughts come out of someone else's mouth," I say.

"Yeah, I know that about you," she says. "That you have that in you too. And what do you know about me? Can you read my thoughts?"

I look in her face, and in the silver light of the moon, her eyes are full of fear and uncertainty. I don't know what's beneath it all, but I take a guess. "You want your life to be a little less crazy?"

"And?"

"And what?"

"You really can't tell?"

"No."

"Then I'll tell you tomorrow," she says. She puts on her clothes and says, "I have to get back. Before he gets too suspicious. And Russ?"

"Yeah?"

"Be at the restaurant tomorrow afternoon. I'll get a table with Charlie. And you'll join us."

That's the last thing she says.

33

I STAYED ON THE BEACH till dawn, drifting in and out of sleep, watching the tide and the stars. Then I went to my room and slept till eleven. I ate breakfast at the restaurant, and I could see Cali and Charlie out on the beach. She got him drinking early, pushing beer after beer into his hand. Now it's 2:00 p.m., and at last they're headed back toward the restaurant.

I sit in a chair by the pool, so I won't look like I'm waiting for them. I don't know why that matters. Maybe because I'm so uneasy, and it's something I can control.

Two workmen in light blue outfits remove the cover from the pool pump in the bushes behind the lounge chairs. They pause and wipe the sweat from their brows as they watch Charlie and Cali approach.

There's a new guest at the bar today. A middle-aged guy in a white button-down shirt with little black palm trees all over it. I didn't see him come in, but he's been sitting at the bar for at least twenty minutes with his head bowed over a newspaper. His back is to me, and his hands are cupped over the sides of his face, like he's trying to tune out distractions and focus on his reading. Or maybe he's trying to hide. Maybe he ran down here like I did, to get away from everything. I don't know why, but he gives me the creeps.

Cali and Charlie take one of the tables on the pool deck, just outside the thatch roof. She gives me a quick glance and then they sit with their backs to me, facing out toward the sea. I walk over to the table and pull out the chair directly across from Cali.

"Mind if I join you?"

Cali looks tired. I can tell from the faint circles under her eyes that she hasn't slept.

She looks at me coldly and says, "Suit yourself."

What kind of rude reception is that? What the hell is she doing? I want to turn and walk away right now. But I sit.

I can tell by Charlie's dark, sullen glare that he's already drunk. I

andrew diamond

just can't tell how drunk. When the waiter stops by, Cali says, "Margaritas all around. On ice, not blended. And no salt." The waiter nods and walks away.

Charlie looks like he might fall asleep. Cali strokes his thigh and says, "Is today going to be a nap day, Charlie?" The sight of her touching him fills me with jealousy.

Charlie perks up and says, "Maybe a nap after we eat. Maybe you'll be nice today and give me a little something."

I could hit either one of them right now.

The waiter brings our drinks. He gives the one with the little green umbrella to Charlie. Cali and I get the other two. I see the little glance they exchange. Cali and the waiter. What was that?

Cali raises her glass and says, "To honor among thieves."

"Here, here!" says Charlie, as he toasts her.

My glass is still on the table. They both look at me until I reluctantly pick it up and join the toast.

Charlie pulls the straw from his glass and guzzles down a few ounces at once. He finishes with a sharp exhale and says, "Whew! That's strong."

As I put the straw to my lips, I watch Cali to make sure she's drinking hers. She is. And she's staring directly into my eyes, trying to tell me something, but what?

The margarita goes down like limeade. There's no alcohol in it at all. I'm about to contradict what Charlie just said, but her stare is fixed on me, and I don't know why. In my confusion, I say nothing.

Cali says to Charlie, "Did you find the key?"

This catches him off guard. "What?"

She pokes at the ice in her glass and says, "Did you find the key? In Russ's room last night? You never told me."

Charlie shoots me a guilty look, and Cali says matter-of-factly, "You didn't, did you?"

Charlie drinks down the rest of his margarita, looking more and more confused. He is definitely drunk. Cali waves to the waiter and says, "Another." Then she drops my USB stick on the table in front of

Charlie and says, "There."

Now I really don't know what's going on. Charlie looks as lost as I feel. He just stares at the USB drive and blinks. "How'd you get that?"

Cali says, "I fucked him on the beach last night, and he gave it to me." She quietly stirs her drink and says, "What's that thing you like to say, Charlie? There's no kind of whipped like pussy-whipped?"

All I can do is stare at her with my mouth half open. What the hell is she doing?

"He's been cashing out left and right," Cali says. "With your friend, Mr. Greene. But I already guilted him into sending you a few thousand."

"Wait, here?" Charlie asks, alarmed. "He's sending cash here?"

"Where else?"

"You two are fucking idiots!" Charlie yells. Then in a lower voice, he says, "You don't ship laundered cash to your own address. Fuck! You dumb asses! Now I'm going to have to bail."

Cali says, "*You're* going to have to bail? Or *we're* going to have to bail? Which is it, Charlie? I'm dying to know."

I can see by the look on his face that he has no idea what to say. As the waiter sets another drink in front of Charlie, Cali looks at me with an amused smile and says, "What's the matter, Russ? You look lost."

Charlie puts the USB stick in his pocket, pulls the straw from his glass, and takes a big gulp. Then something behind me startles her. Not enough for a drunk to notice, but more than enough for the guy she's whipped to pick up on. I turn to see the little DHL truck pulling up to the hotel office.

When I turn back, Charlie says, "You do look a little off, Russ." He's starting to regain his confidence now that he has the key. He's even looking a little smug. And I'm starting to get it now. We're getting back in sync, Cali and I.

It was her in my room the other night. That's when she got the red key card and the USB stick. She's the one who cleaned my wound and washed my shirt.

She's agitated now. Whatever she's doing, whatever her plan is, it's approaching the critical moment. She looks to me for reassurance as she reaches for her drink. She's scared. And I think, "Keep calm, Cali. You can do it."

But she isn't calm. The drink falls in her lap, and she jumps up quickly. The glass shatters on the concrete, and there's panic in her voice when she says, "Russ, get me some napkins from the bar. Now!"

Without thinking, I do as she says. As I dash under the high thatch roof, beneath the slow-spinning fans, the two men in blue over by the pool pump put down their tools. The man at the bar in the palm-tree shirt broods over his newspaper with his head in his hands. Beside his elbow, a little breeze flits at the corners of the napkin on top of the stack, threatening to blow it away.

As I reach for the napkins, a familiar voice says from behind the cupped hands, "Does he have the key?"

I'm about to piss myself.

How did *he* get here?

Jack Hayes drops his hands from his face and says, "Does he have the USB stick?"

"Yes."

"Okay. Walk straight down the hotel drive. She'll meet you at the street."

I turn immediately and head back the way I came. Jack is a step behind me. He puts his hand on my shoulder and says, "Follow the girl, Russ. And stay out of the US. You're wanted in Virginia."

I keep moving forward. At the end of the bar, before turning left toward the hotel drive, I hesitate for a moment. The desk clerk is approaching the table with the package from DHL. Cali isn't there. The puddle beneath the table where she sat is filled with ice and shattered glass. Charlie sits wavering in his seat, drunk and bewildered.

The clerk says, "Charlie Taylor?"

I turn toward the drive. Behind me I hear Charlie's startled response. "What?"

"You are Charlie Taylor? This package is for you, no?"

Charlie yells, "He put my name on it? You put my fucking name right on the package?"

I continue down the hotel drive. In one quick backward glance through the open restaurant, across the bar, I see Jack Hayes and the two men in blue surrounding Charlie.

Cali is leaning against a little black car at the end of the drive. When I reach her, she gives me the keys and says, "Let's get out of here."

34

WE DRIVE NORTH, UP the peninsula, toward the mainland. Cali looks exhausted, but relieved.

She says, "I didn't sleep with him, Russ. I told you I wouldn't betray you, and I meant that."

Then she pulls the envelope from beneath her seat. The one she picked up yesterday from the other hotel. She hands it to me and says, "Open it."

I tear it open as I drive. Inside are two plane tickets to Rio de Janeiro, and a passport. I turn my eyes back to the road and smile. "Rio, huh?"

"I always wanted to go there. We don't have to stay. We can go anywhere. It's all wide open." She nods and says, "Look at the passport."

I open it and check the photo. It's the one Wisp took of me back in San Francisco. But my hair and eyes are the right color.

"I saw your friend when I got back to California. I asked him to make that. Check the name."

"Russell Rey?"

"Mm-hmm."

"Why Rey?"

"That's my name. I thought it might be easier to travel as husband and wife."

As we make our way along the narrow road, she tells me the story of how Jack Hayes got her phone number. "It was connected to your phone after I texted you."

"I told you that would happen. I told you they'd track you down."

"And you made me feel really bad about it."

Hayes called her in California and offered to strike a deal.

"He asked me to transfer a third of the money into a Bitcoin wallet for him and leave a third on the server," Cali says. "We keep the other third."

I think this through for a second. "Wait. How's Jack going to get away with that? The blockchain will show the transactions."

"I know. But no one knows who owns the wallets those coins went into. I did the transfers the other night."

"Was that Jack you were talking to on the phone yesterday? When you ran away from me?"

"Mm-hmm. He told me where to send the money. And when to give Charlie the USB drive. He wanted to close the case and get his money so he can retire."

"How did you get the money?" I ask. "The DHL package for Charlie?"

"I got in touch with Mr. Greene as soon as I left your room the other night. After I dragged you in and cleaned you up. Charlie was passed out in a bush. You guys are idiots when you drink."

I can see in her tired face the toll all this has taken on her. But she smiles at me when she says, "The red key card, Russ. You didn't get it."

"What?"

"When I gave it to Charlie on the beach yesterday. I wanted you to see. You should have known there's only one way I could have gotten it. I wanted you to put it all together. That I had the USB drive, and everything was okay. But you didn't get it."

"What did you do with the cash from my backpack?"

"I mailed it ahead. We can't go through customs with that much money."

As we make our way inland, into the lush green hills, little white clouds drift overhead, their shadows gliding across the road and climbing the trees. She curls up in her seat and rests her head against the window. The color gathers again in her cheeks, and her chest rises and falls in a slow, deep rhythm. I look over now and then, expecting to see her asleep. Instead, she stares through the windshield, and I can see in the movement of her eyes and her changing expression that something is troubling her.

Something is troubling me too.

"Did you know Charlie would be here?" I ask.

She looks down and keeps her eyes fixed on the floor in front of her. For a long time, she does not answer. Then at last, she says, "Yes."

"You okay?" I ask. "You look like you're going to throw up."

"Pull over, will you?"

I pull off to the side of the road, and before I can ask what's up, she unbuckles and gets out of the car. She opens the rear passenger door and pulls out her bag, then sets it down on the trunk. When I get out to see what she's up to, she hands me a laptop and says, "Here."

"What's this?"

"The Bitcoin wallet is on there. Take it."

"What?"

"Take it. It makes me feel sick."

I open up the laptop and she shows me where the file is.

"Check the balance," she says.

"I trust you."

"Do you?" she asks. "I don't want you to. Check the balance."

"Okay." I check the balance. "It's a little over twenty-four thousand in Bitcoin. That's, I don't know."

"Six million dollars," she says. Then she repeats with a tinge of disgust, "Take it!"

I study her stricken face for a moment and ask, "What got into you?"

"I don't know," she says. "Greed, I guess. Charlie left me with that little SD card, with what I thought was the key to what I thought was the vault, and I kept logging in, trying to get that money. But the files were encrypted. I thought he was dead, and then he calls and tells me to meet him down here. I didn't want to come down here. In my head, that money already was mine. I just couldn't figure out how to unlock it. And then you came along."

"Did you plan this all out with Charlie?"

She shakes her head slowly. "No. He just gave me the SD card before he left and told me to wait for you if anything went wrong. I didn't know what was going on until Twilight disappeared. Then I put it all together. That Charlie died and left a bunch of money lay-ing around on one of his servers. I had the key, and the money was mine. All I had to do was take it and walk away. But it was like…like a mirage, you know? Every time you think you're getting close, you find it's a little farther off. You keep chasing, and you keep getting farther from where you meant to be. I never meant for it to blow up into this mess."

I feel some sympathy toward her, but also some anger. "Okay, that night in San Francisco," I say. "That first night…"

"Stop it, Russ!" Now she really looks sick.

"Did you sleep with me just because you wanted my help?"

"Stop it!" Her voice is breaking.

"Because you thought I could get you the money?"

She won't look at me. She's shaking her head and biting her lip.

"I'm just asking for an honest answer," I say. And I'm being pretty damn calm about it, I tell myself. "If you're going to start telling me this stuff, you might as well tell me everything. What would you have done if the money really was on that server? If I got it all for you? Would you have ditched me? Would you have left?"

"You knew something was wrong that night," she says defensively. Her voice is hoarse, and she's about to cry. "You could tell I was having a hard time. That's not how a woman acts when she wants to have sex."

"But you went through with it!"

She looks at me angrily and says, "And I asked you that night why you let yourself be caught up in this. You could have walked away. But you didn't. Why, Russ? Why didn't you just leave it alone?"

"I tried to."

"Well maybe you're a better person than I am."

"Well maybe I'm not. You never killed anyone. Why did you follow me to Virginia?"

"I told you," she says. "I wanted to get you out of trouble. To give you the key so you could turn it over to…whoever, and get back to your normal life. It wasn't about the money anymore."

Then, just to be an asshole, just to dig a little further into her conscience, I'm about to say, "Are you sure it wasn't about the money? Tell me, Cali. What *was* it about?"

But I stop myself, because I've already made up my mind about her. Charlie was right. She can't lie, and she can't hide her emotions. Everything she feels is right there on her face. I love that about her.

She says, "You know, last night, on the beach, when you were going to kill me, half of me wanted you to. Because I deserved it, for dragging you into all this."

"You didn't drag me in," I say. "And I'm glad I didn't kill you. Sex is so much more enjoyable than murder."

Finally, she smiles. "And you can do it more than once."

"Is there anything else I need to know about you?" I ask. "Like, you're one of those black widows that eats its mate?"

She shakes her head.

"Or maybe you're a cop?"

She laughs.

"Okay, so we're all done with confession?"

"Oh!" She lights up. "There *is* this tiny part of me that's just a little bit crazy."

"The part that laughs when her boyfriend is trying to kill her?"

"Yeah, and bites. It's just like…like…" She holds her thumb and forefinger an inch apart. "This much." I look at her face to see how serious she is. She abandons the finger measurement and extends her hands in front of her, about six inches apart and says, "Okay, this much."

"Umm…you know your hands are drifting apart?"

"Are they? God, I love how you notice little things like that!"

"Come on," I say, as I walk back to the driver's door and put the laptop inside.

She picks up her bag and says, "You still want me?"

"What else am I going to do with you? Get in the car."

She runs to the passenger door, tosses her bag in the back seat, then buckles up beside me. As I turn the wheels back onto the road, she leans on my shoulder and gives me a little kiss. The soft touch of her cheek and the mingled scent of salt and coconut in her hair send a tingle through every fiber of my body. I hit the gas, and off we go, winding down through the hills, toward whatever's next in this crazy, messed-up life.

Acknowledgments

Thank you to my beautiful wife, Lindsay, for putting up with me (or without me) during the creation of this book. Thanks again for reading the first draft, designing the cover, and being the one from whom Stolen Time Press steals so much of its time.

Thank you to Kristin Mehus-Roe and Ingrid Emerick at <u>Girl Friday Productions</u> for their help in editing this book. And thanks to <u>Meredith Tennant</u> for proofreading.

About the Author

Andrew Diamond lives in Charlottesville, VA, with his wife and three children. By day, he is a software developer who helps universities and libraries build digital repositories. His first novel, _Warren Lane_, was published in 2015.

If you enjoyed this book, tell your friends, and please leave a review at Amazon.com, Goodreads, or wherever you like to hang out online. All we indie authors have to promote us is word of mouth from readers like you. Your reviews do make a difference!

If you want to keep up with what I'm doing, follow my blog at https://adiamond.me or my Facebook page at https://www.facebook.com/adiamond.me/.

If you want to give me a piece of your mind, you can reach me at andrew@adiamond.me.